~ Magic here!

MAGIC BORN

Book Two Of The Guardian Series

RAYANNE HAINES

SOUL MATE PUBLISHING

New York

MAGIC BORN

Copyright©2018

RAYANNE HAINES

Cover Design by Fiona Jayde

This book is a work of fiction. The names, characters, places, and incidents are the products of the author's imagination or are used fictitiously. Any resemblance to actual events, business establishments, locales, or persons, living or dead, is entirely coincidental.

All rights reserved. No part of this publication may be reproduced, stored in a retrieval system, or transmitted in any form or by any means (electronic, mechanical, photocopying, recording, or otherwise) without the prior written permission of both the copyright owner and the publisher. The only exception is brief quotations in printed reviews.

The scanning, uploading, and distribution of this book via the Internet or via any other means without the permission of the publisher is illegal and punishable by law. Please purchase only authorized electronic editions, and do not participate in or encourage electronic piracy of copyrighted materials.

Your support of the author's rights is appreciated.

Published in the United States of America by
Soul Mate Publishing
P.O. Box 24
Macedon, New York, 14502

ISBN: 978-1-68291-675-9

ebook ISBN: 978-1-68291-648-3

www.SoulMatePublishing.com

The publisher does not have any control over and does not assume any responsibility for author or third-party websites or their content.

This one is for Shelaine

Acknowledgements

I'd like to offer heartfelt gratitude to everyone at Soul Mate Publishing for helping bring this book to life; to Cheryl—editor extraordinaire; to Fiona—designer extraordinaire; to all the writers on the label who have offered so much support; and to Debby for giving me the chance to share The Guardians with you all.

Thank you to the ladies of CaRWA for your friendship and community.

And thank you to the readers and reviewers—for everything!

Chapter 1

She must be losing her touch. Mar opened the makeshift medical office door, only to be swept up into the thunderstorm gaze of Neeren Simine.

The Parthen Kings eyes swirled green, black, and yellow. Wicked. Measured.

His six-foot four-inch frame exuded cool masculinity. Prowess. Sin.

Nonchalance written on every part of his body. He wore tan slacks and a loose white cotton shirt that effortlessly showcased his muscles. His sleeves rolled up above his powerful forearms. His feet were bare. As always.

Show-off.

Mar had been a guest on his island for close to two weeks and only managed to ruffle his feathers a couple of times. She usually pissed people off at least twice per conversation, but with this guy? Nothing. It was unnerving not knowing what he felt. Schooled in the art of diplomacy and secrecy, his face betrayed nothing. He was ice, through and through. She squinted, hoping to decipher something in his high cheek bones. His square jaw. His thick lower lip.

Neeren grinned at her. His yellow eyes remained aloof. "Do you like what you see?"

Mar snorted. Refused to give him the satisfaction of knowing he unnerved her. "Dream much?"

"Double-entendres this early in the day, Maria?"

Of course, she hadn't meant it that way. Trust him to pick up on subconscious spilling out.

Neeren was half parthen and half water elemental. Parthen were shifters (black panther variation) and dream walkers. A race imbued with the ability to enter others dreams and manipulate them. Once inside a person's mind, dream became reality. Whatever the parthen wanted to happen—happened. Pain or pleasure. They wielded their gift with exacting precision. Needless to say, most immortals were nervous around them. The jury was out as to whether they were admired or reviled. Depends on who you spoke to.

The Elementals, a race capable of controlling all the earths elements, were one of only a few with a natural ability to block parthen from entering their dreams. because Neeren was both parthen and elemental he could bypass this natural blocking ability. Could do whatever he wanted to any elemental he wanted. Even kill them in their sleep.

His secret was out now though. To keep peace, he'd agreed to have his dreamwalking abilities bound against the elemental. Mar was the witch tagged to do the binding.

Mar leaned her hip against the door and winked at him. "Funny. Bet you think you're pretty clever."

"Hardly. If I was clever, I'd have figured out a way around this." Neeren narrowed his eyes at her. Baring perfect teeth in a sinister grin.

A shiver raced up her spine and slammed into her gut. Goddess he annoyed her.

Mar pursed her lips. "It's not going to hurt. I never pegged you for a chicken. Tell me, how many bodyguards are standing guard during this little tete-a-tete?"

"Ah yes, that's it of course. I'm scared." He grinned again. "How perceptive of you."

She hated his grin. How his lower lip curled up slightly. Her jaw clenched. Realizing they were still standing in the doorway, she retreated a step to let him in.

He remained where he was.

"Are you coming in or what?"

"I'd rather not, thank you."

She sighed. "Alex wasn't such a baby about it. Just get in here."

He growled. "Yes, well my sister trusts you for some strange reason."

"Look, you two made a deal. It's time to follow through, kitten."

He bowed mockingly. "As you command."

Turning away, she walked into the room. Better than telling him to piss off and not come back. She had a job to do. It didn't include being mocked by some cat.

The walls pulsed. Pushed down on her. She hadn't noticed before. Maybe it hadn't been as glaring when it was just her and Alex, but the space felt claustrophobic. A single bed lay in the middle of the room. A lone, white metal chair beside it. A small wood burning stove heated the room. Her flesh warmed. A pot of herbs brewed over flames. The smell of sage, lemongrass, and rosemary calmed her. The smell of magic.

The room should have felt clinical. It didn't. Magic required energy and intimacy. The strongest magic came from connection. Mar would have to get very, very close to Neeren for the spell to stick. Dread bounced in her stomach. Beads of sweat collected on her forehead. Dripped down her spine.

"So how does this work?" Neeren's voice jarred her back to the present. "Shall I strip and lie down?"

Mar gifted him with her best don't-fuck-with-me stare. The only way she'd get through this torturous afternoon was by maintaining control. Dude had no idea who he was dealing with. She wasn't some wet behind the ears novice. She flexed her shoulders. Smirked. She was one of the most powerful witches on the planet. No joke. No fooling. She'd studied her ass off. Trained until her soul bled. She wasn't the best because she'd been born special. His dreamwalking shit didn't scare her. And no cat was going to dominate her, even if he was a King.

"Oh, kitten, you wish. Go ahead and lay down. But keep your clothes on. This won't take long."

His voice weaved through the room like honey. "You'll find things always take longer with me. I expect you to be thorough, witch."

"Oh good, now you're gonna play the seducer? Lucky me." She rolled her eyes. Twice.

He smirked and glanced away. Like it was nothing. Jerk. She stirred herbs. Placed another log in the stove. Watched fire lick at fresh wood.

The flames roared whenever the King's sister, Alex, entered the room. Mar's new BFF controlled fire and was one of the toughest people she'd ever known. They were best friends though because Alex took no one's shit while still being kind.

Mar liked kindness.

Binding Alex had been easy. Her friend was newly immortal. She'd known about the immortal world for less than a month. When Mar reached into her subconscious, she'd discovered Alex hadn't fully embraced her immortality. Neeren wouldn't be so easy. The guy had been born and raised a King. Considered the most powerful of his kind, he'd spent his one hundred and twenty odd years protecting his people from outsiders.

Her gut clenched as he climbed onto the bed and stretched out his legs. Muscled calves hung over the edge. His slacks pulled taut around long limbs. Even his stupid feet were perfectly proportioned.

Her stilettos clicked her frustration as she stomped across the floor with a pot of herbs. She allowed herself a moment to study him as he closed his eyes. Thick, black lashes swept above his cheekbones. He breathed easy. Ice, she thought again. And too damn masculine for his own good.

Mar licked her lips. "I'm going to have to touch you to do this. I'll reach into your sub consciousness to access to your dream world. Then using magic, I'll lay a block over your abilities. To do this, I'll rub an herb mixture across your forehead and temples. I may have to touch more of your face. There will be a sense of connection." She swallowed. "Don't get any bright ideas about touching back."

Neeren's eyes remained closed as he replied, "I will endeavor to remain passive and non-reactionary."

Mar leaned over his chest. Her hair spilled across his face.

He flinched.

"Sorry," she said.

She pushed her hair off her shoulders and leaned in again. A few stray strands fell across his lips.

He flinched.

She grinned. "Sorry."

"Get an elastic band for fuck's sake."

"I don't have one."

"Hell."

"Suck it up, Norman. It's just hair. Now don't move."

Mar positioned the pot next to his chest, lightly touching his flesh. Placed the fingers on her left hand along his temple. With her right hand, she traced a pattern through the herb mixture. She hummed under her breath. Tracing the exact pattern in a continual motion, until it began to glow. Fire sang. Sweat broke out across her chest. Moisture glistened along Neeren's upper lip. A blue mist rose above the floor. As it reached her knees, she placed her fingers, coated in moist herbs, against his jaw.

He remained motionless.

The chant became a wave. An echo. A siren call. The air vibrated.

Slowly, Mar traced a new pattern across his face. Swept fingers across his cheek, up his nose, over the forehead, and down his hardened jaw. Repeated the movement again and again.

His breathing echoed her chant. Her breathing echoed his. Matched the staccato beat. As they joined, the pattern across his face glowed the same blue as the mist now at her chest.

Mar reached for his mind. Stretched for connections. Searched for pieces of him linked to the elemental. Let the spell weave between her and Neeren so they might become one.

A shadow appeared. Her consciousness pushed at it. Heat bit her. The blue glow on his flesh singed her. His subconscious fought. Pushed back at light seeking entrance to this deep place.

Mar pushed harder. Ignored a burning against her skin. Reached into shadow. Directed light energy. Battered with wiccan power. She would not be stopped. A crack appeared in the gray. She channeled her glow past the barrier Neeren erected.

Pain engulfed her. Agony. Her lungs constricted, trying to hide from the force beating at them. Her limbs weakened. Dizzy, she tried to pull free. Neeren grasped her hand. Held it against his face before she could escape.

"Finish it," Neeren moaned through gritted teeth. Clenched jaw.

This was wrong. She shouldn't be feeling this.

"I can't," she moaned back.

"You have no option now," he growled. "Complete the spell so we can be done with it."

His eyes remained closed. His face glowed electric blue. His entire body illuminated.

Mar forced herself to ignore the burning inside her gut. To ignore the cries of death she heard in his mind. To pretend she hadn't felt his content. She resumed chanting. Louder this time, almost frantic. Watched as the blue glow finally weaved itself into a wall blocking his power.

As soon as it was done, she ripped her hand out of his and fled across the room. "What did you do?"

Neeren sat up. Controlled. Swung his legs over the side. Rested his hands on the edge of the cot. Smiled his knowing smile.

Replied, "What I was born to do."

Chapter 2

Neeren poured himself a glass of his favorite spiced rum and sat on the cream leather couch in his office.

Two hours. It had been two hours since the little witch bound his power. He hadn't expected her to be able to reach as far in as she had. He'd been reading her since they met two weeks ago. Yet hadn't known she controlled so much power. Thought she truly was as flighty as she pretended. He'd been wrong. Someone had erected a barrier over her mind.

He didn't think it was her.

Neeren tossed amber liquid down his throat and rose to stand in front of the window. From this place, he could see across the island out to the water below. As a water elemental, he controlled the water around his home in the Aegean Sea. It did his bidding and kept his people safe. He'd been raised to believe his powers were a gift from the creators.

He downed his rum and stared out to sea lost in old memories.

He'd grown up knowing that he must be kept a secret from the elemental. Those immortals didn't like creatures more powerful than them. Neeren and his sister were far more powerful.

After his father's murder, he'd become a shadow. He protected his mother as she grieved. Protected his island. His people. Remained hidden to the world until he had what he needed to fight enemies within the elemental and win.

That time had come later than he'd prayed for. But it had come. He found his sister, Alex alive and well, living as a human. Together they destroyed the elementals responsible for murdering their father.

To keep the peace, they agreed to have their dreamwalking powers bound against the elemental kind. It didn't sit well with him, but in the end, he'd agreed.

They didn't know what else he was capable of.

But now? Now the witch did. That was a problem.

A knock on the door startled him. He turned from his internal musings and arranged his face into the mask of indifference he was known for. "Enter."

His sister Alex swept into the room like a firestorm.

"What did you say to Mar?"

"Nothing. And hello to you too, sister."

She stepped into his personal space and wagged her finger at him. "Mar is acting all weird and morose. What did you say to her?"

It felt as though there was never a time when she hadn't been there—this sister of his. She was everything now. He was learning from her about how to be more at ease. Apparently, or so she said, he had a reputation for being off-putting.

"I didn't say anything to your little friend."

"Little friend? You sound seriously pompous, Neeren. Can you please stop acting like a jerk around her?"

He stretched his shoulders. "I did not act like a jerk. I simply refuse to play her games or get all wrapped up in her weird behavior like the rest of you do. I let her bind me, under protest I might add, and then I left. What else should I have done? Thank her?"

Alex stepped back and walked over to the liquor cabinet. "No, but you don't have to be mean. And she isn't some little friend either. We're grown-ass women, brother."

"I wasn't mean, sister," he replied with the same amount of mocking censure in his tone. He sat back down on his couch and smiled at her—his blood. "I know you are both grown-ass, powerful, could kick-me-into-the-next-century woman and all . . ."

She interrupted. "Your chauvinism is showing again."

"Would you sit down? I didn't say anything rude to the witch."

He grinned as she plopped herself on the nearest chair and curled her feet up under his knees.

She rolled her eyes. "She has a name. I don't understand why you give her such a hard time. She helped us."

Neeren raised his hands in submission. "Very well, I'll try harder. I know she is your friend, but she disturbs me. I'm not fine with having her bind my powers. I'm not fine with her hanging out on my Island for weeks because she feels like taking a vacation. And I'm not fine with the fact we know virtually nothing about her."

Alex tossed her knotted mass of red curls behind her shoulders and flopped back against the edge of the arm rest. He admired her complete lack of artifice. She was an open book. The witch was like that too. A little wild. So fresh. He wished he could soak in their freedom for a while. Wished he could let go like they did. He was exhausted.

"Grandfather and Collum both vouch for her. And Grandfather has known her forever. Plus, I trust her. She's my friend, Neeren." Alex stared at the ceiling. Her hair brushed against the floor. "Did you ever think she disturbs you because you like her?"

He swallowed his rum slowly so he wouldn't choke on it. The brand—Zaya—was a blend from Trinidad and Tobago. It had sweet and complex flavors of citrus peel, vanilla, spices, and caramel. It had taken him fifteen years to find a rum with the exact flavor combination he preferred. It wasn't the most expensive brand out there. Didn't matter.

He grimaced. "I do not like her. She's a frat girl on steroids."

Alex pierced him with a look that said he'd crossed a line. "Yes, she can be over the top sometimes. But she's incredibly strong. She found you when no one else could. And . . . she's a good person." She handed him her empty glass and stood up. "Be kinder, Neeren."

He accepted the cup. "She must respect my authority here."

Was that pity in her eyes?

As they stared at each other she shook her head. "You have a lot to learn about women."

~ ~ ~

After she left the room, Neeren fell back across the couch. To see what it felt like. It was strange—flopping. He felt like a fool within seconds. He stood, crossed the room, and sat at his desk instead. Started up his computer. Opened iTunes. Slowly scrolled through the music library. Bach, Beethoven, Strauss, Mozart. Further down were Ria Mae, Imagine Dragons, Lana Del Rey. Those came from Alex's library. She'd synced her library with his a few days ago. Told him it would bring him into the real world. What was the real world anyway? Who decided? His world was as real as any other, wasn't it?

Now that he didn't have to hide anymore, he could openly leave his island. For the past twenty-five years, immortals the world over had wondered who the new Parthen King was. There were plenty of rumors about him. Rumors he'd been happy to let grow. But now word was out. A peace agreement had been struck and the story was spreading. The story of him and Alex. He had a face now.

Neeren took a deep breath. Centered himself. Getting carried away wasn't an option. He closed his laptop without turning the music on. Poured himself another glass of Zaya. Strode back to stand in front of floor to ceiling windows. His entire home was built of steel and glass. Light poured in around him. Into every corner. Every crevice. He'd spent his life stuck on this island so the elemental wouldn't find him or his mother. Long ago he'd decided he wouldn't be stuck behind walls. Neeren refused to live like the shadow the world thought he was.

Below him, black cats roamed the grounds. Among them, dancing with her arms raised to the sky, her mahogany hair flying out behind her, twirled the witch. His hands clenched at his sides in response to . . . something he couldn't quite name. She was wild. Seemed to come and go by the rhythm of her own heartbeat. Lived like life was meant for devouring with gusto.

His people stared openly at her. As he did behind tinted glass. Did she know he watched her? Secretly admired her shocking beauty. The cream linen shift she wore did nothing to hide her tiny waist. She was an enigma. This creature of earth. She had as many secrets as he did. The others might not see it. They only saw her big hazel eyes. Her hips swinging with the wind.

She laughed, and his chest tightened.

"Maria Del Voscova." He tasted her name on his lips. Wondered what her soundtrack was.

Chapter 3

Exhilarated and exhausted, Mar wandered into the commercial sized kitchen at the back of the house. She needed a release from the power flowing through her veins. She always felt high after performing magic. Dancing on the cliff edge hadn't helped.

Receiving admiring glances from the male parthen had been cool though.

She routed among cupboards while ignoring startled looks from the kitchen staff. "Don't mind me. I'm starving! Say, you got any Nutella? White bread? The good stuff, you know? I don't want any healthy crap. I need Azucar!"

One older, heavy set woman in a green apron—*Jane? Janette?*—took pity on her. "Try the freezer. We might have months old cream puffs in there somewhere."

"Thanks, Jane!"

"It's, Janelle."

"Are you sure? You look like a Jane."

"It's, Janelle."

"Huh. Cause I could've sworn it was Jane. You should do something different with your hair. You have Jane hair."

The woman's face dropped. "There is nothing wrong with my hair. It's practical."

"Yeeeaaaah. It's Jane hair." Mar raised her hands in surrender. "Look, I'm just saying, you live on a tropical island, you're a gorgeous goddamn shifter, and a kick-ass cook. You should really have Janelle hair—not Jane hair. But you know, just one woman's opinion over here."

Mar lifted hair off her neck. "God it's like a sauna in here. You guys need drapes or something to block the sun. Oh, Kingly One won't put out the money huh?"

Janelle pointed to the freezer and simply said, "Out."

Mar winked good naturedly, headed to the freezer, and began searching for contraband cream puffs. She heard muffled voices outside the freezer. Could swear she heard Jane say something about leaving for a break. She smirked. Bets were Jane showed up to work later with a tight new hair style.

"What are you doing?"

She jumped. Smashed her head on the rack directly above. "Ow. Dammit." She rubbed her head. "Do not sneak up on me. Do you have some kind of sick obsession?"

When Neeren only scowled, she replied, "I'm looking for sugar."

He growled. "I did not sneak up on you. This is my freezer."

"Okay, Negative N. Didn't your mother teach you to share?"

"My mother taught me many things. Such as, don't let strangers take things from you."

Mar laughed and rubbed her head. "Sure, Norman. Whatever. I think after our little morning binding session we're hardly strangers."

Neeren reached above her head, pushed two quarts of sugar free yogurt out of the way, and pulled down a tub of Rocky Road ice-cream.

"What the hell? No fair. You're six foot a million."

"Do you want some?"

She stopped and stared at him. His voice had changed. Become deeper. Teasing. Erotic. The game was different now. Her eyes swung to his mouth before she could stop herself.

"Yes."

He grinned. "I want to know more about your experience this morning. For each answer, I'll give you a spoonful. Deal?"

"You're evil."

"So, I've been told. Shall we begin?"

"In here?"

"I believe you told Jane you were hot. This seems like the perfect place."

He backed them further into the freezer. Stopped mere millimeters from touching her. Warning bells screamed in her head. He was a Tsunami swamping her frazzled mind. Her body leaned in to him of its own free will. Treacherous, needy flesh.

A frozen pig hung from the back-left corner. She concentrated on it. Focused on the bags of frozen vegetables and pizza dough to her left. The cases of fish to her right.

"Sure, perfect. What do you want to know?"

"What did it feel like?" He scooped out a spoonful of the ice-cream and brought it to his mouth.

She stared at his lips. "What?"

"Binding me?" he prompted before swallowing the ice-cream.

"It felt like it always does."

"Not a good enough answer. Take this seriously, Maria."

"Fine. It felt hot and soft. Then it felt angry."

He placed a new scoop of the ice-cream against her mouth. Seeking entry, he rubbed the spoon gently over her lips. Her traitorous breasts tightened. She opened her mouth and swallowed the cream he placed on her tongue. He leaned in closer.

"Does it always feel like that?" he purred in his honey voice.

"No."

He placed another scoop against her lips.

"Why not?"

She swallowed the cream, licking a drop from the corner of her mouth. Stared him directly in the eye. "Because of what else you can do."

He rubbed the cooling, empty spoon along her lower lip again. Stared back. His hooded gaze hot and heavy. "Dear, Maria, you know this is private, right?"

Her tongue darted out to catch the last bits of cream. She smiled at his intake of breath. Thought he could seduce her with dairy, did he? She ignored the twinge in her groin instructing her to lap him up instead of ice-cream.

Mar wrapped her fingers around his to hold the spoon. "Step back, Neeren."

She knew the moment he realized she wasn't falling for his seduction game. The look on his face changed.

His eyes darkened. "What did you say?"

"I protected myself against you the minute you walked out my door this morning, big boy. Now step back, but leave me the Rocky Road."

He tilted his head, but did as she asked. All business, his voice came out clipped. "I need your word you'll keep quiet. This affects Alex too."

"No, it doesn't. You forget. I've been inside her brain too. She can't do what you can."

"She can't?"

Mar sighed. "You heard me, big brother. Little sister isn't like you."

"I am not evil."

He said it with such conviction she almost believed him. Instead she grabbed the ice cream container and scooted around him so the door was directly behind her. "Tell that to all the people you've killed." She sighed. "Look I'm not judging. Lord knows I've seen worse—well maybe equal—I'm just saying."

A scratching noise at the door re-directed her attention. Whatever else she'd planned on saying lodged in her throat as a wrinkled, slobbering face peaked around the door. When the animal saw Neeren it waddled in, practically throwing itself at him. Neeren reach down, picked up the wriggling beast, and started crooning.

Mar choked on invisible ice-cream. "You have a bulldog?"

"Yes," he replied while petting the dog's wrinkled head.

"Is this a trick?"

"No. This is Daisy."

"You have a bulldog named Daisy? You're a cat!"

"Don't stereotype. I adopted her a week and a half ago. She's a rescue."

"Aha." Mar searched the freezer for hidden cameras. "What are you trying to pull over on me? This isn't going to make me think you're less dark."

He sighed while scratching behind the dog's ears. "I admit I will do whatever is necessary to protect my people, including kill. This doesn't make me dark."

"It's the way you kill."

"Yes, I suppose so," he said with no remorse. "Would you like to pet her?"

"What? No."

"Afraid you'll like her, and me a little, if you do?"

"Not gonna happen, big boy."

He scratched the dog's forehead before putting her down. Daisy snorted around Mar's feet and she almost laughed. "You own a bulldog."

Neeren stepped closer. Without warning, he leaned down and licked her lower lip. Her knees buckled. Fire ignited in her belly. Hard. Fast. Before she could react, he placed her fingers in his mouth. Sucked errant drops of chocolate off them. Growled low in his throat.

"Maria, I need you to promise me you'll keep those beautiful lips sealed."

Her head spun. He held her fingers tight. Locked his eyes on hers. Waited. Like stone. Her body raged with want. She pulled her hand back. Refused to look down at her tingling fingers. "Or what?"

A slow smile turned up his lips. "Or I'll have to convince you further."

She refused to ask how. "Why is it so important? A promise doesn't change anything."

"It changes everything. You are bound by your promise. A promise is sacred." He took the carton of ice-cream out of her hands. "Should you break it, it would affect our . . . friendship."

"I don't think I like you—even with your ridiculous little bulldog."

A coldness swept over her as his face changed again. Gone was the seducer. In his place stood a king.

"I don't need you to like me. I need you to make me a promise."

"Fine. I promise. But I'm doing it for Alex. Not you." She grabbed the ice-cream back. "And you don't intimidate me, Cat. Now get out of my way."

Pushing passed him, she strutted into the kitchen with her bounty of stolen ice-cream held high. Daisy trailed behind her, snorting.

Chapter 4

"The leader of the cat pack is watching us again."

Sand sifted through Alex's fingers as she glanced up to where Mar pointed. On the cliff above them stood Neeren. Wind whipped hair about his face. He wore his regular uniform of a button-down shirt with the sleeves rolled up, tan slacks, and bare feet. She found her brother's presence comforting. Apparently, Mar didn't feel the same way.

Alex shrugged. "He doesn't mean anything weird by it. He likes to make sure we're okay." Alex studied Mar under her lashes, thankful for her friendship. Thankful for her knowledge of the immortal world Alex found herself thrust into.

Mar turned to stare at Alex. "Yeah, you keep telling yourself that. Brother darling has a couple screws loose if you ask me. You two are nothing alike, thank God. I mean, dude actually yelled at me at dinner Saturday."

Alex choked on her water. She wondered, not for the first time, if Mar was as wild as she acted. Mar was always up for something crazy. She drank more than anyone Alex had ever met and she always—always pushed buttons. No matter who the person was. Even Alex wasn't immune. It was like the switch telling Mar when to stop was missing. She never stopped.

"You were stripping on the kitchen table," Alex exclaimed.

Mar laughed and flipped hair over her shoulder. "You make it sound dirty or something. I spilled coffee on me and it was burning."

Alex pursed her lips together. "There were other people in the room, Mar."

"I told them I was taking my top off. Is it my fault they didn't leave?"

Openly gaping, Alex said, "Well yes, kinda."

"Whatever. Your brother still needs to pull the pole out of his ass and loosen up a little."

"You just don't like how he looks at you."

Mar recoiled. "Sistah say what?"

"Don't play stupid. Everyone's talking about how he stares at you. You can't tell me you haven't noticed."

"Dudette. You're crazy. Your brother is not looking at me. Also, did you know he has a friggin' English Bulldog? Why didn't you tell me?"

Alex laughed. She searched the cliff to see her brother had moved on. The ocean at their feet churned slightly. Perhaps in response to Neeren's emotions. She was never quite sure how much control he had over the ocean.

Mar snapped her fingers. "Earth to Alex."

"Sorry. I keep thinking about when we met and everything that's happened since."

"Yeah, it's been a crazy couple of weeks," Mar replied.

"It's going to take me a while to get used to all this immortal stuff."

"Sure it is. It'd be nuts if you were like—oh yah this is a walk in the park. You're taking to your power like a fish does to water though." Alex sighed as Mar stroked her shoulder. "You're doing good, friend. Be patient with yourself. The rest of us were born to this world. Give it time."

Alex rested her head on her friend's shoulder as the image of Collum Thronus filled her mind. Collum, her two-thousand-year-old boyfriend, real life dragon, and guardian of the races, departed the island two weeks ago. She hadn't spoken to him since.

"Quit thinking about him," Mar said,

"Oh, come on, you promised you'd stop using your witchy powers to read my brain."

"Sorry to break it to you, friend but it doesn't take witchy powers to know you can't get your mind off ol' dragonballs."

"Well I don't need you to bring it up every time we sit here, okay."

Mar lifted her hands in a gesture of surrender. "Okay. Don't get your Levi's in a knot. I'm just saying if you want to talk to the guy, you should call him."

Alex dug her fingers deeper into the sand. "I am not calling him. He's the one who wanted to go fast. I asked for time and a few dates. I haven't heard from him since."

"Yeah," Mar said. "How horrible of him to give you space." She snorted. "Total looser."

"You don't know what you're talking about."

Alex walked to the water's edge glancing into the shadows looking for . . . something. "He's avoiding me because he doesn't know how to date."

Mar stood, dusted sand off her bare legs and walked to Alex. Alex squeezed her hand. It was still strange for her to call Mar friend. After Mar bound her dreamwalking power, Alex thought she'd be unable to trust her. Somehow it hadn't mattered. Mar wouldn't let it. She'd decided the two of them would be best friends and suddenly they were.

Mar was a Spanish spitfire half of Alex's height. She dressed like a high-priced call girl. Said utterly inappropriate things at the wrong time—even if they ended up being completely true. Alex loved everything about her.

"Collum might not know how to date. But he knows how to love. You gotta give a little too you know."

"I'm not going to worship him, Mar. Adulation isn't what he wants or needs, and it isn't the kind of relationship I want."

"Right. I gotcha." Mar shifted her stance. "Do you have sand up your crack? I totally have sand up my crack." Wading into the Mediterranean Sea, she started splashing water over herself. "He'd obliterate the world for you. Like, insane."

Alex didn't even flinch as Mar jumped from one thought to the next. By now, she was used to it. Probably wouldn't know how to handle her if she didn't.

"No, I don't have sand up my crack, and no he wouldn't. I know he's your buddy and all, but Collum would not obliterate the world for me, not unless it fell under the Guardian's charter of rules and regulations. And I don't even want him too. I want him to take me out on a date. It's simple."

Finished rinsing herself off, Mar walked out of the water and plopped back in the sand next to where Alex stood. "So dreamwalk and tell him."

Alex sat beside her and stretched her toes into the water. She had no intention of going in any further. "I did tell him. I told him about cheap Tuesday movie nights, gummy bears, and wanting to be a part of the human world. He left."

Alex picked up a handful of sand and threw it into the waves. Her fire tattoo writhed against her flesh in agitation. "And I am *not* going to him in his dreams. Dreaming leads to sex and then I'll get all needy. I don't want to go there again. I want Collum to get to know me outside of all the immortal world stuff."

Snorting, Mar said, "A—he's a Dragon. B—he's two-thousand. C—he's *the* Guardian of the Races. All he knows is immortal world stuff. Not to rain on your parade or anything, cause I totally agree he needs to do whatever you say, but I don't know if he can be anything but Dragon-Beast-Master-Guy."

Alex sighed. "I know. I still need him to try." She stood, and reached down to pull Mar up. "C'mon we better get back. What time do you leave?"

Mar waved her hand and sand and grit fell off them. Their towels folded themselves and climbed into the beach bag. "Tomorrow at five in the morning. My flight leaves Greece at noon. Though if your brother had anything to say about it, I'd have been outta here a week ago."

Alex reached down to pick up the perfectly packed bag on their way back to the castle. She wiggled her eyebrows at Mar. "It's because you're cramping his style. His harem won't go near him with you here."

"Well I don't give a shit if they jump him in the great hall."

"Sure." Alex hesitated a moment. "Have you ever had a serious boyfriend?"

Mar winked. "A lot of wishful thinkers out there. But no. I like hot, juicy dates. Nothing serious for this girl."

Alex plodded up the hill as Mar carried on behind her.

"I mean, I been busy perfecting my skills. Guys get in the way. Neeren's groupies can calm down. I'm not clamoring to jump Sir Cat's bones."

Alex prodded, as Mar caught up to her, "Anyone else that might be worried about you while you're here?"

"Nope. I told you. Only boy toys for me."

"I mean like sisters? Brothers? Parents?"

A shadow covered Mars eyes for the briefest second. "No one." She shook her hair. Winked. "I was born from the mouth of magic."

Alex rolled her eyes before replying, "I'm sorry I won't be able to see you off. I have training. Mom and Aunt Quinn are ridiculously strict with my schedule."

They'd reach the top of the path by then. Alex looked back down at the beach. Sand glistened below. The waning sun cast a red glow over everything.

"Are you going to tell her you're leaving?" Mar asked.

"Yes. I hope she understands."

Mar held her hand again and squeezed. "She will. You're her daughter."

Chapter 5

The next morning Mar waited on the dock as Neeren's staff loaded her luggage onto the speedboat. Salt from the ocean clung to her skin. The wind blew her hair about her shoulders. She was dressed head to toe in butter yellow leather that clung to her curves and accentuated the dark hazel of her eyes. She looked good enough to eat and she fucking knew it.

On the cliff edge, stood Neeren. The sun rose behind him as he surveyed the scene. His ebony hair glistened. Her breath hitched as he strode down the path toward her. Really, he sauntered, in no hurry. It annoyed her.

She waved at him. Yelled, "Hi, kitty," and grinned at the collective gasp from his staff. His step faltered, for only a second. She'd take it.

Before the binding, Neeren had always seemed to be around, checking on her and Alex. Brushing up against her. Offering assistance with a glimmer in his eye. He'd even tried having a few flirtatious conversations with her. As far as she knew, women threw themselves at his feet. The entire immortal world heard stories of the secret Parthen King and his harem of groupies. She understood—to an extent. The guy was gorgeous. If you went in for the whole cold as stone, perfectly polished, put the lady on a pedestal, thing.

After the binding, he'd changed. The flirting stopped. His actions became more intentional. More intense. He knew what she'd seen. He didn't have to pretend to be indifferent with her. Every time he spoke to her, she felt like he was claiming her. Tasting her. She couldn't tell Alex. She didn't know what it meant.

Returning to the task at hand, she contemplated her airline tickets. She was scheduled to meet with Collum in Greece for a debrief before joining the other guardians in Vancouver. Mar still felt guilty about keeping the news from Alex.

Mar brushed ocean salt off her leather top. No matter what, she was shopping before any job or visiting occurred. She needed a new outfit for the big intro.

She stared out to the water. Refused to look at the Cat King as he walked onto the dock. Being in his presence annoyed her. She felt his hot breath on her neck. His calm, measured breathing.

"Seriously, do you have no understanding of personal space?" Mar complained, baring her teeth.

She pointedly studied the sea. It was still. As clear as glass. She remembered Alex telling her the sea around the island followed Neeren's emotions. How could anyone be calm all the time? It was disturbing. He didn't lack emotions. She'd felt them. What was it?

"I'm nowhere near you," he retorted.

She turned back, ready to blast him, only to see he was on the other side of the dock. His perfectly manicured, bare feet, poked out from under gray slacks. Knowing she'd have to face him to say goodbye, she squared her shoulders. He stood, feet apart, shoulders back. His hands lazily settled in his pockets. His face chiseled. A slight smile lifted the corner of his upper lip. His hair glistened. Like silk. Like steel. If you couldn't tell he was a panther you'd have to be completely dense. If you couldn't tell he was a king, you'd have to be blind.

Heat pooled in her stomach the same time it surged up her neck. She grimaced and folded her arms across her chest.

Everyone knew the stories of the Parthen King. Even though no one knew who he was, they'd all heard he was a legendary lover with a harem of kittens at his beck and call.

Mar dropped her arms and lifted her chin. No way was she going to feel turned on. "Well, I can smell you from across the dock. When's the last time you showered? I thought cats liked to be clean."

She grinned as a wave hit the dock directly behind her.

Goddess, why was she nervous? She'd been inside his mind. What she'd seen had scared her a little. It had intrigued her as well. Made her realize there was more darkness and depth to him than she'd thought. Maybe he wasn't just a player. She hadn't wanted to know. Could she know what he was and still be a little turned on by him?

His voice carried across the dock, smooth as butter. "You are in fine form today. Tell me, how much work is it always trying to come up with witty one-liners?"

Mar grimaced. "You're mean. The others may not see it, but I do. You don't like being told, no."

He tilted his head to the side, "And you are a child trying to play an adult game, Maria."

"Fuck you."

He laughed. "Are you offering?"

He sauntered across the dock crumbling her resolve to find him undesirable. Muscles pulsed in his legs with each step. He invaded her space for real, this time. Ran one finger down her arm.

She ignored the tingling sensation and stepped back. "Now who's playing a game? You're pissed I bound your dreamwalking power against the elementals. I might be young compared to you. But I'm not a child, *compañero*."

"True. Do you think you will stop me from taking what I want?" He shrugged. "I can still walk into your dreams, little girl."

"Kitty, you have no clue. I'd turn you into a fur purse if you try any shit against my will."

"So, invite me." He leaned in. Behind them water began to rock the boat against the dock.

"Excuse me? Quit pretending you want me. You don't even like me."

"I do want you. I don't have to like you to want you." He nodded to the men on the deck before looking directly into her eyes. Challenging her. "I've wanted your rock hard little body since the day you arrived on my island and asked me to massage your shoulders."

"Is that what this is about?" she exclaimed. "I turned you down and it hurt your special feline feelings. Have you been trying to figure out how to get me in your bed since then?"

He simply grinned at her.

Mar shifted on her yellow stilettos and leaned in until her breasts touched Neeren's arm. "Everyone here thinks you're into me, but I'm just a challenge until the next thing comes along. Let me make this perfectly clear. I don't have sex with strangers or playboys. You're both."

Around them the sea began to foam. The staff loading the boat had disappeared. The captain headed below deck. The dock was deserted. Even the birds sought other shelter.

Neeren leaned into her breasts. A sinister smile curled his lips. He towered over her. Placed his hands on her hips. Stood perfectly still while staring.

"I'm no stranger Maria. You've seen who I am. I think you like it." He leaned down, lifted her hair off her shoulders and licked the side of her neck.

She forgot to breathe. Her lips parted. She swallowed quickly. He smelled like temptation. Goddess, she was tempted. Her feet remained rooted to the deck. Moisture flooded her mouth. "I told you not to touch me unless I asked you to."

"Ask me."

He nibbled sensitive muscles on her neck. His left hand kneading the soft flesh at her hip. His right tightened in her hair.

"I'll give you whatever you want. Ask me." His voice purred.

Her nipples tightened. She felt tipsy. Flush. Scorched where his hands kneaded. She turned her head. Only the slightest bit. It was all he needed. His growl burned into her stomach. Moisture slammed into her belly. His fingers gripped her.

He covered her lips with his. They were soft and hard at the same time. Insistent. Heat poured over her flesh. She'd never felt anything like his lips. She whimpered against his mouth.

He nibbled her lips. Licked. Bit them. Added more pressure until she opened her mouth. He moaned as he slid his tongue between her lips. Pressed one palm against her breast and slowly pushed against the hardened nipple.

Whimpering she leaned against his hand.

"Maria. Give me everything," Neeren's voice was guttural, dark.

With a flash of clarity Mar remembered what she'd seen in his mind. What he could do. She wasn't fooled. She'd had enough dark people in her life trying to take.

She pulled away and straightened her shirt. Took a moment to catch her breath before speaking. "I'm not doing this."

He stood in front of her perfectly calm as the world raged inside her chest. Waited. Like they had all the time in the world. Made no move to pull her back.

Mar flung thick hair over her shoulders and glared. "I know you, Neeren. I haven't told anyone because you're Alex's brother. I'm not putting her at risk because of your crazy shit." Her voice rose an octave. Came out strained. "You enjoyed hurting them."

Neeren took two steps back. Glanced at the water before focusing intense eyes on her face. The sea quieted. "I'm not defending myself to you."

"You enjoy killing."

"I'm a hunter. What do you expect?" Neeren closed his eyes and when he opened them again they were blank, emotionless. He was back to being king.

He pulled the purse off her shoulder and placed it in the boat. "You think you know me? I know you too. You like playing games." His lips parted on a slow grin. "I'm willing to play."

"Screw you," Mar replied. "I don't want to play anything with you."

"No? I can already smell how much you want me. You don't have to hide it."

Anger laced her voice. "I'm not willing to be a member of your harem. How could you not know that yet? Figure shit out, kitten."

A predatory smile curved his lips. "Done. I accept the challenge."

"What are you talking about? I didn't issue a challenge."

He reached out. Took her hand to help her on the boat. "You asked me to figure you out. I accept. Since I'm not locked on this island any longer it should be easy." He gently stroked along the flesh at her waist. "You'll see me soon, little witch."

His men wandered back onto the platform as Mar stood flabbergasted. She watched at a complete loss as he passed instructions to his men. He'd bested her. She didn't like it. She'd take his challenge. Twist him up in so many knots he'd beg her to let him run back to his island hideaway.

Chapter 6

Alex cleared her throat. "I'm leaving in the morning with Quinn."

"What, honey?" her mom said from across the gym.

She tried again. Aunt Quinn escaped the gym a few minutes before, leaving it to Alex to tell her mother they were going back to Victoria.

"I'm leaving in the morning with Quinn." She stumbled at her mother's shocked look. "I miss my job and my home in Victoria. It's beautiful here. Really. Maybe you and Neeren can come visit me."

"This is your home now. You will be safe here."

"I don't need to be safe here anymore, Mom." She begged her to understand. "I was raised among humans. I'm not comfortable here. I . . ."

Gray interrupted her. "What can you possibly mean you aren't comfortable here? Everything is taken care of. You're a princess."

"I know." Alex studied the gym floor. The skylight ceiling. Weapons glistening along bamboo walls. Each item painstakingly polished after a training session. Just as the grounds were groomed after each outdoor session. From day to day, you'd never know, she, her mother, and aunt ripped the earth apart with wind and fire. The Island offered perfection. Everywhere. Everyday. It was suffocating her.

"I miss my job. I'm a really good journalist and I want to go back."

Gray pursed her lips. "Journalism is beneath you. I

blame Quinn for this. She always had an interest in human work." She turned her back.

Alex stared out the glass wall to the sea beyond. Everything here was immaculate. There were no heavy walls. No dark colors. This castle felt a little like how she imagined heaven would. Everything soft. Clean. Warm. White.

Black panthers roamed the estate, standing out with glistening ferocity. Alex wondered if Neeren planned it that way.

Alex tried to reason with Gray. "It's not Quinn. It's me. I was raised in Victoria. I studied hard to get my degree. I want to use it. We're out of danger. I need to go back."

"It's my fault. If I'd brought you here sooner this would feel more like your home."

Alex shook her head, but didn't deny it. She walked over to her mother and wrapped her arms around delicate shoulders. Quinn said Gray was like a porcelain doll. Her mother lost everything twenty-five years earlier. She'd been brutalized. Her husband murdered in front of her. Her child ripped away from her. She was getting stronger physically. It would take much longer for her emotions to heal. If they ever did.

Alex squeezed her shoulders. "C'mon, Mom. I love you. Everything you did, you did to protect me. I understand. I'll love you forever for giving me a normal life. It's a life I enjoy."

"You are destined to be one of the strongest warriors in the world. Your powers exceed almost everyone except for your dragon and brother. If you stay and train, you'll be untouchable."

Gray hung her head. Her voice came out like a whisper. "Others will always come after you because of who you are. You're never going to have a normal life."

Alex tipped her head back and sighed. She'd known Gray wouldn't like this, but she still had to go. Neeren walked in the door as she prepared to convince her mom to come with her.

"Your friend, the witch, has departed," he blurted out.

"Not now, Neeren." Gray sniffed.

"What is going on? Mother, why are you crying?"

Just great, now she'd have to deal with Neeren in savior mode. Alex steeled herself for his inevitable reaction. "I'm leaving with Aunt Quinn in the morning. I told Mom and she's upset."

"Okay."

"That's it? Okay?" Alex's voice rose on the last word.

"I never thought you'd stay here forever."

Her mom pouted. "Well I did. This is our home."

Neeren walked to his mom and touched his forehead to hers. It always amazed Alex at how easily he could calm her.

"This is our home, Mother. I thought for a time it could be Alex's as well. But it isn't. Her place is where she began with her dragon." He lifted his face and smiled at Alex. "I promise there will always be a place for you here, if you want or need it."

Alex smiled. "I thought you'd freak out. You always talked about how it was our destiny to rule together."

"It is our destiny to rule together. I understand you might not do so entirely from here." He smiled a secretive smile. "I am also interested in seeing what the outside world can offer me."

Alex eyed him suspiciously. "You're fidgeting. You never fidget. You're a statue. What's going on?"

Her mom chimed in. "For heaven's sake. He's thinking about all the women he can meet out there." She wandered out of the room mumbling under her breath. "This is all Quinn's fault."

Alex slapped her brothers shoulder. "Are you planning on bedding the rest of the population now that you've made your way through the Parthen?"

He rubbed his left shoulder and raised a single brow. "Watch it, little sister. You're tougher than you look."

"Very funny. When did you start using sarcasm?"

"I'm taking cues from you and other visitors."

"This is about Mar, isn't it? You want to visit her, and you think letting me go will pave the way for you to do so."

"I am"—he shrugged—"undecided about the witch."

"She thinks you're too intense. You need to back off."

"Like your dragon has? You asked him to do so and now you haven't heard from him. Has this helped his case?"

Flames crawled up her neck. Her lips flattened into a straight line before she answered, "What goes on between Collum and I is none of your business."

"Maybe what goes on between the little witch and I is none of yours."

"See how little you know about women." She poked her finger into his chest. "I'm her best friend. Everything about her is my business."

Alex stood on her tiptoes and looked him right in the eyes. "Please tell me you didn't do anything creepy and stupid."

"I do not do creepy and stupid things."

"Riiiight, you keep telling yourself that." She pushed her tangled hair off her face. "God, now I'm going to have to call and apologize for my brother." She gasped. "Did you get handsy? Don't tell me you got handsy."

"I did not get handsy." He cleared his throat. Shoved his hands in his pockets. "What do you mean by handsy?"

Alex threw her hands in the air and spun away. "Crap. You did. For a guy who's supposed to be legendary with ladies, you are so dense. You better not have put a strain on my friendship or you're in a lot of shit, brother."

He righted himself and raised his brow again. Using her birth name, he replied, "Alexedria, you worry for no reason."

Before she could comment, her mother and Quinn rushed back into the room looking satisfied.

"Guess what," Quinn squealed. "Your mom is coming for Christmas."

Chapter 7

Mar stepped off the boat onto the bustling dock, becoming instantly enveloped in the big sights and sounds of the Greek people. Loud men laughing with other loud men. Beautiful women smoking cigarettes on the corner. Teenagers squealing with flirtatious delight. The scent of bitter coffee hung thick in the air. Coffee capable of holding up your spoon and coating your gut.

Broken marble pillars lay haphazardly strewn around the dock. Thrown on a whim by Gods with no further use for them. Their ancient energy vibrating within everyone who spoke. These were a people of history. Of legend.

Collum waited with hands folded across his chest. Legs apart. Every bit the legend Greek people whispered about in the dark. Mar waved. Smiled. She'd never had a big brother. It was almost eerie how quickly Collum fit the bill.

"Hey, Puff. Howz you?" Mar yelled across the dock.

Collum sighed but walked toward her smiling. "You have everything?"

She pointed to the luggage behind her. "All here."

"Three bags, Mar? How did you end up with three bags? You were only on the island a couple weeks. And we came with nothing."

"Seriously, dude? Those are carry-on. I've been living with three pairs of shoes for two weeks. Those cats are shit shoemakers."

Collum grimaced. "Don't tell me you went shoe shopping."

"Well of course I did. Once the big crisis was over, Alex and I did some sightseeing. It's a pretty cool little island she has there. Aside from the terrible shoe stores." She noticed his quick intake of breath at her besties name. "Yeah, Alex took me to all the places. Alex sure is a great lady. Smart. Funny. Tough. That Alex—what a woman."

He interrupted her. "I get it. I'm a dick. I haven't called. She asked me to back off. I did."

"Back off. Not disappear, dumb ass."

"Enough. I'll handle my relationship on my own."

Mar laughed at his pigheadedness. Poor guy had no chance. "Whatever you say, Puff. But don't come crying to me when it all blows up in your face because you waited too long to call."

"I'll endeavor to keep from doing so."

"Good, cause I'm team Alex all the way."

Collum scowled. "Did you tell her you were asked to be a guardian?"

"You know I didn't." She punched him the chest. Received a few odd looks from passersby. "It was a shitty thing to ask of me."

"If she accepts, you'll be able to soon enough."

"She's going to be even more pissed at you when she finds out."

"I know. Now hand me your bags."

Mar threw her bags at him. When he'd asked her to join the guardians she'd jumped at the chance. Being asked was one of the highest compliments of her life. She hoped Alex also accepted, and forgave her for keeping the secret. But Collum had been adamant. Being a guardian was a secret you carried with you to your grave. Secrecy was what kept them alive. As far as the world knew, Collum was the only guardian. It needed to remain so in order for them to effectively do their jobs.

Mar preferred to live a private life anyway. She had her own secrets. Having a team at her back would be nice for a change.

"Wake up, Mar." He snapped his fingers in front of her face.

"Sorry." She grinned. "Thinking of all the shoes I'm going to buy here. Greek sandals—oh la la."

"There is no time for shopping."

Her stomach flopped. "Excuse me. I don't think I heard you correctly. Cause I know you didn't say I can't go shopping."

"You heard me correctly."

"No, I really didn't. I need warrior clothes, buddy. Unless you want this guardian performing feats of intrigue in patent leather pumps and a pink bustier."

He snorted. "You're telling me you don't own sensible clothing."

"Um, none here." She fixed him with her toughest scowl. She didn't pout—ever. "I need clothes befitting my first mission."

Collum didn't blink, but he did give in. She'd consider it a win.

"Fine." He threw up his hands. Suitcases and all. "Head to the Kolonaki neighborhood. They have the best mix of luxury and local shops in Athens. Meet me at the apartment when you're done. You remember the address?"

Mar jumped up and kissed his cheek. Thankfully he bent down a bit to make it easier on her. Six-foot six-inches tall behemoth. "Do I? I never forget a thing. See you later, Puff."

~ ~ ~

Three hours and three thousand dollars charged to his expense account, later, Mar knocked on the door to Collum's Greek residence.

Collum opened the door scowling. "You're late."

She scowled back. "Didn't know I had a curfew, boss."

"What the hell did you buy?"

"Seriously, boss, you don't want to know. Just know I needed it all."

"Quit calling me that," he snapped.

Mar grinned. She still had it. "Sure thing, boss."

He scowled at her again but wisely said nothing else.

She followed him as he turned his back to her. "Hey, aren't you gonna help me carry these?"

"Nope."

"Jerk."

From the set of his shoulders, she thought he might have grinned. She hitched bags over her arms and pushed past him.

"I'm drinking your most expensive booze. All of it."

"You ship out at six tomorrow morning."

Mar pushed his office door open and threw her bags into the nearest corner. She ignored the antique furnishings; The millions of dollars of Greek artifacts lining the walls. She'd seen them before. Besides, see one dusty porcelain statue, you seen'm all.

She stomped to the liquor cabinet. Rooted through until she spotted a bottle covered in dust. She pulled the cork and took a swig. The liquid curled in her mouth. She spit it out before swallowing.

"What the hell?"

Except for a slight crinkling around his eyes, Collum's face remained impassive. "Vermouth. I don't make a lot of martini's. Now, if you're done destroying my carpet can we discuss your mission?"

"Already? Thought I was going to Vancouver to meet my new superhero teammates first?"

He rolled his eyes. "Some serious shit is going down now and I need you elsewhere."

Mar sniffed bottles on the top shelf, finally settling on a sweet-smelling bourbon. She plopped herself on a chair in front of the fireplace. Regally patted the one next to her. "Sure thing. I'm ready. What's the scope?"

Under her lashes, she studied Collum as he poured his glass. He was a fine specimen. No one could deny it. But a little too, been-there, done-that for her liking. She couldn't even rile him like she really wanted to. It was like he was always in on the joke. Fun but a little less satisfying than when she really blew someone's mind. Maybe it was because he was over two-thousand years old and a dragon?

He'd never own a bulldog. Would go for a wolfhound or something. She shook her head. Now why the hell had that thought entered her mind?

Collum's voice pulled her back to the moment at hand. He handed her a portfolio. "Five high-ranking immortals from different races have disappeared. My intel suggests they're in Madrid, Spain. The vampires are involved. Someone's making a play for more power."

Mar closed the portfolio and folded her hands across her lap. Her heart raced. "I might not be the best person for this one."

"I disagree. You are the only person I trust with this." He leaned over and grabbed her hands. "Look, I know this can be scary, overwhelming even. But you were asked to be a guardian for a reason. I have faith in you."

As he grinned she wondered if he realized he looked even more intimidating when he smiled. Either way, the smile wouldn't soothe her. Not if vampires were involved.

"You're Spanish. You're a relative unknown. You're cute enough to come across as no threat."

"Yeah, but . . ."

"We need you on re-con. I can't go. The other guardians are booked. Jason and Idris are busy with other things. Diana is in India and will be for the foreseeable future. I need you to ask a few questions. Go to a couple parties."

"I do like parties."

"The cover is you're working for Marcus Wu, VP of Televale Industries, researching potential Spanish partnerships in the media industry. He's been recruited to help us gather more intel. You're an intern. A highly valued one." He winked.

"In other words, people will think I'm his mistress checking stuff out for him in case he wants to break away from the family business?"

While she waited for him to reply, Mar placed the portfolio on her chair and poured another bourbon. Amber liquid splashed against the crystal glass. She gulped it back and poured again.

"People will think I'm a bed-hopper. I bought ninja clothes."

Behind her, Collum replied, "This is the job, Mar."

She squirmed. He had no idea of the risk she'd be taking. And she couldn't tell him. She loved Collum like a brother. The thought of losing his friendship because of her secret, terrified her. "Fine, but don't expect me to like it." She threw back another shot of bourbon before saying, "I'll see you later, after I go shopping for the appropriate sleazy outfit."

"You fly out in three hours," he reminded her.

"How very spy-like of me. Flying out in the cover of darkness."

"Just make sure you're back in time. And eat something for goodness sake."

"Yes, Dad." She flopped back in her chair.

Who would've thought she'd end up here. Friends with The Guardian. Besties with his lover. She'd never expected a Parthen King with a bulldog to be a part of the picture. Thought she'd be alone her entire life.

Mar grinned. "You know what? I'm good with what I have. I'll shop for what I need in Madrid. It will fit with the cover anyway."

She laughed at Collum. "People have a way of seeing what they want to see with me. They'll want to see a rich, Spanish girlfriend. So that's what I'll give them."

He raised his glass in a toast. "Take'm to school, Mar."

She took a deep breath and prepared to launch her future. "Plan on it, boss."

~ ~ ~

The air on the plane was suffocating. It had been years since Mar set foot in Madrid. She could hardly fathom why she agreed to do it now.

A four-hour flight. Far too long and unbearably too short. They'd only taken off and she was already suffering. Collum had purchased a first-class ticket. Thankfully she wasn't squished between other passengers, but she also couldn't use magic to ease her discomfort. The guy across the aisle was a big ol' Spanish dude dripping in gold. She knew the type—thought every woman on earth was mad for him. Spent every night alone. She pushed the call button on her chair.

A posh flight attendant appeared and asked Mar in Spanish, "Can I help you miss?

"Si, Una botella a augua por favour."

When the woman returned a minute later, Mar popped a valium, chugged the water, and settled in to her cubicle for the duration of the flight. She closed her eyes, adjusted her shoulders, and placed her headphones on to block the noise of the crew and passengers.

Five minutes later someone nudged her shoulder. She patted them away. Turned to her other side. The nudging continued.

"Vete ya estoy durmiendo," she said.

"I know you're sleeping. It's why I'm here."

The scent of oranges filled her nostrils. She jolted up. Came face to face with Neeren. "You jerk. I told you not to enter my dreams. What are you doing?"

He leaned over her, placing both hands on the sides of her chair. Her gut clenched. Green eyes, the color of summer. He licked his lips. His eyes narrowed.

"I wanted to see you."

Butterflies fluttered inside her ribcage. "Why?"

"To kiss you."

"What?" Her stomach dropped, and her toes curled.

He twirled a lock of her hair around his finger. His other hand remained on the arm rest. "It's okay. I'm a dream. You can kiss me, then pretend it wasn't real when you wake up." He grinned at her. "I'm risk free."

She thought about it. For a hot minute the idea made sense. She could have a little taste. Wake up pretending this had been a normal dream. But they both knew it wasn't. If Neeren was in her dream, it's because he'd placed himself there. It was as real as if he was sitting on the plane.

She glared at him. "I told you I won't play this game. Do you want me to curse you?"

He laughed. The sound was sinful. "No game. I'm giving you an out. You want to taste me. So, do it." He leaned in. His hot breath tickled her neck.

She dug her nails into the chair to keep from grabbing him and making a fool of herself. Her body leaned into him of its own accord. Breast to magnificent, rock hard, chest.

"Yes, baby." He lifted his other hand to stroke her arm.

The word baby brought her back from the edge. He called her Maria. Not baby. She wasn't one of his harem and she wouldn't be seduced like one.

She pushed against his granite chest. "My name is, Maria, asshole. Don't call me, baby."

He tilted his head and stared. Like what she said meant something.

She barely refrained from kneeing him in the groin. "I don't like you. Remember?"

He sat back on his haunches. "Keep telling yourself this . . . Maria." A devastating grin curled his lips before asking his next question. "Why are you going to Madrid?"

"How do you know I'm going to Madrid?"

He pointed to the airline ticket sticking out of her purse. She shoved it back down. So much for being a sleuth.

"Stop snooping. Where I go is none of your business."

"I've decided to make you my business."

She almost called the flight attendant over to complain about his bothering her. But of course, it would do no good. They were in her dream. In truth, she was sound asleep in her flight cubicle. Old rich dude probably snoring next to her.

An errant thought interrupted. Was she talking in her sleep? "Hey, does this conversation happen in the waking world too?"

"What?"

She could tell she'd thrown him off balance with her question. Good. Time to take her power back.

She teased him, "Slow, kitty. I asked you, if we're talking in my dream and it's supposedly real, am I talking in my sleep?"

"No. No one else is privy to my being here. As far as the rest of the plane is concerned you are sleeping peacefully."

"But if you cut me or something, I'd bleed?"

He looked appalled. Outraged. Her stomach fluttered again.

"I would never hurt you." Anger glittered in his eyes. Green summer turned to a thunderstorm. "Maria, do you think I would hurt you?"

She took a deep breath. It was now or never. "I've been in your brain, Neeren. Have seen what you can do. What you've done. For you, hurting people is as easy as breathing."

And there it was. Anger shifted to something else. Not regret. She'd been hoping for regret. He sat back again. Pushed the sleeves of his black sweater off his forearms. They were muscled. Covered in soft black hair. His skin tanned. She studied his hands. Would they be hot against her skin? How many times had he wrapped them around someone's neck and squeezed?

"Look at me, Maria. For me, offering death to some is easier than breathing." He gently cupped her chin. Made her face him. "They hurt my mother. Tried to rape her." He closed his eyes. Inhaled air on a long sigh. "They deserved it."

Tears stung her eyes. "I'm sorry. I'm so sorry. But to do what you did? Surely there was another way."

"What? A more humane way to kill your enemy? Be real. What bothers you is I turn you on. You want me, even knowing I can and will rip my enemies mind apart, and that I'll take pleasure in doing it."

A ragged breath escaped her aching chest. "You killed twenty parthen—an entire campsite—with one thought. They were awake and aware, Neeren. The last thing they saw was you smiling at them."

"I fucking hope so." His lip curled into a sneer. "Tell anyone you wish, Maria. I hid myself for close to a hundred and fifty years to protect my mother and sister. No more. If you want to tell people I can kill shifters and humans alike by thinking it, for fucks sake do it, and stop lording it over me."

She bit the inside of her cheek. "I saw you. You were cold, calculated. There was no feeling. It was like you weren't there. Like killing is as easy as tying your shoes."

"No. It requires much less effort. I was born to be a hunter. A killer." He shook his head. Like he was disappointed in her. "You felt what this power feels like when you bound me. That was a fraction. A minuscule moment. I live feeling this immense power every fucking second. The only way"—a haunted growl tore from his throat—"the only fucking way my people survive is for me to be in control of every emotion I've ever had. That is my life."

The blanket on her lower legs covered her like dead weight. He could kill any shifter or human with a thought. By blinking his eyes. Yet the first time they'd met he'd tried to cop a feel. Had been trying ever since. Maybe he wasn't evil. The thought crashed into her brain with the force of a freight train. It didn't matter. She was a witch. A human. That put her at risk. She had enough to deal with. Mar sat up and pushed the blanket off her feet.

Her eyes begged him to understand. "People who swore they loved me have hurt me before. Because they couldn't control themselves. Or wouldn't. I can't take that risk again."

"I'm not them. I won't take the blame for what they did."

He stepped back, leaving her with the distinct feeling she'd just lost something important.

He shook his head. "You can believe me or not when I tell you I don't hurt innocents. I'm a hunter. I will kill again. I'll do it in any way I need, to protect my people. And I'll be rock solid."

He turned from her to listen to something in the distance. "Your plane is landing soon. You need to wake up. When you do, remember that I'm not the one who hurt you."

Before she understood what he was doing, he leaned over and kissed her. His soft lips pushed against hers. Gentle. Careful. Electricity shot through to her core. Her lips opened on a moan. He pushed his tongue into her mouth.

He tasted like a summer thunderstorm. Like fresh air. The calluses on his hands scratched her skin. Tingling reverberated straight into her tightening nipples. She whimpered. Arched against him. He leaned in, deepening the kiss. Rocked his body against hers. Her fingers gripped the back of his neck. He purred. A jungle cat feasting.

She feasted back. Let all her confusion pour into the kiss. His mouth felt like a lifeline. Like safety. The thought poured through her like warm milk and cinnamon. The smell of oranges wrapped around her. For a moment, she felt a contentment she'd never known.

The kiss ended before she was ready.

He pulled back on a sigh. Stroked her hair. Whispered against her cheek, "I'm done playing. Goodbye, Maria."

The flight attendant shook her awake at the same time as the pilot's voice came over the loud speaker saying they were preparing to land. Tears poured down her cheeks.

"Oh, *Mi Ami*. Did you have a bad dream?" the woman asked.

Mar didn't know how to answer. She'd got what she'd wanted. Hadn't she? Neeren was gone. Why did that thought tear a hole in her chest?

~ ~ ~

Check-in at the hotel was relatively simple. Admiring glances came fast and hard, at least until Mar told the clerks her booking was under the Wu family. Afterward, there was so much bowing and scrapping it was all she could do not to gag.

The hotel was, of course, the best money could buy. Appearances must be kept up. It was a good thing the guardians budget was unlimited. Neeren would probably think it was a hovel.

In true Spanish style, the rooms were small but elegantly decorated. The bedroom walls reminded her of a Seville sunset. Lush pillows framed the bed like an artist's pallet. Merlot carpets covered the floors. A bouquet of roses sat on the side table and filled the room with the scent.

It was six in the morning and she was wide awake. She laid on the bed. Tried to close her eyes but images of Neeren were tattooed to the backs of her eyelids. She punched the mattress. Covered her head with a pillow. Her stomach growled. She rolled to the edge of the bed. If she couldn't sleep she might as well eat. A walk on the main street might burn off her extra energy. That's what she'd do. She had to do something other than stare at the walls.

The cell phone buzzed behind her head. She swatted blindly for it and pulled it to her ear.

"You've reached Mar," she said, thinking it was Collum checking in.

Neeren's voice came through instead. She almost dropped the phone.

"You landed safe? Why didn't you call me?" Annoyance rang in his voice.

Mar rolled her eyes. "I don't have to check in with you."

"It is considered common courtesy, Maria. I'm sure you knew I'd be wondering."

"No. I didn't. It never occurred to me to call you. Seriously. Why would you care?"

"You are Alex's friend. This makes you"—he quieted for a moment—"important. Someone should check in with you and I believe you have no family."

She cringed. "What makes you think that?"

"You did not speak of a mother or father during your time at the island and I have never heard you on the phone with anyone. I assumed . . ."

She cut him off before he went too far. "Well don't assume shit. You know what they say when you assume right. Makes an ass out of you and me."

He snorted on the end of the line. "What a ridiculous statement. Very well, Maria. You have tons of family you simply do not wish to talk to me about."

"Both my family, and what I want to talk about, are none of your business."

She almost felt him roll his eyes. She knew she was acting petulant, but she couldn't stop herself.

"You have arrived safe?"

She sighed. "Yes. I've arrived safe. I'm hungry though. I can't sleep, and I have killer jet lag after the flights from Parthen to Greece and then to here in Madrid." Now why did she tell him that?

"Go to Salvador Bachiller Jardin Secret. It is on the fourth floor above the shops on Calle Monstera, not far from the Gran Via. You'll love it. It's mostly locals and they have decent coffee."

Surprise raised her voice. "I thought you'd spent your life hidden on your island. How do you know about local haunts in Madrid?"

"I said I spent my life hiding. I did not say I'd never been anywhere."

"Not the vibe you give off."

He chuckled. It was a soft sound.

"It was important people remained ignorant to my occasional sojourn off island. There were times I'd disappear for a few days to myself. As far as anyone knew I was meditating in the caves in the south side of the island."

"I think Alex and I drove there one day. It's beautiful. Ragged and barren with all that volcanic rock."

"The south has always been my favorite part of the island. The way the waves crash against the cliff edges with raw intensity."

She couldn't believe he was confiding in her. It was . . . nice. It made him seem normal. Not that she'd ever tell him. "Where else have you been?"

"Only Europe. Never anywhere in Asia or the America's. I would like to see the mountains in Canada—where Alex came from."

He paused again and she had the sense he was testing the taste of his words before he spoke. "Would you like me to visit you in Madrid?"

She rested her head on the pillow. His voice was soft, lulling her into thinking they were having a normal conversation. It wasn't true of course. He was a killer. She needed to remember that. What if he lost control around her? Like her Mother had.

"Maria?"

She sat up. Stuttered, "No. No I don't want you to come here, Neeren. You told me you didn't want to play games. Neither do I. You aren't right for me."

"You don't know that."

"You invaded my mind on the plane. I told you not to enter my dreams, but you did anyway. Almost as soon as you could."

"I did."

"Why?"

Silence hung in the air as she waited for his answer. Distance colored the sound of his voice when he finally answered. "Because I could."

Disappointment crashed over her. "Because you could? Really?"

"Yes."

His voice came across cold, controlled. A reminder of why she couldn't be with him.

"Well, you can't come here. I don't invite you. I'm busy and I don't want you here."

"You are lying to yourself, Maria."

"Wrong, kitten. You don't know anything about me." She stood up. Paced the small room. Dug her toes into the carpet. She flicked her wrist and the wrinkles on the bed disappeared. Magic skittered across her fingertips. "I'm here on a contract and you'll only get in my way."

"I can help you."

"You think I'm a plaything. I don't need your help," she bit out. "What I'm doing is important and it matters to me. You don't."

She almost apologized. The truth was he'd begun to matter a little. But her course was set. She couldn't risk him getting involved. Couldn't risk trusting him. She'd trusted darkness before. It almost killed her.

This time she heard his sigh. "Very well, little witch. I will leave you alone." Ice crystallized his words.

Tears burned at the back of her throat. The sounds of early morning traffic echoed through her window. A car horn blasted. Spanish swearing erupted as an irate pedestrian told off the driver of the car. It was the sound of life. Of chaos. It was how she blocked out the silence of death. The silence of her childhood.

She bowed her head as she spoke. "Thank you. Don't come to me in my dreams anymore either."

"You have made this clear."

She pulled the phone away from her ear. Maybe if she concentrated, his face would appear on the screen. It would be rock hard, she knew. His eyes would be emerald shards. They would look at her with disdain now. There would be no heat. That was what she wanted. Wasn't it? To end whatever this was before it began.

"Good. As long as we're clear." Her voice caught. "Look I . . . I gotta go. Breakfast, remember? No hard feelings. Bye, kitten."

She hung up before he could say a word. Before he told her another story. Before she caved.

~ ~ ~

Ten minutes later Mar surveyed the sleeping city. Quiet before the sun rose. In an hour, the streets would be filled with life.

The streets of Madrid had a music all their own. The people were her people. Her culture. Breathing deep, she let the early morning air fill her lungs. Soon it would be too hot to think, let alone wander. Explore now. Air-conditioned shopping later.

It'd been six years since she'd been here. Another ten years before then. Her Nonna and Nonno owned a little shoe shop she visited often as a child. When they felt it necessary to remove her from her mother's presence for a while. She didn't like to think about those days.

Salty tears burned behind her eyes. No. She wouldn't cry. Not now. She stopped crying for her mother a long time ago.

Isabella—the woman had never been a real mother. Always seemed jealous of the power Mar wielded. Even at a young age it had been evident Mar would be more powerful than almost any of the Wicca before her.

In the end her mother found what she'd been searching for. A swarm of death followed. The details were shaky. Mar'd been so young. Her grandparents murdered. Her mother at fault, yet screaming for revenge. Bouts of insanity and lucidity. Blood.

Terror takes on many faces. Isabella wore them all. There were days Mar loved her so hard. When the woman recalled she was a mother. The other days . . .

Thankfully the American branch of the Wicca council got Mar out when they did. She'd spent ten years with them. Ten blissful years.

When she was eighteen she decided to return to Madrid and see if it still held memories. The witches, with the help of her ancestors, cloaked her. Blocked her mind from any intrusion as a way of trying to keep her mother at bay. The block remained in place to this day.

Secrets. She held many.

An appreciative whistle brought her back to the present. She smiled at the group of young men who whistled at her. Still drunk. Likely on their way home from a party the night before.

She waved. Yelled, "Hi, boys" at them. Red-faced, they ran the other way with embarrassed laughter. Her lips curled with humor. Keep them off guard. Always a good motto to have.

As she looked around she realized she'd gotten herself lost. Madrid was a maze of endless cobblestone side streets and back alleys, filled with ancient brick buildings, and mom and pop shops. She tried to find her bearings. The traffic from the Gran Via a faint whisper. Mar had no idea if she was facing north or south. She was lost on an empty street filled with early morning shadows.

Unease crept up her spine. The hair on her arms stood on end.

Two old men wearing moth ball covered suits and bolero hats entered from the other end of the street.

She waved them over *"Disculpe? Dónde puedo encontrar la Calle Monsterra?"* They looked at her with glazed eyes. She tried again in English. "Calle Monsterra? I'm looking for a secret coffee shop on the fourth floor of a building there."

They continued to stare blankly ahead. A shiver raced down her spine. She shook it off. Tried a final time. "My friend told me of this place. Do you know it?"

The sound of heels clipping against cobblestone rang out behind her. A dragging noise followed. Her blood turned cold. Understanding settled in her bones. They'd found her. So quickly? She'd been stupid. Careless.

She spun toward the sound. Arms raised. Magic poised on the edges of her fingers. Ready to fight with everything she had.

A woman dressed in black stood at the edge of the shadow with a baby in her arms. One hand wrapped around its neck. Beside her, a young woman with silent tears running down her agonized face; held in check by the fear of her child's imminent death.

Ice filled Mar's veins as the woman spoke. "Maria Del Voscova. We've been looking for you."

"What is this? Some kind of shitty prank? Did Andrew send you?" Mar asked, trying for the mistaken identity ploy.

"Come now or I kill the child. Right here. Right now." The woman's words were clipped. Measured for full effect.

Mar knew she meant it. This kind had done so before. Would do so again. Liquid terror poured through her bones. Fleeing should have been the priority. Escape before more of them showed up. More always showed up. But she had to save the kid.

The Vamp sneered.

Her mother had taught them well.

Mar threw her shoulders back with fake bravado. "Great. She sent the welcoming party I see. Couldn't come up with something a little more original? A baby? Really?"

"I have orders not to kill you. I'm allowed to kill anything else." The vamp inclined her head to the infant in her arms. "Do not temp me."

Mar noticed the length of her fangs. She was an old one. A strong one. Obviously, they were determined this time. She rubbed the tips of her fingers together. Felt the pull of the magic inside her.

"I can feel the spell you're attempting to weave. The air reeks of your magic. Do not push me, child," warned the vampire before dragging one long finger nail along the infant's leg.

The smallest drop of blood appeared. A tiny cry tore from its throat. The mother fell to her knees, begging for the return of her baby. The old men sidled closer.

Mar dropped her hand. Memories of other dead children clouded her mind. Her mouth parched. Her bravado turned to dust.

"You are to be returned." Vamp bitch stretched out her hand. One finger coated in blood. "Come before it's too late for this one."

"What's your name?" Mar asked quietly.

"Melisandre. Come closer to me."

"Do you know why she wants me, Melisandre? She wants to steal my life. To imprison me inside her."

Melisandre shrugged lithe shoulders. "Why should I care. I have my orders."

"Give the child to her mother and I'll join you. I can't promise I'll come easy though. You're asking me to die for you."

Melisandre sneered at her. Death hung in her eyes. Hair the color of ice flowed down her back. "Make this easier on yourself."

"Yeah, well dying is never easy, is it?" Mar pulled the magic back to her fingers.

Melisandre shook her head and handed the child over. "Bite it," she said to the young woman at her side.

The crying woman raised her head and grinned. All tears were gone. Mar knew then they had tricked her. She'd seen what they wanted her to see—a bereft mother. Before she could react, the vampire lowered her head to the child's neck. A wail bounced off the building walls.

Mar dropped to her knees like a stone. "Stop. Stop," she screamed. "Stop. I'll come!"

Melisandre flicked her hand at her partner. She ceased her feeding.

"Tell me you stopped her in time," Mar begged. Grit dug into her knees. Ice wrapped itself around her throat.

Melisandre inspected her finger nails like nothing had happened. Like they weren't discussing the life and death of a baby. "The infant is alive for now. Once I return you, it will go on to live a long and healthy life. It is your choice."

Mar's shoulders slumped. Regret racked her body. She put her hands out in front of her and closed her eyes in surrender.

Neeren's face appeared. His haunting face. His thunderstorm eyes. He wouldn't know what happened to her.

Sure, Collum would send people if she didn't check in after a couple days. By then it would be too late. He wouldn't think to worry about her earlier. No one would. No one knew her past.

Fuck that.

As the vampire reached for her, Mar swung up her clasped fists. A direct hit. Vamp dropped like a stone. Spinning to the left Mar used magic to hurl the infant from the other vamp's arms. It flew easily through the air and landed safely on a small patio three stories up.

Lead vamp and the other rushed her. So it was to be brute strength? Mar swung with everything she had. Blocking blows, both magical and real, while flipping through the spell book in her mind. She threw out a protection spell to soften the blows raining down on her back.

The two old men on the other side of the alley shifted to young vampire warriors and rushed her. One wrapped cold arms around her neck attempting to choke the life from her. Mar tore at rock arms to no avail. She'd never defeat them this way.

"Don't kill her," shouted the lead vamp. "They need her alive."

The pressure on her windpipe eased. Mar searched her mind for a magical weapon. She spun a shadow spell to block them from prying human eyes. Then she let them beat her. Placed her hands on the earth rather than try to block the blows. She called upon mother earth. Called for her ancient protection. For life to wipe out death. Roots burst up from between cracks in the pavement, wrapping around the feet of her four assailants. Vines crawled up their arms and around their waists. The blows stopped as the four fell to the ground.

Heaving, Mar pushed herself off the ground and dusted her legs off. She grabbed a shard of tree root and plunged it deep into the male vamp who'd been attempting to strangle her.

He faded to dust as his companions struggled against their bonds.

Mar sneered at the lead vamp. "Not so tough after all hey, bitch." She raised her hands to plunge the makeshift stake into her chest.

Even as Mar spoke the words, the vines holding her adversary rotted and fell from her arms. Death destroying any life that tried to touch it. Vamperilla raised her hands in time to stop Mar's blow. She clasped Mars neck and squeezed. The roots holding the remaining two vamps gave way as quickly.

Iron bands were clamped around her wrists as Mar struggled for air. Magic pulsed through the metal. She'd be unable to defend herself in any way with these on. It was one of the first spells she'd been forced to learn. How to keep a magical being from calling forth their power. She collapsed, angry at her stupidity and cockiness.

Melisandre removed her hand and grinned down at her. "I told them you would be easy to bring in."

"Check your shit, bitch. That wasn't easy on any of us. Especially dust boy there." Mar inclined her head to the dust swirling on the concrete by her feet.

Melisandre laughed. "They knew the risks." Her voice as cold as the dust settling in Mar's veins. The vampire flicked her wrist again. A mist wafted through the street. When it dispersed, the baby crying on the patio shifted to a small fluffy cocker spaniel. It wriggled contently from its perch, oblivious to the danger it'd been in.

Mar slumped in defeat.

"We've been learning," Melisandre said.

"No. You're nothing but a vessel," Mar retorted. "My mother's been stealing power and placing it in you—for a time. Don't kid yourself into thinking you have any magical power."

The woman nostrils flared. "You know nothing."

"I know you'll be dust soon enough."

Melisandre took an angry step toward her.

Mar winked. "Careful now. You don't want to upset, Isabella." She lifted her chin a notch. She wasn't giving up yet. "I've hidden long enough. Take me to my Mother."

Chapter 8

Neeren hung up the phone. He leaned back on his pillow. Placed his arms behind his head in satisfaction. He'd heard the catch in Maria's voice. She could pretend if she wanted but he knew he'd cracked her armor. What he still couldn't figure out was why she was so unwilling to try something with him.

So, he killed people. So, what. He only killed those who deserved it. He knew what death felt like. He'd died a million times over after his father had been murdered. His dreams racked with images of his baby sister being offered death before life. Watched his mother turn into a shadow. Her entire existence became a living reminder of death.

He could kill his people with a thought. He lived with this enormity every second of his life. Not a moment was he unaware. Not a fucking moment.

He knew what death felt like. He didn't meter it out lightly.

Besides, every one of Maria's friends killed people. Even Alex. He refused to believe that was the reason.

Daisy snored at his feet. He pulled the slobbering beast up to his chest. She sunk in. Snuggled against him. Snored loud in her contentment. He still couldn't believe Alex had talked him in to adopting the dog. They'd found her two days after the battle with the elemental. Alex had been searching online pet adoption sites—apparently, this was something humans did when they were stressed or bored. Daisy's ridiculous face popped up on the screen. They'd both laughed at her. He'd made some offhand comment about wanting to scratch her belly. The next thing he knew Alex emailed the adoption agency in Greece and he was the owner of a seven-year-old, overbred English bulldog with breathing problems.

Quinn flew to Greece the next morning to pick up the animal. Neeren expected the dog would want to be around Alex or Quinn. Nope. For some reason, it wriggled right up to him, started pawing at his leg, and whimpering to be picked up. So, he did. He picked the damn dog up. Now he couldn't get rid of it.

He scratched her behind the ears and she snorted in gratitude. The dog had had a rough life. She'd had six litters stolen from her. Had lived in a concrete prison before the rescue group found her. Neeren knew what it was like to be caged.

Yet the dog still wriggled her behind when she met someone knew. Still barked and squirmed in joy. Having her around gave him hope. It was ridiculous. He'd never tell anyone. Prayed one day he'd feel lightness too. Hope.

Maria brought out sparks of hope every time he was around her. With her antics. The way she argued with him. The way she put him in his place. The way his desire for her numbed the throbbing power in his mind.

He wondered if she would like his bedroom. She'd seemed to admire the rest of his castle. This spot was his oasis. As open as the ocean. His bed floated above the floor in the middle of the room. Held by invisible wires from charred beams attached to the ceiling. The floor was made of the same charred wood panels from the old boat house.

He and his father spent countless hours there, oiling the boats, talking about what it meant to be a man. A leader. After his death, Neeren ordered the building burned to the ground. Thankfully he'd come to his senses in time. Put the fire out before everything turned to ash. All the wood was charred though. It was right to have the wood in his room. It was a reminder.

With a final rub of Daisy's belly, he climbed out of the bed, and pulled on trousers and a white cotton shirt. There was work to be done. His kingdom wouldn't run itself.

~ ~ ~

Neeren carried his morning coffee into his office. Sunlight poured in through floor to ceiling windows. Priceless works of art lay scattered along the floor. One entire wall was covered in books. He'd read every book on those shelves. Everyone from Dante to Margaret Atwood. One year, he'd locked himself in this room and read. 2001 had not been good for him. It was the only time he'd given in to his grief. His mother barely survived it.

His desk, a piece of art itself, melded with layers of silver and bamboo, sat in the middle of the room. No clutter covered the surface. His Mac computer lay in the center of the desk. He booted it up and turned on iTunes. After scrolling a minute, he chose Lana Del Rey. Let her voice wash over him as he started his day.

The coffee was strong. As he sipped, memories of Maria bragging about Glenn's coffee surfaced. Glenn worked for Collum and was revered among the immortal world for his coffee. He did more of course. Anyone who thought otherwise was a fool. His sister mentioned Glenn and Collum were close. He didn't know of anyone else who could say the same about that dragon.

Below him, waves broke softly against the shore. The sea was clam today. For too many years he lived in turmoil. No longer. The island sighed. He sighed with it.

Quinn and Alex left the night before. He'd miss their vibrant energy, but he was a solitary man. He wouldn't mind a few days alone before removing the cloaking from the island. He didn't have to hide anymore. It was an exhilarating thought.

An easy knock on the door pulled him out of his reverie. He turned the music down. "Enter."

Talon Breton strolled through the door. Neeren grinned at the man. They'd known each other since childhood. Used to chase the girls in skirts around town. Talon now ran the university. He was a large bear of a man with chestnut hair—a rarity on the island. Most of the people who populated the island were shifters of the panther variety. Talon was an eagle. His family had been here forever. His father ran the university before Talon, and had been friends with Neeren's father.

"We haven't spoken in some time. How are you?" Neeren asked his old friend, clapping him on the shoulder.

"Did they all leave?" the man asked in his easy style.

Neeren laughed. "Yes, they all left."

"About time."

Talon sat on a cream couch in the corner and Neeren laughed again. Talon was the only being on the island who'd ever treated him as an equal. He'd been a good friend. Had never cared Neeren was king. Talon was also a recluse. They would often go for months without speaking.

"So, tell me about everyone," Talon said. "What's your sister like? What about the petite brunette always hanging around her? The students say she led the dragon here."

Neeren's gut clenched at the mention of Maria. He still tasted her lips on his lips. He sat beside his friend and offered him his coffee. Talon didn't drink. Had never touched alcohol.

Neeren grinned. "My sister is perfect, of course. Strong. She will make a good queen if she desires it."

"And the witch?" Talon asked. He sipped the coffee, nodding his thanks.

Neeren found himself stalling. "The witch was . . . confusing. Wild. Aggravating. I still do not know what to make of her. I couldn't reach into her mind. There is a block."

"But you want her?"

"Yes, I do. Why the interest? You've never cared before."

"There's been talk. That she affected you. You seem lighter than before. I noticed as soon as I walked in the room."

Neeren paused. He leaned back on the couch. "I am unchanged."

"Were you just listening to pop music?"

"Yes."

"And you have a pet?"

"Yes. But the poor beast needed me."

Talon laughed. "Neeren, old friend when I walked in this room you clasped my shoulder. You never show such easy affection. Ever."

"What are you talking about? We have been friends since childhood."

"And since your father's death, we haven't hugged. Not once." Talon sipped the coffee as Neeren cocked his head.

"My people touch me all the time."

"You never touch back. Not unless you're fucking someone." Talon smirked.

Neeren stuttered. "I . . . That can't be correct."

"It's okay. You have your reasons. Now, though. People talk. They say you've been seen watching the witch."

"My sister has been here." Neeren straightened his pant pleat. "If I have been watching her it is only because she spends time with my sister."

"Friend, stop lying to me. It's a good thing. It's time you came back to life."

"You know I cannot lose myself over her. You know the consequences if I do."

"You can lose yourself a little." Talon shook his head. "You've had this control beaten into you, your entire life. Liking a woman will not mean the end of your control."

"What if it does?" Neeren rarely showed weakness to anyone. But he trusted Talon with his life. With all his secrets.

"If you lose control I'll be there to stop you. As I promised when we were eight."

Neeren glanced at the floor. Rubbed his feet on the oiled wood. The coolness driving an ease into his body. It's why he never wore shoes. He needed the grounding connection with the earth like he needed water to breathe.

Talon stopped him back then, when Neeren had been on the edge of destruction. All because of some temper tantrum. His parents refused to allow him to go on a school field trip to Greece. Neeren hadn't fully understood at the time why mother and father kept him sheltered on the island.

He'd despised his father after realizing he couldn't leave because of who his father was. Cursed him. Screamed that he wished he'd drown. His father started choking on water. Coughing it up. Talon punched Neeren in the face. Knocked him out before his dark thoughts killed his father.

Thank God he'd recovered. Neeren still remembered the haunted look on his father's face. Control training began that day. Meditation. Martial Arts. Sensory deprivation. Everything they could think of. Talon had been his best friend and confident ever since.

Talon's blunt voice interrupted his thoughts. "You going to visit her?"

"Yes. She's in Madrid on secret business. I will go see her in a few days. Give her some time."

"Why wait?"

Neeren grinned. "I didn't wait. I joined her in her dreams and she is upset. Plus, she keeps harping about me killing my enemies."

"Really? But that's what you do with an enemy. You kill it."

Neeren threw his hands up. "Exactly what I said."

"Is she squeamish?"

"No." Neeren laughed. "She is tough. Strong. Doesn't take hell from anyone."

"Well then, she's probably just playing hard to get. Go to her in her dreams again tonight."

Neeren uncurled his long legs and walked to the window. The waves broke softly on the shore. He was in control. Everything was as it should be. "I will wait a day. I'll go to her tomorrow night."

~ ~ ~

He couldn't wait another whole night.

It was two in the morning. Images of Maria behind his eyes kept sleep at bay. He threw his restless legs over the lightweight gray canvas chair. Dark water churned below. The north wall fireplace warmed his skin. Spring on the island was a perfect combination of warm days with cooler nights. Madrid would be hot with no ocean breeze for Maria to cool herself with.

Had she found the secret garden restaurant he'd told her of? Had she even looked? He was surprised to realize he missed her presence. His island missed her. The water missed her. She brought joy to a place too long steeped in grief.

She wanted him. He smelled it on her every time she came near. The musky scent of desire. A deep, full bodied scent. Almost gritty. The smell of her power. Maria was no girl. On the plane, she'd nearly undone him. Pulling away from her was one of the hardest things he'd ever done.

The day had dragged on unbearably. After Talon left, he'd presided over a morning council session. It would take many more sessions to come to a consensus on how to handle the influx of trade meeting requests. The other races had wondered about the Parthen homeland for centuries. The island had been cloaked the minute his father found out his mother was pregnant with him. One hundred and twenty-five years of solitude for both Neeren and his people. That was over now. The tribe looked forward to renewed trade with other immortals. Still, many were nervous about what it would mean for their way of life. No one wanted a huge influx of commercialization.

He'd always wondered if the islanders held it against him; their forced retreat from the world. Over the years, they assured him a quiet way of life was what they all wanted. The meetings today confirmed most of the council preferred their isolation. They felt safe—superior even. After all, Parthen was a paradise uncorrupted by outside influences. The discovery of his sister changed everything.

He'd skyped with Alex just after dinner. She'd harassed him mercilessly about coming to visit. Her words still rang in his ears.

"Come see me soon, okay."

"I will," he'd promised.

"I want a scheduled time, Neeren."

"I will join you in August when the council breaks for the late summer session."

"August is months away."

"You left, sister. I do not have the same freedom. When I visit, we will sit beside your ocean and listen for those killer whales you told me of."

"You'll love them. I'll buy craft beer, and greasy fries. We'll hang on the beach all night. I miss you."

The call lasted over an hour. It still amazed him she lived. He'd believed her dead for over fifteen years.

September twenty-first was the day Neeren's grandfather Domhall found him and Mother. He told them of Alexedria's escape with the help of the dragon king Collum Thronus, and her life lived as a mortal. Maria's magic allowed his grandfather to find them. Domhall hired her to create a locater spell without telling her why. Maria set more in motion than she'd ever know.

Anticipation sat like a rock on his chest. His little witch was utterly annoying. Janelle, his head chef, jokingly referred to her as chaos uncorked. He agreed. Maria was utterly alive.

He made his way to the bathroom for a cool shower before visiting her. Needed the water on his skin. Needed to block out everything but the connection to his water element.

At exactly three in the morning he lay down on sheets the color of a muted sky. Maria would want more color, he thought. She was lush. Dramatic. Fierce.

He closed his eyes. Slowed his breath. Focused his thoughts to a single pin-point. Her name. Maria. His fingers flinched once before his body became weightless, like a cloud in the room. Moisture hung heavy in the air. Cocooned him. In a moment, he would be with her.

Something stopped him. He pressed lightly. Too much pressure would kick him back to a waking state. An electric current pushed back. A blackness. Not Maria, though it carried her magical essence. Had she blocked him? She'd been serious? She didn't care about him?

Awareness crashed in with the weight of a drowning man.

Before he'd even opened his eyes, he leapt out of bed. Grabbed his cell phone. Dialed her number. No way was he texting. The phone rang. Once. Twice. Three rings before going to voice mail.

"Fuck."

He breathed deeply and dialed again—slower. With precision. Water swirled at his feet. Maybe she was simply slow to wake up. Unless she set the ringer to silent? The phone wasn't off. If it was, a message would come on saying the person he was trying to reach was unavailable. The voicemail clicked on.

Her honey voice said, "Sorry, babes. I'm off doing cool stuff. No time for a convo. Leave a message and I'll holler back. Later, bitches."

He growled in to the phone. "Really? You erected a magical block?"

He hung up and threw the phone against the mattress, which was utterly unsatisfying. His howl pierced the night air. His feet splashed through the film of water now covering his bedroom floor.

The ocean crashed against the rocks. Large waves churned. He padded back to his bed and retrieved the phone. Dialed the number again. It rang three times. His water element raged through him. Icicles dripped off his fingers, dropping like bullets to the floor. Her voice came back on voice mail again. "Sorry, babes. I'm off doing cool . . ."

He pulled the phone from his ear. Snarled. Counted the seconds before the beep. "Pick up the phone. Maria."

Words spilled out his mouth uncontrollably. "Ignoring me won't change what is happening between us. I am calling you back at exactly eight am."

He slammed the phone down again. Ice water covered the floor to his ankles. His fingers were texting before he knew what he was doing . . . *You are acting like a child. Pick up the phone . . .*

He hit send.

"Fuck."

He smashed his hands into his robe and left the room. The ocean beckoned. It was the only thing that would calm him. He needed to get out of the castle before he did something even more stupid. Like calling her back . . . Again.

Chapter 9

"Tell me again what you told my supervisor?" Alex looked in the mirror at her aunt. They'd been home for two days. It felt like they'd never left.

Quinn, in a pale pink velour track suit, sat on the edge of her bed, laying out outfits for Alex to choose between for her first day back to work. She sipped tea out of a chipped blue mug while studiously examining each article of clothing. So far, they'd eliminated the gray wool pantsuit and the lilac top with cream flowers on it.

"I told them your birth mother had been found and needed an immediate blood transfusion because she'd been in a horrific accident." Quinn picked up a red suit and showed it to Alex. "What about this one?"

"I'm not wearing a power suit on my first day back. I don't know why I'm even stressing about this. Everyone else will be in jeans and T-shirts. The journalism room is filthy. It's mostly old guys in stained sweaters. And I'm just a junior reporter. I'm lucky to even have a desk."

"Dress for the job you want," Quinn replied.

Alex faced her aunt directly. "What I want is to blend in. Look at me. I look different. Everyone's going to notice. I don't look like someone who's given a blood transfusion."

Her aunt waved away her concerns. "No one is going to notice the changes. We do because we're immortal. Humans won't. At most they'll think you look healthy and relaxed. They'll sense a change, maybe. Will be drawn to you without knowing why."

"That's what I'm worried about. I don't want anyone asking too many questions."

"Trust me, darling. You're worried for no reason."

Her aunt sifted through the pile of clothes on the bed. All of them gifts from Neeren. Each piece of clothing cost more than her car. Alex brought home ten percent, including the ruined lilac dress she wore the first time she dreamwalked to Collum.

Despite the fact that they were immortals, Alex and Quinn lived a modest, middle class life. Quinn controlled wind. Alex controlled fire. Alex was also a Parthen princess. The Parthen were a race most others equally reviled and respected. Though they were renowned for their emotional control, they stayed mostly to themselves. But you didn't want to mess with them—with her. Alex was one of them now. Maybe if she reminded herself often enough it would feel real.

As her aunt sorted through the pile, Alex noticed a piece of pale blue silk pop up. "Stop. That one."

Quinn pulled out the piece Alex gestured to and passed it over. It was a full sleeved, three-fourth length tunic dress with slits up the side. It was gorgeous. Understated. The color shimmered like the ocean outside Neeren's castle. It was perfect. She'd wear it in tribute to her family on her first day back to work. She normally dressed more casual but maybe her aunt was right. Dress for the job you want.

Quinn nodded in approval. "It will cover most of your flame tattoo. And if you add an old pair of denim jeans with Peter Pan boots it will be perfect. I'm pretty sure there's a dark blue cashmere sweater in there somewhere too."

As Quinn rooted through the pile the phone rang.

Alex grabbed it off the bedside dresser. The caller ID came up as private. "Hello," she spat out quickly, assuming it was a telemarketer.

"Morning, babe."

Her breath caught in her throat.

Quinn quietly left the room.

He said nothing else. She waited but he remained silent.

Unable to bear the silence Alex said, "It's been almost two weeks, Collum. Why are you calling me?"

"To wish you a good first day back to work."

The deep timber of his voice cut right to her uterus. She shook off the sensation.

"I haven't heard from you for ten days," she reiterated.

"Yah. I told you two weeks. Couldn't hold out that long."

"Not even a text?"

"I had to go underground unexpectedly." He paused. When Collum spoke again it nearly undid her resolve. "I've been researching movies."

Alex sunk to the edge of the bed. Her flesh a puddle on the pile of clothes. His voice was aged whiskey. Firewood. Sex.

"I miss you," he said.

Alex's heart leaped. "You could have called me before now."

"No, lover, I couldn't. Communication with me would've put you back in danger. Thought you deserved a break, Kit Kat."

She sensed him smiling into the phone receiver. She groaned. "You aren't funny."

"I'm a little funny."

I need to leave for work soon. I can't talk long."

"Want a ride?"

Her spine straightened. She pushed red tangles out of her face. "Where are you?"

"Outside your house, babe. Like I said, I missed you."

She jumped up. Sprinted to the bedroom window. Almost took a nose dive as she tried to untangle herself from the clothes around her feet. She pulled the shear curtain back.

There he was. Leaning against his hummer. Looking like a god. Looking every inch the dragon he was. She'd forgotten how power exuded from his every pore.

His hair was longer. It hung around his shoulders in soft waves. He wore dark green cargo pants, shit kicker boots, and a black T-shirt that clung to every muscle. Collum had a lot of muscle. At six foot, six inches, two-hundred-fifty pounds, he took up space.

Because he was King of the Dragons he had little interest in blending in.

Because he was Guardian of all immortals he held more power than any creature on earth.

He turned his head and caught her eye. "Let me take you to work, Alex love."

"You can't just show up here, Collum."

His sinister grin curled her toes. He raised his left hand. She'd missed it before because she'd been so busy studying the rest of him.

"I brought you a Caramel Corretto from Starbucks."

Son-of-a-bitch. "Fine, but I'm only coming down for the coffee."

Chapter 10

Collum's dragon roared as it caught site of Alex at the front door. Her red hair blazed behind her. Smoke wafted out the ends. Her tattoo writhed against her flesh. Collum could see the ridges under her clothing—peeking out from the blue silk wrapped around her body. The flame strained toward him. Fire to Fire. His beast struggled to break free.

His woman was near.

She rushed across the distance and snatched the coffee out of his hand. Gulped back at least a quarter of it. Groaned her pleasure.

His fingers itched to touch her.

All business, she said, "Thank you for the coffee. No. You may not drive me to work. I'm not showing up in your hummer with you by my side. Not when you're dressed like Rambo on steroids."

He almost laughed again. Fuck, he'd missed her. Her temper. Her tight ass. Her caffeine addiction. How she loved to tell him off. Her strength. It was her fire. It permeated every part of her. As he thought it, his beast growled low in his throat.

Alex jumped.

"Sorry, babe. He wants you right now." Collum stroked the mass of crimson tangles now smoking with heat. His voice lowered an octave. "You look fucking gorgeous."

A soft moan bubbled under her breath.

He invaded her space, caressed her cheek with his other hand. "I missed you."

She turned her face slightly into his hand. Exhaled. "You have a funny way of showing it."

"You told me you needed time to think. I gave you time."

"Not even a text?"

"Thought it was what you wanted. Hated every second of it." Collum shifted his hands to her hips. Leaned in to whisper against her mouth. "Let me show you how much I missed you."

She moaned. The scent of her desire filled his nostrils. He gripped her hips. Waited.

His body responded to every part of her. His Alex was no simpering girl. He'd never get enough of her. There was no reigning in her glory. She was molten energy. Heat poured off her skin in waves. She'd never back down. Not to him. Not to anyone.

Alex's violet eyes had a cat like quality since her transition. They flashed yellow at him now. "Show me."

Fire exploded in his throat. He growled again. Lifted her to lean against the Hummer. "That's my girl."

Collum ground his mouth against her as their tongues collided. He was past the point of taking time. Of being gentle. He wrapped his left arm around her waist to hold her in place. Pushed his right hand into her pants to grasp the slickness.

"Wrap your arms and legs around me, baby."

She groaned against his tongue as he pushed his fingers into her wetness.

"My coffee. Take my coffee," she begged.

"Drop it. I'll buy you another fucking coffee later."

The liquid splashed to the ground as Alex wrapped her arms around his neck. The minute he felt her do so he pulled her legs up around his waist. Carried her to the other side of the vehicle, away from the house. He held her against the door of the Hummer. Ground himself against her. She arched her back, thrusting her breasts into his chest. They kissed like wild things.

When Alex pulled his shirt off, he roared with unconfined pleasure. Her hands driving fire into his chest. He ripped her silk tunic, out of control with the need to touch every part of her flesh. Her breasts mocked him, hidden behind her white lace bra. He ripped her bra open with his teeth. Suckled her breasts like a lifeline.

She gripped his neck, moaned. Writhed against him. He shoved his hand back inside her pants. Pressed his palm in a circular motion against her clit as he shoved two fingers inside her.

She came quickly against his fingers. Her nails slicing into his back.

He lifted his head to the sun and roared fire. He'd never get enough of her. Would kill anyone who tried to harm her.

As his lover floated back to earth, Collum kissed her forehead. Her cheeks. Her eyes. "I love you so fucking much, Alex. Skip work and come home with me."

She leaned her head against his shoulder and sighed. Kissed his neck. Rubbed her hands along his arms. "I missed you."

"I know, babe. I'm sorry. I couldn't come before now." He shrugged. "Work."

"Really? What kind of work?"

He paused. "That's what I want to talk to you about. It's important."

Steel entered her voice. "Well, I can't miss my work."

"What if you had a new job?"

"What? At one of your subsidiaries? Glenn looks after everything for you. Besides I like the job I have." Alex blushed. "And now, thanks to you I have to change."

Collum laughed, undeterred by her annoyance with him. "Red is your color. Put on something red."

He set her back down. Straightened her ripped top. "I'll wait here to drive you in. We'll stop at Starbucks on the way. Talk more."

"Um no. No, you won't. I told you, I am not showing up to the paper in a hummer. This is Victoria, B.C., Collum. City of living green. We'll get lynched."

"Fucking environmentalists. Unless they're all riding home-made wooden bikes, living in a grass hut, they better not look twice at me."

She smacked his chest and walked back toward the house. "That's why you aren't driving me there."

"Wait. Before you leave out here alone, I need you to answer one question."

She turned back. "What?"

"Do you prefer chick flicks or action movies?"

Chapter 11

At Eight fifty-seven in the morning, Alex pulled into the paper's parking lot in her old, beat to shit Jetta.

She jumped out of the car, raced across the lot, and hit the inside of the building at eight fifty-nine. Her ass hit her chair at exactly nine o'clock.

Half the desks around her remained empty. Journalists were notorious for showing up at strange times on and off throughout the day. She didn't have the luxury today. One minute past nine the intercom on her desk phone buzzed.

She snatched the phone before it rang a second time. "Hello?"

"Good morning, Alex. Mr. Tanner would like to see you in his office please."

Who was Mr. Tanner? "Sure thing. Be right there. Umm, where is his office?"

The voice on the other line sighed. "Fourth floor. North west side. Corner office. Natalie will check you in when you arrive."

"Right, I'll be right up, Thank you." The voice on the other end hung up before Alex finished speaking.

The flames on Alex's skin wriggled in agitation. Her chair scraped against the floor as she stood. She smoothed her jacket trying to calm her nerves. Alex already regretted listening to Collum. Why the hell had she decided to wear a red suit jacket with her jeans?

She nodded to the other staff as she waked through the office. Most of them remained hunched over their computers typing furiously, or desperately searched under candy wrappers and assorted moldy mugs for files. God, she loved the smell of sweaty journalists and stale coffee in the morning.

She ran the stairs to the fourth floor rather than take the elevator. Since her transition, she needed more exercise than normal. She'd always been a runner. The weekly training sessions on the island with Quinn, Gray, and Neeren helped keep her even. Now that she was back she'd have to up her exercise game.

Alex pushed open the door to the executive offices main lobby. She cleared her throat to gain the attention of the plump woman manning the front desk. "Hi, I'm Alex. I was told to come up here to meet with Mr. Tanner?"

Natalie—Alex presumed this was Natalie—looked up from her screen, gave Alex the once over, straightened her shoulders, and narrowed heavily shadowed blue eyes before replying, "Take a seat and I'll see if he can see you."

"He can see me. He already called and asked me to come up," Alex reminded her.

Natalie pursed her lips. "Well, I still have to check. Take a seat."

Alex bristled but sat down. If she was going to continue to work in the human world she'd have to accept this form of treatment. Resting-bitch-face-Natalie didn't know Alex was a powerful immortal princess. Besides she'd never felt comfortable with servants attending to her every need back on the island anyway.

Alex might not enjoy women like Natalie, but she understood them. The woman probably had a husband and three kids to look after at home. After putting in a nine-hour work day for a male boss who treated her like a servant. This space was Natalie's castle. She had power over who entered and when. Alex could deal with it.

She took a seat on the 1970's lime green sofa and crossed her legs. She realized she still had on the blue Peter Pan boots. Alex took a mental inventory. Blue boots, red jacket, green couch. Great. She probably looked like a Christmas tree. She was never taking fashion advice from Collum or Quinn again.

Natalie buzzed the intercom. "Hi, Carol. Alex from the basement is here to see Mr. Tanner. Is he available?"

Alex heard Carol sigh before speaking in a condescending voice on the other end of the line. "Yes, Natalie. He's expecting her and is on a tight schedule. Send her back."

The line clicked off before Natalie could respond. Alex refused to smile. She was on Nat's side now.

Natalie spoke with a little less confidence. "He'll see you now."

Fuck that, Alex thought. Natalie needed her kingdom. No way was Alex taking it from her today. She leaned in and spoke conspiratorially. "Thanks. Carol's in fine form today, huh. Way to wreck the Monday."

When Natalie nodded, Alex sauntered over to her desk. "So, when did Mr. Tanner start?"

"Three weeks ago." Natalie glanced around the lobby to make sure no one was eavesdropping. "He's great. It's Carol you gotta watch out for."

~ ~ ~

It was a long walk to the east side of the building. At the end of a long hallway sat Carol. She wore a honeysuckle colored suit. Her blond hair expertly coiffed around her face. Her desk spotless. Her French manicure absolute perfection. Maybe mid-fifties? Self-consciously, Alex shoved her tangled curls off her face. Why hadn't Quinn thought to remind her to put her hair in a stupid ponytail.

Before Alex could speak, Carol said, "He's waiting. Go in," and promptly turned back to her work.

Alex glanced at the four closed doors in her immediate vicinity. Not one had a name plate.

Carol sighed and pointed at the door to her left. "In there. Move it."

Alex jumped. She doubted anyone ever made Carol feel small or shitty. Was sure even the aforementioned Mr. Tanner did whatever she said, as soon as she said it.

Moving quickly, Alex opened the door and entered the private office. Behind the desk, his back to her, Mr. Tanner stared out the window. His office was as filthy as Carol's was clean.

Old coffee cups littered every surface. Two half-eaten sandwiches lay on the desk. The only other chair in the room was covered in stacks of paper. In fact, every piece of furniture was covered in paper. The floral sofa by the book shelf. The side table with the old printer. Piles of books and papers towered precariously in every corner. Alex grinned, immediately at ease.

Salt and pepper seasoned his hair. Broad muscled shoulders stretched a non-descript gray sweater. He turned. Her pulse quickened with unease. He had a chiseled jaw and full lips. His dark eyes filled with curiosity. As he spoke the air shifted. Alex drew back.

"It's okay. I'm not here to hurt you." He smiled. "I promise."

Alex tried to decipher the strange sensations bombarding her. "Who are you? What are you?"

"My name is Jason Tanner. I'm a vampire." He pushed the papers around on his desk. "But I'm not interested in your blood."

Jason laughed and then raised his hands in surrender. "Joke, Joke. Well, not the vampire part. Come to think of it, not the not wanting your blood part either."

Her new boss smashed his hands into his hair. "That came out wrong."

Alex called to the fire in her hands.

Jason shrugged. "Dammit. I'm bad at this. Please sit down. I'm a good guy. Just happen to be a Vamp."

Alex inched backward. Hoped he wouldn't notice. Glanced behind her to see how far the door was. Big mistake. When she turned back he stood directly in front of her. He grasped her hands before she could raise them. The flames on her body writhed, heating her skin.

"Please," he said, considering her eyes. "This is about business. Nothing else. I'm not here to fight you." Jason released her hands. "Collum would kill me if I tried."

Alex's voice rushed out on a wave. "Column, what the fuck does Collum have to do with this?"

"Your boyfriend is my boss." He pushed the papers off the chair. "Now will you please sit and let me tell you why I asked you up here?"

She remained where she was. Tried to pick up something from his gestures but couldn't get a read.

"It's because I'm dead."

"What?"

"You can't figure me out because I'm dead. No soul. At least not the kind you can sense." Jason grimaced. "I'm just saying it because I've run into this situation a lot." He retreated behind his desk and waited. "Please sit down. We have a lot to talk about."

Alex pushed her hair of her face, called sparks to her fingertips, and sat in the chair he offered. "Okay. Talk. Start with how Collum is your boss. If you try anything I'll burn this room to the ground."

She leaned back in the chair and crossed her arms. "I'm pretty sure vampires can burn to death."

Jason leaned back as well and rested his arms on the desk. "True. But the lovely Carol is an ice-queen and I don't think the fire would get very far."

Alex leaned forward, fascinated. "You're kidding. I had no idea."

He laughed. "Oh, you sensed something. You just didn't know why she seemed so cold. It's because you're new and still learning to trust yourself." He snapped his fingers. "I can help with that."

"How? Don't forget to include Collum in your story."

"The big man? He's my boss." Jason flashed a charismatic grin. Stretched his arms wide. "I'm a Guardian."

Alex's heart raced. "Bullshit. Column is the only guardian."

"Technically not quite true. Column is leader of the guardians. There are five of us. Or I should say, there were five of us. Your grandfather was a guardian until the tragedy with your mother. Then there is myself, a renegade wolf named Idris and a faye warrior Diana."

She shook her head. "Column and Domhall would've told me."

"They're not allowed to tell you, I'm afraid. You don't get to know unless you're one of us."

Her skin tingled. "Why are you telling me now?"

"Because, we want you to join us. Domhall and Collum both recommended you. Idris agreed. Diana said she doesn't care." Jason winked. His lips split open in a wide grin. "I'm your new mentor."

Alex's chest tightened. Sparks flew out of the light sockets. "Collum never said a word of this to me."

Jason nodded. "Right. Well. I think he wanted to this morning. Didn't work out the way he hoped." He leaned back in his chair and crossed his hands behind his neck. "Do you want some coffee. I can ask Carol to bring us some. She might even do it if she's in a generous mood."

"No, I don't want coffee." Alex lurched to her feet. "I wanted to come back to my job and be a journalist. I wanted to be normal. I don't want to a be a guardian."

Alex clutched her head in frustration. Rampant emotions were spiking in her brain and she had no way to hold them back. As fire climbed up her neck the lamp on Jason's desk exploded.

"Let's take a breather." Jason pushed his chair back from the walnut desk, walked over to the door of his office, and opened it slightly. "Carol, can you bring me two glasses of chamomile tea please? Maybe add a splash of whiskey."

As Jason shut the door, Alex heard Carol grumble, "I'm not cleaning that up."

He pulled his office chair over broken glass, next to the one she'd vacated, and gestured for her to sit again. "I still remember waking up and realizing I was a vampire. It was ancient times. Thirteen-hundred and sixteen to be precise. Black Death was ripping through Europe. I was from a noble house. I was twenty years of age, set on a course of academia and then, bam. It was over. I was a vampire. Reviled the world over. Filled with bloodlust."

Burning closed Alex's throat as he spoke. A single tear fell from the corner of her eyes. She wanted to be normal. She wanted aunt Quinn to be normal. Wanted her mother to be normal.

Jason's words echoed Alex's deepest fears. "All of those people. Your new friends. Your family. They were born knowing who and what they were. You had dreams. Goals that had nothing to do with immortality. Trust me I get it. Even Collum, with all his love for you, won't."

He lightly touched her hand. "Collum recognizes your confusion. The man wants to help. The dragon isn't sure how."

Jason retrieved the drinks from Carol as she discreetly entered the room. He pressed a cup into Alex's hand. Printed on the side of the mug was a picture of a pug dog sitting on a sofa. Written under the picture were the words, *Have a Pawsome day*.

Alex laughed through tears falling freely down her

cheeks. Jason was the first person to put into words what she'd been feeling. The first to admit he'd felt the same.

"How did you manage it?"

His eyes flickered. "It gets easier. You discover ways to continue doing what you love. This existence gifted me with time to learn everything I ever wanted. I've studied every legend. Every scripture. I know every prophecy. I travel and work in whatever field I feel like studying. It's been a good life." He punctuated his last words with finger quotes.

"You don't have to walk away from humanity. Or from following your path. Mine is seeking knowledge. Yours, I believe, is unearthing corruption. It's one of the reasons I became a guardian when Collum asked me. It's why we all think you will excel as a guardian."

Alex wiped her eyes, sipped her tea. There was more whiskey in it than tea. She'd have to thank Carol later. "I don't want to give up my life yet."

Jason nodded. "You don't have too. Maybe let yourself be okay with broadening it."

She swallowed and asked, "What do you want me to do?"

Chapter 12

Blood caked Mar's hands. She'd been clawing at her cage for two hours. Her nails were chipped. Her fingers raw. The blood wasn't entirely hers though. She might be small, but she knew how to fight.

When she'd woken up in the cell, anger burned like ice in her veins. Freaking vamps had drugged her. A chloroform cloth pressed to her mouth when her attention had been on Melisandre. Bitch was going to pay for putting her there.

As soon as her shackles were removed by the vampires, Mar landed a couple good punches. They'd wanted to kill her. Malice poured off them in waves. Orders were orders though. Mar knew her mother would never let anyone hurt her... Good Ol' Isabella would want that honor all to herself.

They locked her in a medieval dungeon built into rock. Mystical energy pulsed along the edges of her cage. She was as bereft of power as she'd been with her shackles on. Obviously, her mother had been practicing.

Mar was left in the cage with the clothes on her back and one thread bare blanket. A moldy, single cot sat in one corner. A stained bucket tipped sideways in the other. Dim lights flickered on and off. Her purse mocked her from a half-broken table on the other side of the narrow corridor.

Her cage was one of several in the damp basement. Water trickled down an exterior wall. Lichen grew in corners. The place stunk like rotting shit. Goosebumps covered her skin. At the end of the narrow corridor, a thick metal door stood ominously. Occasionally a scream reverberated through the cavern.

If they were going for spooky, they'd succeeded. Personally, Mar thought they'd read one too many Vampires-for-Dummies books. Trust her Mom to take it to the extreme. I mean honestly, what self-respecting vampire lived like this?

"Bitch is so gonna owe me a new manicure when I get out of here," Mar complained to the shadows.

Laughter echoed from the other end of the hall. "Darling girl. You're as feisty as ever I see. How I've missed your zest."

Mar cringed. "Isabella. Been a while. Too bad it couldn't be longer."

"Don't be rude. I made sure no one hurt you. You can at least call me, Mother."

Her mother rounded the corner. As regal, as dark, as demented as Mar remembered. Jet black hair hung poker straight down Isabella's back to her knees. Her eyes were black too. Empty. Bile burned the back of Mar's throat.

Isabella walked fingers along the outside of Mar's cage. Tapped blood red nails against metal. "You wound me. I've spent years searching for you. Really, to have ignored me for so many years?"

"Sure," Mar quipped. "Next time you want to murder my grandparents in cold blood I'll make sure to put out the welcome sign."

"You think you know everything. You know nothing. I saved you." Isabella clamped her hands around iron bars and stared into Mar's eyes. "Now I need you. We're about to achieve everything we ever dreamed of."

Mar grabbed the bars by her mother's hands. Rage racked her chest. Disgust. She knew what her mother was. She'd always known. Who cares if details were fuzzy.

"Yeah. Thanks, but no thanks. I'm not interested."

Her mother's eyes narrowed. "You don't know what I'm offering."

Mar tasted pennies in the back of her throat as bile rose.

She swallowed her nausea. "Pretty sure I do. I don't want to share anything with you, Isabella."

"Mother," she screeched. "You will call me, Mother."

Isabella reached through the bars and clasped her wrists. Mar should have remembered how easily her mother could be set off. It was too late to change anything now.

Lost in her madness, Isabella squeezed. "You have no idea what I've done for you. There is so little time."

The bones in Mar's wrist cracked. She screamed as waves of agony spread through her body. "Stop."

"Why do you fight me so, Maria?" Isabella ranted.

"Mother," Mar begged. "Stop. You're crushing my wrists."

Confusion crossed Isabella's brow. She looked down. Dropped Mar's hands like they were burning brands. Mar snatched her hands back. Her wrists hung limp. Black bruises were already appearing. A whimper tour from her throat.

Isabella wailed like a child. "What have I done? Why do you always make me lose control?"

"Sure, Mom," Mar said through gritted teeth. "This is my fault."

"Stop arguing with me." Isabella shook her head. Madness haunted her eyes. "No. No, I'm not mad at you. I will fix you. I can. Do you want me to fix you, darling?"

Tears poured down Mar's face. She tasted salt on her lips. Tasted the memory of all the other times Isabella fixed her. After every wound. After every spell she'd practiced on Mar had failed. The devil lived inside her mother.

"Yes, Mother. I want you to fix me."

"I'm sorry. I'll make it better." Isabella pulled a chain from around her neck. The key to the cage glistened.

Mar had one chance. She needed her mother to open the cage. The lock clicked. Isabella stepped inside. Mar dropped to the earth moaning. Her mother lunged to catch her. The door hung open.

Isabella reached for Mar's hands. Wrapped them inside her own. Burning agony racked Mar as her mother held her hands and chanted. Slowly the bones knitted themselves back together. The action felt like a burning spike repeatedly jamming into her flesh. She almost passed out from pain. Almost.

As the last of her mother's chanting ended, Mar shifted slightly. Flexed her fingers inside her mothers. Wrapped them around Isabella's smaller hands. Held her tight. As they stood together Mar pulled her hands up, gripped Isabella's head, and brought it down while ramming her knee upward. Bone connected with bone. Her mother dropped like a stone.

Mar knew she'd pay for that later. Likely with a broken leg, or shattered knee. For now, it was enough. She pushed her mother to the side and grinned when Isabella fell like dead weight onto the cement floor.

There were camera's everywhere. With luck, Mar'd have a couple minutes before guards reached her. She scrambled over her mother's body and rushed for her purse. As she dumped the contents on the table her cell phone fell out with a clunk that sounded like heaven. Thank fuck they'd been too stupid to take it.

Multiple text message covered the screen. Neeren. He'd never give up. A low battery light flashed. One bar. There was no time to call. Mar hit reply. Prayed to every goddess she knew. Every ancestor. Typed—*The vampires have me. Contact the guardians*—Pressed send, and smashed the phone against the rock wall.

Behind her, footsteps pounded down the long-blackened corridor.

Mar calmly walked back into her cell and sat down on her filthy cot. She spoke directly to her awakening mother. "It's okay, Mother. I forgive you for what you are about to do."

~ ~ ~

Four male vampires rushed the cage. Three tackled Mar on the bed while a fourth picked Isabella up off the floor and dragged her dead weight from the cage.

Mar covered her face with her hands as best she could. Practice makes perfect and she'd had a lot of practice defending herself. Blows landed like dumbbells against her arms. Chest. Head. Purple and black bruises would set in soon.

"Enough!" Isabella's voice rang out in the cell.

In front of Mar an unlucky vampire turned to ash. Isabella stood behind him with teeth bared. She wiped a drop of blood from her broken nose.

"No one touches her," Isabella said to the remaining vampires while snapping her nose back into place.

They nodded quickly and stepped away from Mar.

"Tie her up you idiots. Or do you want her having another go at me?"

Her mother paced the cell. As soon as Mar was secured to the bed, Isabella walked over and gripped her chin. "Who did you contact?"

Mar stared into her mother's eyes. Her clear, sane eyes. Had she been played?

Fake it till you make it— "What are you talking about, Isabella?"

"Don't play stupid with me, Maria. I know you didn't come to Madrid for a sightseeing visit. I also know you've been making friends with some very important players." Isabella gripped Mar's chin harder and leaned in. "Now who did you contact?"

Mar ripped her head out of her mother's grasp. Stared at her defiantly. "No one. The phone was dead by the time I reached it."

"And when should we expect, no one, to reach us? I'll put out something special to welcome them." Isabella laughed at her confused look. "I have immortality. He wants fire."

Mar struggled to breathe. "What Fire? Who wants Fire?"

Isabella flipped her hand in the air. "You'll see. We know you've been hanging around with that holier than thou, Dragon. His time is over. Our time is now. When should we expect him?"

Mar collapsed against the wall. Relief washed over her body in waves. For a moment, she'd thought Isabella meant, Alex. Collum? Well he could take care of himself.

Mar studied her mother. She looked different. Sane. "Who is the mysterious, he, and how come you aren't insane? Last time I saw you, you were a raving lunatic."

Isabella laughed. It was a low, throaty sound that echoed over the walls. "You haven't seen me in over a dozen years, Maria."

Something like censure lay under her words. Maria's hackles rose. "Are you admonishing me, Mother?"

"Well, I mean really. Not to reach out to me? I could have been dead for all you knew."

Mar blinked. "A—you're evil, and B—you're already dead."

"Quit being so melodramatic. We have much to talk about. First we have to get through this."

"What are you talking about?"

Isabella glanced at the shadows. "I'll come see you after you've had a chance to calm down a bit." She walked out of the cage but turned back to Mar before locking the door. "Also, I apologize for hurting your wrist. Sometimes I glitch. I'm trying to get better."

Chapter 13

Alex gripped Jason's arm as she stepped out of the limo sheathed in velvet. The forest green dress they'd picked fit like a glove, complimenting her runners figure. Her legs peeked through a high front slit as she walked. Full length sleeves covered the flame tattoos. The deep V neckline dipped to her navel. She'd never worn anything so blatantly sexual in her entire life.

This dress was different from anything else she owned, including the clothes Neeren purchased for her. This dress was about owning her body. Her sexuality. Herself.

In three-inch gold heels, she topped six feet. Her loose hair flowed down her back like fire. Blood red lipstick and black mascara completed the look. Power flowed through her blood. Feminine power. She was strong, sexy, and in control.

Jason winked at her. "Collum is going to lose his shit when he sees you."

Alex grinned wickedly. "Are you sure he'll be in there?"

"Oh, he'll be in there. He's looking forward to introducing you to immortal society."

She blushed. "But only as the daughter of Gray Taleisin, right? No one is to know about our relationship."

"Yes. People will be more likely to open-up to you if they don't know about your relationship with Collum. As soon as word of your mating spreads, they'll clamp up."

She'd never understand why everyone was so afraid of Collum. She shook her head. Flames licked her back as she did so. Alex grinned and walked arm in arm up the red carpet with Jason. Her stride sure, strong. Heads turned. Her name a whisper among the other guests. The story of her resurrection spread quickly.

No expense had been spared at this party. Jason explained earlier it was a high-ranking political event. A bit like a Presidential fundraising dinner in the mortal world. Alex might even see some people she'd always thought were mortal.

Apparently Brad Pitt was a descendant of Thor. Which made sense when she thought about it. And Angelina Jolie? An ice demon from a world called Ungor. It never would have worked out.

Alex marveled at how her world had changed. Over one thousand candles lit the path to the front door. Centaurs bowed low on their front knees as guests filed past. Massive iron doors thrown open. As they approached, a fairytale came alive inside the house. Flowers of every color hung from the ceiling. Waterfalls, suspended in mid-air, filled the room with moist fragrant air. More candles floated in every corner of the great hall. Fairies flew around the room carrying large trays of champagne.

Jason tugged on her arm. Alex turned to him breathless.

He winked again. "Not all bad, hey?"

She grinned from ear to ear. "No. Not all bad."

The room was a sea of navy suits and champagne glasses. Alex stood out from the crowd. Admiring glances followed her across the hall. As they took their places at a table of eight, Jason quickly introduced her to the other guests. They all nodded politely. Interested in this new elemental. Alex struck up easy conversations. Several people asked about her brother. There was a lot of interest in Parthen's solitary king and when trade with the island would open.

One seat remained empty. Collum would arrive later as befitting the Dragon King and one true Guardian.

Jason wore a light gray suit. His tie slightly askew. His hair tousled. He looked like a night librarian. Much of it was an act. His clothes. Persona. Alex'd gleaned much already. There was a lot more under the surface with Jason. No vampire was that nice.

He'd explained her job tonight was to ask as many naive questions as possible from everyone . . . but especially from the vampires. She was to play the newbie card, while trying to dig up as much info as possible about the vampires. They were hoping a vamp would let their guard down enough to let something, anything, slip about missing immortals and who was killing them.

Collum believed it all related to a turf war. Someone hoped to amass enough power to take over. They'd need a lot of kills to make it happen. He'd sent Mar to Madrid to check things out. Idris was in Romania talking with the Old Ones. Alex had been charged with seeing what she could find out tonight.

Dinner was about to start when Collum walked in, dressed in a charcoal three-piece suit fitted to perfection. A slight checkered pattern shifted as his muscles stretched under the fabric. His dark, wavy hair rested like silk against his shoulders. Liquid fire caught in Alex's throat.

Every candle flickered as he walked past. Each guest stood, then bowed. Collum's face was hard. Granite. Ancient power cut along the line of his cheekbones. He greeted a few guests. Shook the hand of the elemental elder, Lachon Findel. The two chatted briefly.

Alex's tattoo crawled against her flesh. He who created fire, had entered the room. A slight murmur carried across the hall as Collum walked to his table. He looked like Ares. God of War. Conqueror. His eyes narrowed when he saw her. A promise of sin in their depths.

Alex tossed her hair behind her back. Instinctively thrust out her breasts. Her skin tightened. She licked her lips. He stalked across the hall, ignoring everyone. When he reached the table, flames in the candelabra flared. It took everything she had not to reach for him. Fire slammed against her chest, begging to break free and reach him.

"What are you wearing?" Collum snarled.

A picture of him ripping the dress from her body tore through her mind. Alex bit her lip as heat racked her body. "Do you like it?"

"My only love," he growled. "You are a fucking goddess."

The ends of her hair ignited. He reached for her.

Conversation at the table exploded. Soon, everyone in the room knew the Dragon had called the Fire Elemental, his love.

Beside them Jason sighed with frustration. "Well, there goes that idea."

~ ~ ~

Two hours and no regrets later, Alex and Collum left the party hand in hand. They'd shrugged off the disastrous beginning. Collum quickly introduced her to the assembled guests as his girlfriend. Inwardly, Alex cringed over the word. Secretly waited with baited breath for him to mess up and say, Mate. When had she started to think of herself that way? They were supposed to be taking their time, waiting—like modern relationships dictated. Being with him in public had changed something. Maybe, she thought for the hundredth time, waiting was ridiculous.

Not once had she imagined wanting to be with a man like Collum. How childish of her. How naïve. Alex had discovered he was so much more than a dragon king. He was also funny, loyal, and thoughtful. And kind. Endlessly kind to those he cared for.

They danced the night away. Made out in alcoves and laughed like teenagers. It might have been the best night of

Alex's life. She'd failed in her first mission. Neither of them cared. Now, they leaned against his BMW arm in arm.

"You should have told me about the guardians before," Alex admonished him.

Collum nodded. "I should have. I'm doing a few things wrong. Trying to figure out what it means to share myself."

"And you made Mar keep a secret from me. Not cool."

"Yep. I blew it." Collum curled his fingers around hers, driving warmth into her palm.

"What if I'd said I didn't want to join your elite band of spies?"

The corner of his upper lip curled with humor. "We're a little more than spies, lover."

"Right. You rule the world. Answer the question please."

"You're my mate. I'd have changed the rules. Still might."

Her chest fluttered at the word, mate, on his lips. "No more secrets?"

Collum had the good grace to look apologetic. "I mean, I'm two thousand, babe. I've done a lot of stuff. It's gonna take a while to fill you in on everything."

Alex looked up at the night sky. He'd stared at this sky before humanity existed. A cool breeze lifted the hair off her shoulders. She sighed. Understanding him wasn't going to be easy.

Loving him would be.

Alex pulled Collum's head down and kissed him. He gripped her waist. Kissed her back. It wasn't a desperate need for each other rocking them this time. It was gentle, and frivolous—hands touching intimate places between bouts of laughter.

The other guests gave them a wide berth as they walked to their cars. Alex certainly wasn't an unknown anymore. After tonight, word of her parentage, and relationship with Collum would spread like wildfire. She was certain by midday tomorrow every immortal would know the new Parthen

Fire Queen had captured the heart of the Dragon King. It was better. Alex was no good at subterfuge. If Collum still wanted her to be a guardian, her role would have to be something other than re-con.

Collum grinned at her. "I guess we blew that didn't we."

Alex melted, then swatted his shoulder. "I didn't blow anything. You walked in and caused an uproar."

He slowly pushed his hand inside her dress and massaged her breast. "What did you expect when you wear something like this around me?"

"Self-control, Collum," she stuttered on a moan as his finger flicked her nipple.

The air around them shifted. Collum removed his hands from her dress and leaned back on his heels. Inner light pooled in the center of his dark eyes. He pulled a box out of his pants pocket and lifted the lid. A blinding solitaire diamond as large as her thumb glittered back from the blue satin coating inside.

"Marry me, Alexedria. In your human church. On a mountain top. Wherever you want. Marry me."

Alex's breath beat like thunder in her chest. Electricity shot through her legs, leaving them weak. It surprised her much she wanted it. How quickly she'd realized she was meant for him. The word, *Mine*, flashed through her thoughts. And it was true. He was as much hers as she was his. This was real belonging. Not ownership, but knowing deep in your bones your soul has always been the companion of another.

Her voice was rock solid as she answered. "Yes, my dragon. Name the date."

Fire blazed in his gaze. Collum pressed the ring on to her finger.

"I'm going to fuck you against this car," he growled in her ear.

Her knees gave out as his hand pulled her skirt above her knees.

Behind them someone cleared their throat loudly. It was enough to bring Alex back into the present. She frantically pushed Collum away.

Collum growled low in his throat before turning to their intruder. "What?"

Jason appeared out of the darkness. "You two really need a room. But first . . . Collum we need to talk about what happened tonight and come up with a new strategy."

"Not now. Fuck off."

Embarrassment flushed Alex's skin as she hastily shoved her skirt into place. "Collum. Go talk with him."

Collum stroked her cheek. A promise of forever clearly shining in his eyes.

Yep, Alex thought. Marrying this guy. "It's true," she said. "We totally blew it. You better talk with Jason about our next move. I'll meet you at your hotel, okay." She grinned at Jason.

Collum sighed, straightened his suit, and handed her keys to the BMW. He kissed her nose. "I won't be long."

~ ~ ~

Alex admired Collum's frame as he and Jason walked away. God, when had she become a love-struck fool? She blamed Collum for being so freaking gorgeous it hurt to look at him.

She fumbled with the keys in the dark, trying to unlock the car door. Collum had parked near the edge of the lot. Typical male—worried about someone putting a dent in his car. Nice for making out. Not so nice when trying to find the lock in the dark. On her third try the keys fell from her hand.

"Shit." Alex groaned.

She almost called Collum and Jason back but they'd moved on quickly. Alone in the dark, she shook off a foreboding shiver, hitched her skirt up, bent down, and searched for the missing keys. Gravel bit into her knees. Her heels twisted her ankles in an unfriendly angle.

Blind in the dark, Alex sifted through dirt under the vehicle. "Unbelievable. Stupid shit."

Behind her, someone giggled.

"Need some help?" asked a young female voice.

Alex smacked her head on the outside mirror as she jumped up. "Ouch, goddammit. Sneak up on a person why don't you."

She rubbed the back of her head while searching out the faceless voice. It was so dark now Alex could only make out a silhouette. Very thin, average height.

The female voice cut through the dark. "I have a flash light on my cell phone. Here."

Bright light flashed into Alex's eyes.

"I'm Brita. Lose your keys?"

Alex blinked "I dropped the stupid things trying to unlock the car door."

"Where's your friends?" Brita asked.

Something in the lilt of her voice put Alex on edge. She replied cautiously. "They went to get my coat."

Brita shrugged her shoulders. In the glow from the flashlight Alex made out short hair. The bottom half of her head was shaved. The top half glued up in tiny spikes. She wore a silver mod style dress with knee high boots. Very hipster, Alex thought. She looked about sixteen years old.

"Yeah," Brita said. "My dad went to get the car and told me to wait out here. I don't know why he couldn't park in the lot like everyone else."

The tension in Alex's shoulders eased a bit. "What kind of car does he drive?"

"Oh, some old guy Mercedes." Brita waved her hand in annoyance.

The fist of tension around Alex's chest released its tight grip. This was a kid, not an assassin. "Men. Can you shine light around the bottom of the car?"

Alex bent down a second time, careful to steer clear of the mirror. On her hands and knees, she directed Brita to position the light to shine under the car. Alex refused to think about the damage she was causing her beautiful dress.

"I think I see them. I'm gonna have to stretch. Can you shine the light under further?"

"Sure thing." Brita kneeled beside her.

A sharp prick at the back of Alex's neck stung like a bee sting. Burning ice seeped under her skin. Muddled her thoughts. Her hand froze. Then her body.

Brita laughed. "Seriously? It was that easy? Wow. The dragon picked you? You need to get your shit together."

Alex fell to the ground in a heap as her arms gave out. The little bitch dragged her further into shadow. Before passing out, two errant thoughts ripped through Alex's mind. One—she was desperately and completely in love with Collum. And two—what was with her and getting attacked in parking lots?

Chapter 14

Neeren grunted as he raised sixty-pound dumbbells above his head. He'd barely slept. It was now five in the morning and he was in the gym with Talon.

"Just call her," Talon said.

Neeren thrust the dumbbells again. His form was off. "No. I made a fool of myself after talking with you last time. I acted like a stalker."

"I'm sure it wasn't that bad."

"Well it wasn't seductive."

As Talon laughed, heat flooded Neeren's face. He added more weight, jerked dumbbells above his head, dropped them, and sat up.

He briefly closed his eyes before confiding in his friend. "Truth is I like her. I've never had to prove myself to someone before. It is . . . bothersome."

More laughter burst out of his friend. More heat crawled up Neeren's neck.

"Poor you. You finally have to do more than crook your finger for a girl to come running. It's part of life. Suck it up and try to win her."

Neeren shoved his hands through his hair. "She would not answer my texts."

"So, try again. Maybe she was sleeping. You did call in the middle of the night. Not smooth."

Neeren contemplated his space as he contemplated his unexpected desire for the little witch. The gym took up eight hundred square feet on the houses lower level. Filled with every workout machine imaginable, he spent early mornings here. Routine. Control. How easily he lost it around Maria.

Of course, even here every wall was made of glass. The north wall retracted, opening onto an outdoor track. Currently he faced east, and as sun rose over the cliff a tingling warmth settled in his bones. Long ago he'd positioned the bench he sat on to catch the morning rays. He waited patiently. Offered silent thanks as the sun softly bathed him in a pool of morning light. Talon sat beside him and handed him a bottle of water.

"I've created a beautiful place, haven't I?"

Talon slapped his back. "You have. There is no more beautiful island in the world."

Neeren tossed the water back. Energy radiated up his spine. The sun called to his panther. As it did every morning. His bones prepared to shift.

He placed the bottle on the floor. "I'm going for a run along the cliff edge."

"Are you going to call her?"

Neeren stretched. The ocean beckoned him. "Yes, old friend. I will call her . . . after I run and regain my self-control."

"Well then," Talon replied as he pushed Neeren out of the way. "Race you to the beach."

Neeren gave his friend a head start before slowly shifting into his panther state. Muscles tore. Claws extended. Bones snapped. Lengthened. Black fur quickly covered his skin. His eyes burned yellow. Fevered. His jaw twisted. Neeren breathed easy as his lungs expanded and his body reknitted back together into a five-hundred-pound black panther. He exalted in the feeling of his feline body. Let power flow through him. He was King. He would win his witch.

A low growl sounded in the back of his throat. With

a kick of his massive hind legs he ran with the wind and overtook his friend.

~ ~ ~

An hour later, exhausted and refreshed, Neeren opened the door to his bedroom. A sense of calm replaced his earlier doubts. Daisy still snored at the foot of the bed.

He scratched behind her ears and shook her awake. "Go find Janelle in the kitchen. She has your breakfast waiting."

As though the dog understood, she stretched and jumped off the bed in search of kibble. He shook his head and headed for the shower. As he walked past the bed he noticed the light on his phone flash. He checked the clock on the nightstand. Almost a quarter after six in the morning. He lunged for the phone.

As he read the text, tremors shot through his body. His heart-beat thrashed in his ears. Black spots swam in front of his eyes. The text had come in forty-five minutes ago. Forty-five fucking minutes. When he'd been running to forget her. The words screamed at him from the screen— *The vampires have me. Contact the guardians.*

There was only one person she could mean.

Swallowing his anger, he dialed the number for Collum Thronus.

Collum answered on the first ring. "Neeren, I was just about to call you." Collum's voice came across the line harried.

Neeren cut him off. "Something has happened."

"How do you know?"

"Maria sent me a text." Neeren paused. "I retrieved it only a moment ago."

"Maria?"

Something in the dragon's voice pushed through Neeren's terror. "Yes, Maria. Why were you about to call me?"

"It's Alex." The dragon's voice hitched. "She's been taken."

Neeren fell to the edge of the bed. Rage coursed through him. "Maria has been taken as well. Start from the beginning. Leave nothing out."

"It's a combined attack. What happened to Mar?"

"I have no fucking clue. She sent me a text saying the vampires have her, and to contact the Guardians. Since you are the only goddamn guardian I know, I called you. Now what the fuck have you gotten Maria and my sister mixed up in?"

Collum growled into the receiver. "I discovered your sister missing an hour ago. We were supposed to meet at the penthouse. When she wasn't there I called your aunt Quinn. She hasn't seen her either."

"And?" Neeren prodded. "What aren't you telling me?"

"Both Alex and Mar were working undercover for me. I've been trying to locate a rebel group of vampires killing immortals." Wood shattered on the other end of the phone. "This is my fault. I misjudged the desperation of this enemy. What I can't figure out is how they knew I was looking for them."

Neeren ground his teeth together. "And you picked those two to help you?"

"Alex and Mar are unknown. They were supposed to be re-con duty only." Collum growled over the line.

Neeren's knuckles whitened as he gripped the phone. "My sister is a twenty-six-year old journalist, you idiot. And Mar is a very loud, very flamboyant, witch. She's not a goddamn spy.

"They're more than you think. They were perfectly safe."

"Bullshit. You have a leak, Thronus."

"I fucking know," was the clipped reply.

"I'm coming to Vancouver now."

"No. Meet me in Madrid. That's where they'll be."

"You better be fucking sure about this, Thronus."

More sounds of splintering wood and shattering glass echoed over the line as Neeren waited for Collum's reply.

"The bastards want me. I'm the threat. Not Alex. Not Mar. And they'll want me on their home turf—Madrid."

Neeren threw clothing in a bag as the two confirmed details. "What hotel?"

"The Royal Madrid. On the Gran Via."

"Good. I will meet you there in . . ." Neeren checked his clock again. "Three hours."

There was momentary silence on the other end of the line.

"I can't get there for at least six." The words sounded like they'd been ripped from the deepest hole in Collum's chest. "If they hurt her . . ."

Neeren knew Collum meant both woman. And he agreed. If either of them were hurt Neeren would rip their captors beating hearts from their chest. And he'd do it with the world watching.

"Wait," Collum said. "Why did Mar call you?"

Neeren gripped the dresser with his free hand. The wood crumbled beneath his palm. "Because, Thronus. She knows I'm falling in love with her."

~ ~ ~

Half an hour later Neeren was in the air. Talon would keep an eye on things while he was gone. Especially Gray. When Neeren told her what happened, she'd broken down, screaming and clawing at him. It was too much. Trauma was not something her heart could handle anymore. For years, she'd thought her dead child had been ripped from her womb. Finding Alex had given Gray a sliver of life back.

Neeren knew if he lost Alex he'd lose his mother to her demons. Talon would keep Gray sedated if he had too but Neeren had to bring his sister home, alive. He was going to smash that dragon's face in when he saw him. Whatever he'd gotten Maria and Alex mixed up in could cost them their lives.

Darkness nearly swallowed Neeren twenty-five years ago. After his father's death. His baby sister's death. His mother's breakdown. He'd survived to care for his mother and their people. If Alex was lost to them this time. If Mar was? Talon would have to put him down before he lost control. What he'd said to Collum was true. He was falling for the little witch. She brought a chaotic light to his life. It touched a part of him that even finding his sister hadn't touched.

Neeren wanted to grow old with her.

He leaned back in his seat. Now where'd that thought come from? He was immortal. As a witch, Mar wasn't. Yet, for him immortality meant nothing but living in shadows. Perhaps he should grow old in the light with the witch. She reeked of life and abundance. The essence of her spirit felt like cool water. It mattered little he knew virtually nothing about her. It mattered less her mind was blocked. Whatever she hid meant nothing. Maria would share when she was ready. When she'd needed someone, she'd reached out to him. That told him everything he needed to know.

Fear knotted itself into a ball of ice in his gut. He would find her and destroy whoever took her. And then he would make her his.

Chapter 15

A vein pulsed in Mar's temple as she stared at her friend. Her mother's henchmen had thrown Alex in with her less than an hour ago. Alex's beautiful gown was dirty and torn. Her body slack. Mar cursed the vampires to hell and back. They'd laughed about how easy it'd been to capture the dragon's girlfriend. Mar almost pitied them. They had no idea what awaited. Her mother massively screwed the pooch this time.

As her friend stirred, Mar rushed to her side. Shoved Alex's knotted hair off her face. A small bruise marred one cheek.

"Ssshh, you're okay."

Alex's eyes fluttered open. She moaned softly and rubbed her hands over her face. "Where are we? What happened?" Her eyes settled on Mar's face. "Mar? Don't tell me they got you too."

Mar kneeled and grabbed Alex's hands. She grinned with sympathy. "Wish I could, BFF. Can't. They got me too."

Alex looked frantically around. "What about Collum? Is he okay?"

"No clue. I've only seen you. If I had to hazard a guess, I'd say they captured us to draw him out."

"So, where are we?"

"Madrid."

Alex bolted up then clutched her head. "Really? They must have knocked me out with a heavy sedative. They grabbed me in Vancouver." Her eyes glanced around the cell. "I fell for their charade and got captured like a complete fool."

"Don't beat yourself up about it. At least you aren't dead," Mar offered. They're just using you to get to Collum anyway. No sense dying trying to save a guy that can incinerate this whole building with one breath."

"How stupid are they?"

"Ah you know. Pretty stupid." Mar grimaced. Alex was lucky all they did was knock her out. "Anyway, they fucked up. I managed to get word to Neeren. He knew I was in Madrid. I'm sure he's already contacted Collum."

A single eyebrow on Alex's face lifted. "Really? You managed to contact Neeren?"

Heat crept up Mar's neck. "Yeah, so what?"

"Nothing, just strange you contacted him and not Collum."

"Yeah, well," Mar stammered. "Neeren knew I was in Madrid and I only had a couple seconds to send a text."

Alex raised her eyebrows again but thankfully said nothing else to Mar about it.

"Can't you do a spell or something and get us out of here?" Alex asked.

"Nope. Sorry, sister. My magic won't work down here. A spell is blocking all magic. Can you try using your fire?"

Alex flexed her fists. Sparks fizzled at the ends of her fingertips. Uncertainty crossed her face when nothing happened. She rubbed her chin and grimaced. "Nothing. And it's freezing."

"It's okay," Mar assured her. "I'm sure the spell blocks all power—magical or elemental." She leaned her head against the cell bars and yelled, "Hey, assholes, how about central heating?"

Alex rubbed her arms. "Do you have any idea who they are?"

It was the question Mar dreaded above all others. One she had to answer. She tried, but couldn't bring herself to look Alex in the eye. Instead she studied the cell floor.

"Actually yes. They would be my mother and her henchmen." Mar's eyes fluttered up involuntarily to gage Alex's reaction.

Alex frowned. She opened her mouth, but nothing came out at first. She rubbed the back of her neck. The struggle to understand plainly written on her face.

"Your mother is in league with the Vampires?" She finally spit out.

Mar square her shoulders and rocked on her heels. Panic seeped into her chest. Only her ancestors knew the truth. A few ancient witches in the American coven. "Well, see, the truth is my mother *is* one of the vampires. And it's not only Collum they want."

And instead of turning away from her or looking at her with revulsion like Mar feared, Alex simply let out a slow breath and said, "Maybe you should start from the top."

So Mar did. She sat beside her best friend on the filthy cot and told her everything. She told Alex about her childhood. About her mother's anger over her lack of magical power. How she'd resented her only child and abused her because of that resentment. How the vampires came one day and offered her mother a choice. And about Mar's belief that Isabella murdered her parents for power.

Through it all, Alex listened quietly, gently squeezing Mar's hand every few minutes. The simple gesture meant more than Mar would ever be able to articulate.

When Mar finished, Alex asked, "Did you see her kill your grandparents?"

"Of course not. I heard it all, though. I still have nightmares?"

"Why didn't she kill you?"

Mar wiped tears from her eyes. "What?"

"Well I mean, if she killed her parents for power. Why didn't she kill you?"

"I don't know." But the question brought back an old forgotten memory. "I remember after it was all over she drove me out to a field, held my hand for a minute, kissed my cheek and left." Rage swept over her. "She kissed my fucking cheek after killing them."

Alex grabbed Mar's hand. "Look I ask too many questions. I know. But it makes me a good journalist. And right now, you need to ask yourself why your mother didn't kill you as well. Why drop you off somewhere?"

Mar shook her head and pulled her hands back. "You're trying to give her the benefit of the doubt. My mother abused me regularly. She murdered her parents."

"Tell me about your grandparents."

Mar shrugged. "They were quiet, kind people. They owned a shoe shop in Madrid. I used to spend a lot of time with them there."

"With your mom?"

"No. She'd drop me off whenever her boyfriend came around."

"That it?"

Mar fought for memories, but they were covered in shadows. She remembered her grandfather's smile. Her grandmother cooking. A lot of Mar's memories were covered in molasses. No doubt because of the trauma she'd faced as a child. "I . . . I don't know. Things are dim."

Alex wrapped her arms around her. Mar sank in gratefully.

"Hey. It's okay. We'll figure it out."

~ ~ ~

Mar and Alex pulled apart as footsteps sounded down the hall. Mar struggled to regain her composure. A man who looked like a disheveled librarian strode toward them with a familiar, mocking look on his face. Piercing pain lanced through Mar's head. Shadows crept along her memories.

Alex gasped. "Jason?"

He spread his hand wide. A sinister smile turned his face dark. "You caught me."

Isabella appeared beside him. She rubbed his back. "It's about time you returned, my love," she purred.

Jason pushed her off. Fixed Mar with cold eyes. "Little, Mar. I've been looking for you for a long time."

Mar mimicked his actions. She spread her arms wide and twirled. "In the flesh, fucker. Who are you?"

He clutched his chest in mock agony. Bared his fangs. "I'm hurt. Don't you remember your Uncle Jason?"

Mar's world spun. Memories battered at her brain. Memories of another man. A swarthy man. Her father? Memories of Isabella pulling him away from her. Of Runes and Rituals. Blood.

Mar fell to her knees as memories shifted to those of her mother and Jason wrapped around each other in bed. Of her mother screeching at Mar to get out. She remembered being dragged to her grandparents and begging Isabella not to leave her again. Of quiet conversations between mother and grandmother. Isabella urging them to leave before it was too late.

Mar clutched her head whimpering at the onslaught of horrific memories.

Jason's maniacal voice echoed in the chamber. "What's wrong. Is your carefully constructed world falling apart? Did you forget about what dear old dad set in motion all those years ago?"

Mar fought for her hold on reality. "I . . . I."

Jason taunted her. "Go on. Let the memories in. Those stupid American witches never should have blocked them anyway. You should know who you are. Stop believing you're something more."

Isabella pulled at his arms. "Enough, Jason. Let me welcome you home properly." She rubbed herself against the evil creature in front of Mar. "Now is not the time. Steps must be taken before we meet the dragon."

Jason grabbed her mother's arms, pulled her in front of him, and smashed his mouth on hers, all while starring at Mar.

Nausea rose in Mar's throat. A cold sweat racked her body. She seen this before. Him kissing Isabella, while starring at her. Across the dinner table. Across the room. Like she was his property.

"Yes," Jason said to Isabella. "Come and welcome me home properly." His eyes flicked between Mar and Alex. "Then we'll decide what to do with our bait. And our little prophecy."

Isabella's lips flattened into a cold line. She gripped his hand and pulled him down the hallway. "Five minutes with me, my love and you will forget they even exist."

~ ~ ~

"What the fuck? What in the actual fuck?" Alex screamed.

As the memories continued to pour in, Mar pushed herself off the cold ground to lurch to Alex's side. Images from a life of torment bombarded her. Her knees gave out as wave after wave of agony sliced through her chest.

Alex wrapped arms full of life and heat around her.

"I don't know what's going on, but that son of a bitch is a goddamn guardian," Alex shouted.

A forgotten life crept to the surface of Mar's mind. Images of her father attacking her, crowded among those of her mother desperately trying to pull him off. Of Jason, knocking her father to the ground and kicking him in the head. Mar rubbed her neck where an echo of teeth piercing flesh lingered.

Her father was a vampire. The revelation rocked Mar to the core. She'd been running from evil her entire life. Yet, all along it lived inside her. What had Isabella done?

Alex shook Mar's shoulders. "Come back, Mar. Come back."

"My father was a fucking vampire," Mar whispered. "He killed my grandparents. I remember everything."

Alex pulled her into a fierce bear hug. Squeezed Mar like her life depended on it. "It's going to be okay. We'll find a way out of this."

"Nothing is okay. All these years . . ." Panic clutched her chest. "I have vampire blood. Fuck."

Mar gripped Alex, afraid she was losing it. Was she having a heart attack? Could a half vamp have a heart attack? "My mother is with Jason. I remember them falling in love. Isabella wanted to run away with him. But he refused."

Mar smacked her head with open palms. "There's something I'm still missing." She wrenched herself away from Alex. "Why would she block my memories?"

"Maybe she was trying to protect you."

"Oh, come on. You saw her. She's not like your mother. You hit the jackpot with both your adopted mom and your biological one. I got stuck with evil incarnate. Don't kid yourself. Isabella tortured me plenty on her own. You saw her. She was wrapped around that fucker."

A low wail poured out of Mar's mouth before she could stop it. "I hate her."

The struggle to come up with something kind, or wise, or even sympathetic to say was clearly written on Alex's face. But of course, there was nothing to say—other than they were royally fucked.

Mar continued, "And how the hell did Isabella conceive me if good ol pops was already dead?"

"I have no clue." Alex rubbed her face. "This whole immortal world is new to me. You're the expert. The most obvious guess would be magic had something to do with it."

Mar laid on the floor. Ignored the cold and wet. Ignored the pebbles biting into her legs and the pain in her back. She covered her head with her hands. Memories crept past barriers put in place so many years before. Once a landslide starts all you can do is ride it out and hope it doesn't kill you in the process.

She inhaled stale air. Despair was a scent she was familiar with. She smelled it now. People lost their lives in these rooms. Her mother and Jason had a hand in it.

"Why don't I crave blood? I mean, if I'm half vampire shouldn't I crave blood? I'm disgusting," Mar wailed.

Alex plopped down beside her. Her hair tickled Mar's nose. "Look at me."

Mar shifted toward her friend and groaned. "I'm seriously gross."

Alex gripped her hand, warming Mar's frozen fingers. "You aren't gross. Look at me. I'm half elemental and half parthen. It doesn't mean I have all the powers of both. Obviously, because your mother was alive when you were born you took on her traits and not those of your father."

"Maybe."

Alex snapped her fingers. "You aren't sensitive to sun. I've never met anyone who loves to suntan like you do."

Mar sniffled, but perked up. "Right. And I fucking love garlic."

"Of course, you love garlic. You're Spanish. See. Whatever enabled your mother to conceive you must have altered how your vampire side presents itself."

"Pulling at strings, bestie."

Alex pulled Mar up. "Mar, you know this might mean you're immortal."

Mar punched the wall. Blood spurted from cracked and blistering knuckles. Bright red drops splashed against the stone floor. "Fucking vampires."

Chapter 16

Five thousand—that's how many steps Neeren counted while pacing Mar's room, waiting for Collum to show up. Neeren checked in as her body guard an hour ago. Thankfully, Collum called in advance to adjust the booking. It'd taken all his self-control not to rip out the front desk staff's throats, while they took their sweet-ass time confirming his identity. Today was the wrong day to test the patience of a man who'd never dealt with human paperwork before.

Mar's room smelled like coffee and bourbon. The scent evoked images of mahogany hair falling through his fingers. Clothing lay strewn around the room. Five pairs of stilettos were chucked haphazardly in the closet. Her makeup was spread across the bathroom—a brush lying in the sink. Her bedcovers rumpled in a ball.

Maria was a slob. Neeren thought back to the stark order of his room. She'd hate it. No, she'd simply change it.

Rain fell outside. The staccato beat of water on the hotel deck sounded like an erratic heartbeat. Light, then heavy, then light again. On the street below, people squealed in delight. Neeren hated their delight. Their naivety.

Whoever took Maria hadn't even tried to make it look like she'd run off on her own. They wanted to be caught. He clenched his fists. It took all his control not to wish pain on an innocent. One wrong thought and the bellboy could end up dead. It was best if he remained in the room.

Neeren perched on the edge of the bed, pushing a pile of black silk off to the side. He fingered the bubblegum pink lace bra and blouse brushing against his thigh. Who had she planned on wearing them for? Cold sweat covered his brow. The room was suffocating him. The thought of someone harming Maria was suffocating him.

He rushed to the window, gripped the edge with claws he could no longer contain, thrust his head out the window, and gulped in humid air. The ledge crumbled under his grip. Concrete dust flittered to the ground below. Nausea made his stomach role. The last time he'd felt this helpless was after his father's death. When he'd watched his mother curl up in a corner and slowly lose her soul. Neeren pushed claws through his hair. Despair chewed at his gut. He wouldn't lose Maria or his sister.

Neeren snapped to attention as a thunder clap from behind the door carried through to the street. The dragon was here.

Neeren rushed to the door, ripping it off its hinges in his haste. All the pent-up worry and anger gnawing at his gut exploded at the sight of Collum Thronus. He smashed his fist into the man's jaw. A satisfying crunch of bone on bone reverberated in the room. Collum's head snapped back but the fucker remained on his feet.

"You piece of shit. Give me a reason not to kill you right fucking now," Neeren snarled through bared teeth. Muscles pulsed in his back, hands, and face. He was on the edge of turning and letting his panther loose.

Collum looked at him with haunted eyes. There was no fight. No anger. Blood dripped out his broken nose.

"I need you to help me," Collum begged before stumbling into the room and falling to his knees.

It was then Neeren realized Collum shouldn't have arrived for another three hours. He lifted the man off the floor and flung him on the bed. "Did you fly here in dragon form? Why didn't you come in a plane?"

"Couldn't wait. We need to find them." Collum gripped his hand. "I can't lose Alex."

Neeren recognized terror in his eyes. Felt certain it was mirrored in his own. He pulled his hand back. "I need you whole, Thronus. What do you need to regain your energy?"

"Water. Food. Red meat. As much as you can get," came the ragged reply.

Neeren ordered room service. One of every entre on the menu. "I'll pay an extra five-thousand euro each, directly to you and the chef if everything is up here in ten minutes. The bloodier the meat the better," he growled into the phone. "Don't even think of starting another meal before you finish this order."

He slammed the phone down, grabbed a pitcher off the counter, and filled it with tap water from the bathroom. Thrusting it under Collum's face, he growled again. "Start explaining. I need to know everything if I'm going to be of help."

Collum grabbed the pitcher and gulped half the water down. He wiped his mouth with the back of his hand. Fixed Neeren with a stark and calculating stare.

For the briefest moment Neeren felt as though he were being assessed. Measured.

When Collum spoke, each word resonated with gravity. "The immortals know me as, The Guardian. In truth, there are half a dozen of us around the world. We are the keepers at the gate, my friend. The last defense. The holders of balance between immortal and human kind. Even those who think they know—don't. My power is legion above them all. Gifted by the Gods. Over the last thousand years, I quietly recruited the strongest, smartest, most moral among us and asked them to join me. If they agree they must vow to become a shadow. No one can ever know what they do. Ten days ago, I recruited Mar. Three days ago, I recruited Alex."

Stunned, Neeren leaned against the wall in the small room. He shoved itching hands in his pockets before he smashed the man's face again. Fury lanced his chest. The pitcher of water bubbled in front of him. "You asshole. You would sentence them to a living a lie."

"No." Collum sighed. "I offered them the power to change the world."

Neeren studied the man in front of him. A man feared. Revered. Almost a God. All he saw was a man broken by the thought of losing his love. "They are not dark like us. They are light and life. You steal that from them with this request."

"And I believe you're wrong. Their innocence makes them stronger than any of us."

A knock interrupted Neeren before he could reply. He pulled the door open and two bellmen pushed in carts heavy with food. He pulled a wad of bills out of his bag. Thrust money into their hands. Collum stopped him before Neeren pushed them out the door.

"Come to me," Collum called.

The men's eyes glazed over. They walked to Collum on stilted legs. His voice turned to liquid oil. Hanging heavy and thick in the air. "You will forget what we look like. You saw old men, American tourists, in this room. Nothing else. Do you understand?"

As they nodded mechanically, understanding crept in to Neeren's consciousness. The men left the room, chatting about Americans and the good tip they received.

He studied Collum. "So, you have a few more secrets."

Neeren received another assessing look before Collum replied. "I do. Your sister is aware."

"Tell me."

Collum shoveled food in his mouth with little regard for decorum. "Mind control. I carry the power to make any immortal or mortal do exactly as I say. They can't lie to me. Must follow my commands. If I want you to forget this conversation, you will."

A tug pulled at Neeren's temple. A tingle at the back of his neck.

Collum's upper lip curled. "I can help you control what's inside you, too. If you want help."

"Stay out of my brain."

"I can't read your mind. Reading your emotions? Simple. You're strung tighter than a violin."

"I am in perfect control."

"You keep telling yourself that."

Neeren reached for calm. "I do not need to tell myself anything."

Collum shrugged. "Just saying. I've had two thousand years to learn. You're what a hundred and twenty-five?"

"Sure."

"Look. We're family now. I'm offering my help. Take it or leave it. I don't much fucking care." He shoved rye bread thick with butter into his mouth. Swallowed.

"I do not need your help."

"You don't trust me yet. I get it. You will soon enough."

Neeren sneered. "And yet, still you have a leak. Someone you trust betrayed you, Thronus, and you had no clue."

Collum grimaced. "Touché."

"Why do you need soldiers if you're so powerful? Why Alex and Maria?"

"Because, a thousand years ago your grandfather reminded me I wasn't a God and told me I better make some friends before the world turned against me."

Nothing surprised Neeren anymore. Having grown up the way he did, sequestered the way he was, he had no expectations of anyone. "Domhall is one of you," he stated rather than asked.

"He was," Collum said around a mouthful of steak. "Until the day your grandmother died. After anger and insanity took hold I couldn't trust him to make the right choices anymore."

"And Alex understands what you can do?"

"She does. It's also the reason I need her and Mar." He paused.

Neeren waited. He was good at waiting.

"During the battle we fought on your island two weeks ago I sentenced the rogue elemental Taurin Gondien to one hundred years of living death by drowning. With each death, each rebirth, the cycle begins again. When he finally crawls back to earth? When one hundred years are up? I'll take his head."

Neeren whistled. "Sadistic."

"He is a vile creature. He killed your grandmother. I loved Kaylen like a sister. Everything wrought upon your family is tied back to that fucker. Domhall knew. I did it for both him and I. For all of us. But . . . it was revenge. Plain and simple."

Neeren sneered. "This doesn't fit with your code of honor, I presume."

"No. It doesn't." Collum's voice hung heavy, emotionless. "I invited your sister and Mar to join the guardians because I'm losing my morality. My conscience. I need them to keep me in check."

Neeren slumped beside him. His own demons breathing in his chest. "You have become a killer."

"I've always been a killer. I never used to find it satisfying."

An unexpected release of tension caused Neeren to smile. Don't worry, old man. You'll be fine." He lifted one of Collum's chicken fingers. "I already own a slobbering bulldog named Daisy because of my sister. And Maria has me raving like a lovesick teenager over voicemail."

The two men grinned at each other for the first time since Collum entered the room.

"You and Mar, huh?"

"Yes. She is holding back." Neeren chuckled at the irony. "On account of me being a killer. But we are inevitable I think."

Collum pushed his food away as his cell phone rang. Color returned to his face. He answered with a curt, "Tell me." As he listened to the reply on the other end of the line his face darkened and the heat in the room rose by several degrees. "Tell Idris to contact Glenn. I want them both in Vancouver tonight. Neeren and I can handle things here. And, Carol . . . " He blinked once. "Burn his house to the ground."

Collum hung up the phone. "We found the leak." Flames ignited in his eyes. "He disappeared the same night as Alex. He's the man who called me away from her for a fucking meeting."

Collum threw the tray across the room. "I should've fucking known. He's a vampire. One of the vamps we've been looking into must have gotten to him."

Neeren walked to the window. Flexed his claws. "How do we find him?"

"Well, buddy. He used our woman as bait. He'll find me. The good thing is, he doesn't know who the fuck you are."

Neeren paused to study The Guardian of the Immortals. "Are you looking for morality, Thronus?"

Collum pushed the tray of food aside and rose to his full height. The two of them barley fit in the small room. "I'm looking for vengeance. When you get the chance, I want you to kill that fucker any way you can."

Chapter 17

"Lunchtime, kids."

A battle-scarred vampire slapped warped metal trays against Mar and Alex's cage before pushing slop through the bars.

"You'll need your strength for what's to come," he warned before limping away.

Mar staggered to her feet. "Wait. Where's my mother? I need to talk to her."

"Too late for talk," he mumbled without turning around.

"Help us," Mar begged.

His gait slowed and his back stiffened. "I don't help lost causes." He pushed through the door.

Alex reached for her hand. "We'll figure this out."

Mar squeezed Alex's warm fingers. Her best friend looked like shit. Red tangles plastered around her face. Last night's mascara smeared on her cheeks. Her glorious emerald dress torn and muddied. Still, at that moment, she was the most beautiful person in the world.

A slow trickle of water echoed in the chamber. The damp-filled silence of their prison was getting to Mar. She ached—deep in her chest. She ached. Her brain hurt from the onslaught of memories. From struggling to recall more hiding at the edges of her consciousness.

The door at the end of the hall creaked open. Four guards entered, followed by Jason Tanner. Her beloved uncle. Ache turned to quiet courage.

Mar kissed Alex on the cheek. "It's time. Don't fight this."

"What are you talking about?"

"They're coming for me, bestie. For my magic. It's what they've always wanted. It's how they win."

"We're here because they want Collum."

"They get him by using my magic."

Alex gripped her shoulders and shook her. "You look at me. We can fight this."

Mar twisted away. "No. You can't. Stay out of whatever's about to happen. I mean it."

"She's right, Alex. It isn't my intention to hurt you. I actually like you," came a reply from the end of the hall. "Step away from your friend."

Jason sounded almost regretful. Mar wished it was enough. The key scraped in the lock. Mar smiled at Alex. "Don't fight them. You don't have your power right now and it would kill me if they hurt you because of me. You still might make it out of here."

Alex grasped at her arm. "I'm not letting them take you."

As the cage door swung open, Mar pushed Alex behind her while begging Jason, "give me a minute." After his nod, she turned back to her friend. "I've been running from this shit my entire life. They took me for a reason. It's time to face mommy dearest and get this over with."

"No. We stay together," Alex cried.

Mar sighed. "Nah, we don't. Not this time."

Mar pulled away, tightened her fist, and smashed it into Alex's jaw. Her friend slumped to the ground. Mar caught Alex before her head hit the cement and laid her on the moldy cot.

"You're a good friend," Jason offered.

"Yeah, well, I don't need her getting killed trying to fight off your goons."

He sneered. "Follow me. I want your magic before sundown."

As Mar crossed the threshold, a spark of magic flittered through her chest. She forced a nervous bubble of anticipation back down her throat. The familiar tug of her ancestor's magic butted up against the power holding them apart. Hope lifted her chin. She would face this as she faced everything in life—with fucking style.

"Wanna let me in on the plan, Stan?" Mar asked.

Jason stopped in front of a large metal door and turned to answer her. "Yes. You should know. Today we transfer your magic into your mother. It's why you were conceived." His eyes glazed over. His voice passionate as he intoned, "She who is born of magic will be sacrificed to the vampires. Her blood shall make the queen."

Agony stole Mar's breath. The fist in her gut was back. Smashing into her. Stealing air. She doubled over. Struggled for her sanity through pain. "Isabella knew when she conceived me?"

Jason stroked her hair. "Your father was but a tool. The prophecy foretold his seed would bring forth the child. You are also a tool. Nothing more."

Too stunned to move Mar let Jason pet her like a dog. "Your mother is the true prophecy. She would bear the half-vampire child. She is the one true queen."

Mar wriggled her fingers, grasping at sparks of energy flittering to her. She forced her mind to stay in her body. To stay aware. To ignore the pain. She'd known pain before. This was no different. She righted herself. Flinched back from his petting hands. Mouse bones and gravel crunched beneath her feet as she shifted her stance.

"So, I only exist because of a prophecy?"

"Indeed. When I found Isabella she'd already learned of the prophecy from a banished sorcerer." He clapped his hands like a child. "You mother is brilliant. Her intelligence and thirst for knowledge. A worthy companion for me. We were meant to rule. She would bear the child and walk with the undead. Then, once you were old enough, strong enough, she'd take your magic into her to complete the circle. You were always meant to serve a purpose."

Bitterness choked Mar. "How long did it take to convince you to turn her?"

He glared at her. "There was no convincing. I'm in charge here. Isabella is made by me and so must follow my every word. Together we will rule."

He pushed the heavy door open to expose a stark white room filled with medical equipment. A polished marble floor glistened beneath her feet as Mar entered the space. Two metal gurneys were pushed together against the far wall. Her mother lay on one of them with an IV in her arm.

Jason waited patiently for Mar to look her fill. A group of nurses stood in one corner prepping what looked like a surgical tray filled with various instruments.

Confusion crinkled the corners of her eyes. "What is this?"

Her mother's toneless voice carried to Mar like death. "Your blood. It must be passed from you to me. Once Jason begins the spell, the transfusion will begin."

"Like shit," Mar said.

As she backed away an armed guard blocked her retreat. Tingles raced up her arms and into her chest. Magic re-entering her body felt a bit like pins and needles after your leg fall asleep. Fear of bringing attention to herself kept Mar from shaking her arms. She could wait. She'd bring these bitches to their knees. An unconscious smile crossed her lips.

Isabella smiled back. Her eyes darted from Mar's hands to the nurses. Mar followed her mother's glance. The nurses were terrified, she realized. They were human.

"What are Pollyanna and Little Sue doing here? Don't have any decent vamp docs?" Mar taunted."

"You're of human descent. Isabella thought it best to take precautions and invite human nurses to be part of this historic event," Jason said.

Mar raised a mocking eyebrow. "Invited?"

"Yes. Invited and paid handsomely I might add."

An assessment of the room showed little to no options for escape. Until her magic was up and running again, Mar was a sitting duck. Or a stuck pig, depending on what they were planning.

Isabella spoke from the bed, effectively dousing Mar's enthusiasm. "We are aware your magic is returning. This space is free from the spell cast over the rest of your accommodations."

Her eyebrow raised again. "Accommodations? I'd like an upgrade. I prefer five-star."

Her mother ignored her. "If you try anything to help your elemental friend, she will suffer the consequences. Do not try."

Isabella's dark hair cascaded like a poisoned river across the gurney she lay on. An overwhelming urge to yank it out by the roots filled Mar.

"You know what, Mother. Fuck you." Mar turned to Jason. "And fuck you too, errand boy."

His blow knocked her off her feet. She landed on her hip on the marble floor. Blood dripped from a split lip. Jason towered above her. Rage contorted his face. Gone was the ruffled librarian.

"I'm nobody's errand boy, little girl." He signaled to his guards. "Put her on the table."

From her place on the floor, Mar turned questioning eyes on her mother. "How many times throughout my childhood has this happened? How often did you let him abuse me?"

Isabella's stricken voice carried across the room. "You don't understand."

"I don't understand? Me? You bitch!"

Before her mother could answer, Jason gripped Mar's hair, forcing her face up. He slapped her. Hard. With an open palm. The ring on his hand sliced her cheek open. He licked his lips before bending down and licking blood from her cheek.

"You are a tool," he warned. "And you will respect your mother, or I'll break you until you do."

An image of Neeren's grinning face flashed through the black dots swimming in Mar's head. His outrage at the idea of hurting her. Him crooning to his ridiculous dog. Filling a breakfast plate for his mother. Laughing with Alex.

Mar slumped forward as the guards lifted her. Hair shadowed her face. Her only hope lay in breaking the spell. She searched her memory banks for a spell to isolate and block powers. Raced through a maze of magic in her mind. Flipped through spells like one does a paperback novel.

A hand gripped her chin yanking her face upward. Jason ran a finger across her bloody lip, smearing the blood along Mar's jaw. "Pay attention. The only freedom offered you is in this room. Don't put Alex's life in danger. One wrong move and my men have orders to put a bullet in her brain. Not even a great fire elemental can survive that."

Without thinking, Mar swung her fist, connecting with his jaw. His head snapped back.

She glared at him. "You're a piece of shit."

A cold smile cut across Jason's face. He rubbed his jaw. Something dark flickered in his eyes. He stroked his hand over her shoulder. Gripped her ribcage. "Do you want to play, little girl."

"Enough," Isabella said from the bed. "No more."

With what seemed like herculean effort, Jason released her. Blood red eyes burned into Mars. The only thing keeping her safe was Isabella's word.

Guards dumped Mar unceremoniously on the bed. Secured her hands and feet with metal bands. As the cold metal bit into her flesh, revelation exploded like a bomb. No matter what Neeren was, he'd never do this. Not to her. Not to any innocent. Mar knew it as surely as she knew to breathe.

The next thought came furiously on the heels of the first. Could she somehow reach him? He was close. With any luck, he'd gotten her message and contacted Collum. Neeren, she knew in her gut, would come. Her head swam with the memory of his kiss. The love he'd shown his sister. He'd come no matter what.

Once more she flipped through spells in her mind. Blocked out Jason yelling at the nurses to find a line and prep for a blood transfusion. She focused only on finding a locater spell. A way to find Neeren. The needle pricking her skin nothing more than a gnat. She shook off Isabella's cold fingers trying to grip her hand.

From above, Jason said, "All her blood comes out. Every drop goes to Isabella."

Focus was needed. If Mar let herself think about what was happening she'd falter. She allowed her conscience to float above the woman about to bleed out on the gurney below.

Isabella's insistent fingers rubbed against her. A sense of urgency crept into her subconscious. Mar flipped spell pages until a beam of light highlighted one spell in particular. Triumph jolted through her as she realized the simplicity of the spell required. Of course. She needed only to show him the way. Mar silently mumbled words calling forth an ancient magic to spin a strand of connection between herself and Neeren. She unraveled a roll of thread in her mind. Like she was sewing, or fishing. Threw the line again and again. Pictured Neeren.

Beneath her breath, Mar intoned, "He who will find me, be found. Let this thread light the way."

She gasped as the spell struck true. A wave if intense sorrow and anger flowed into her so fiercely a tear fell from her cheek. Whether it came from him or herself she didn't know. A vision of Neeren sitting on her hotel bed, holding her leather jacket overtook her senses. His head jerk up as their internal eye connected. Power surged through Mar, arching her back off the bed. His roar pulsed in her mind. She smiled. They were connected now. Alex would be safe. He would find her. Neeren never gave up.

~ ~ ~

Mar re-entered her consciousness to Jason's rhythmic chanting weaving an ancient spell. She thrashed against her bonds. Whipped her head back and forth, fighting against the icy feeling penetrating her veins.

Isabella's gaze catching her own. Mar swore anger flashed in her mother's eyes the briefest moment before being replaced by Isabella's stoic, half insane gaze.

The click of a machine sounded like a battering ram in the sterile room. A thick brown band pulsed around Mar's arm. Squeezed. Released as it milked her. Blood circulated through her veins into the tube. One pulse per second. Sixty pulses per minute. The sound of her death sentence. She fought against despair. They wouldn't steal her life.

A soft voice entered Mar's mind. "Give yourself a chance. Slow the flow of your blood."

Startled, Mar gazed at her mother. Isabella's face remained impassive. Barely recognizable. Weakness settled over Mar's bones.

"It's time. Concentrate. You can do this."

Isabella's voice was kind, insistent, raw. The voice of someone who fought for her child once a long time ago. An image flashed behind Mar's eyes. Of her mother holding her as a child. Kissing her cheek. Stroking her soft hair, as wet warmth lingered on her cheeks.

Mar fought through the haze in her brain to reach back telepathically. "I can't do this, Mommy."

"Yes, you can. Remember the games we played as a child. The hiding games. The breathing games. Breathe, Maria. Disappear into yourself and all the pain stops."

More images flowed in unchallenged. How had she forgotten? Every time father left the house, she and mother practiced protection games. Sometimes pain had been involved. Her mother always saying, "We do this now so you'll know how when it's time."

Was it time? Mar felt herself fading. Her fingers and toes were numb. An ache cascaded into each joint.

"Maria!" Her mother's voice blasted in her brain, drowning out the machines beeping, the nurse's voices, Jason chanting. The sound jolted her awake. Mar concentrated. Breathed like she'd been taught.

Slow breaths. In all the way to your belly. Out through your nose. Count to ten. Count to twenty. Count to thirty. Each breath longer. Draw it out. Slow your mind. Slow your blood. Mar remembered it like a ritual. Her mother's younger voice, repeating it over and over. Making sure Mar held each breath longer. There was a song they sang. Mar hummed it under her breath. "Thick like wax. Thick like oil. If my blood does leave, it does spoil."

Mar's blood heated. Thickened like lava. A spark returned to her chest. Around her, nurses scrambled. The band on her arm squeezed. The machine beeped erratically. Her blood thickened in the tube.

Forty Seconds. One Minute. Keep breathing. Thick like wax. Thick like oil. One minute, twenty seconds.

Jason's voice bellowed in the space. Bounced off walls. The chant became a battle cry as he desperately fought against the protection spell Mar weaved. Her blood became glue. Stuck to her bones. Like wax. Like oil. Coated. Coagulated in the tube.

Jason grabbed her shoulders. Screamed into her face. His frantic eyes scalding her. "Stop what you're doing." He shook her. "Look at me! Stop this or your friend dies."

Two minutes. Breathe. Hold yourself. Her mother's voice was loud, like a song in her blood. "Weave protection around you. He can't stop you."

Jason slapped Mar's face. Punched her shoulder. Spittle flew from his mouth as he screamed, "Stop, you stupid bitch."

Chaos exploded behind the door. A roar as loud as thunder shook the walls. Screams followed.

Mar opened glowing eyes. Magic flowed through her every pore. She stared in to Jason's terrified eyes and let her breath out.

Neeren was there.

Chapter 18

Neeren rammed the full five-hundred-pound weight of his panther body against the door to the basement dungeon. A swath of recently deceased undead now black dust behind him. Their decayed blood covered the walls and coated his black hide. Next to him, Collum removed the head of the last vampire guarding the door.

The moment Neeren connected with Mar back in the hotel room, he'd begun running, bellowing for Collum to read his thoughts and follow him. Even before they reached the alley behind the hotel, his body had split. Bones breaking and knitting back together. By the time the transition was finished, his voice was little more than a guttural growl.

Neeren in warrior form was five hundred pounds of muscled black panther, with silver spikes on his back, and claws as long and thick as Kukri Machetes. Those claws tore meter long slashes in the roads as he and Collum raced to reach their women.

In this form, Neeren's control over water was at its strongest. He channeled the element as they ran. Called on rain to cover the five blocks directly around he and Collum. Blanketing himself and Collum in cloud coverage. At top speed, they appeared like nothing more than shadows in clouds.

The storm raging inside him was less easy to control. Neeren fought to keep his rage from locking on to any unsuspecting human. Filled his mind with thoughts of Maria.

He followed the glowing thread leading him to Maria with a singular purpose. Legs, with muscles as thick as tree trunks, propelled him to an abandoned church in old Madrid. Lighting spun and flickered around the yellow slits of his feline eyes. Knowing Collum had his back, he didn't bother with recon. The glow from Maria was weakening. Neeren's heart pounded outside of his chest. His claws easily tore the church door off its hinges.

He and Collum were met by ten undead. A laughable number. Neeren used his claws, his spikes, his teeth. Whatever was necessary to destroy anything in his way. Collum, half-shifted to his dragon form scorched the remaining few.

This was easy work—sending their enemies to hell. As undead fell, dust coated the pews. If the human's God did exist, he would judge only vampires for desecrating his hall.

Neeren launched himself against a thick oak door leading to the basement. The glow showing him the way flickered once, then twice. Agony ripped out his chest in a roar as he launched himself again. The door shook, and with an audible groan, gave way.

Another ten vampires waited. Neeren gnashed his canines together. Let silence wrap itself around him. Control. With deathly precision, he jumped into the crowd. Slashed his huge claws through the necks of Maria's captors. Crushed decapitated skulls under his paws. He fought with utter control, as he always did. Swung vampires off his back like they were gnats.

Deep below, Alex's voice carried, yelling something about Mar.

Neeren raced down stairs, decimating everything in his way until he reached the ancient cavern below the earth. Water leaked from fissures in walls. Bubbled and spewed around them.

Collum leaped over two vampires to reach Alex. A blade glistened in his hand as he took their heads.

Thunder rumbling deep in his throat, Neeren stalked

three remaining vampires like prey. He backed them against the wall.

He tried to form human words in his feline mouth. "Maria?"

When they shook their heads in confusion, Neeren raised a paw and sliced open the neck of one vampire. The undead's eyes bulged in his head, hands clutching his neck against the rush of black blood before turning to dust.

Neeren turned his giant head to the final two creatures standing. He growled again. "Where? Maria?"

A gunshot exploded in the small space. Alex screamed. Neeren spun, concerned she'd been injured. Pain tore through his shoulder. The jolt knocked him back a step. An old Vampire covered in scars stepped out of the shadows and pulled the trigger of an old Glock.

A second shot hit Neeren in the hip. His howl rocked the cavern. He twisted his enormous body and launched himself at the shooter, latching on to the man's neck. As blood lust gripped Neeren he shook the broken body like a rag doll. The man sighed as he turned to dust.

"She's behind the door. Neeren, she's behind the door," Alex screamed, pointing to a massive metal door at the end of the hallway. He swung his head her way. "They have Mar in the other room. Hurry!"

By then Collum had taken the other two opponents out. They lay in a gurgling puddle at his feet. As their blood pooled around him, Collum began tearing apart the bars to Alex's cage.

"Don't come in the cage, Collum. It's spelled to drain your power," Alex yelled.

Collum continued to rip metal bars from the earth. "There ain't no spell, if there ain't no cage, babe. Stand back."

Neeren launched his massive body toward the other end of the hall. Blood poured from gaping wounds in his left front shoulder and right hind leg. He shook his head at the gnawing pressure in his shoulder. A weakening light called to him from beneath a crack in the door. A deep roar wrenched up from his gut. He slammed his body against the door. Thick metal groaned.

He smelled Maria's fear but also her anger. She wasn't broken. He wouldn't lose her. Neeren rammed the door again. A dent appeared but the door remained steadfast. From above the cavern, Neeren heard the footsteps of a dozen or more vampires. He turned to Collum, frantic. They were running out of time.

Collum growled. "Alex and I got them, buddy. You save Mar."

Calling on his water element, Neeren pulled moisture up from the earth. The water listened. As it always did. Burst up from the earth and broke through cracks in walls. Flowed toward him like a river. Like a wave. Rushed to his four paws and wrapped around his body. Neeren rose on his hind legs as water pulsed with life. He slammed his giant body back to the ground and water crashed into the door. Coating it. Layer upon layer. Shaping around the hinges. Pushing into the key hole.

A magnificent groan ripped from his throat and the water froze in place.

Turning to Collum, Neeren growled, "My. Kill." Then he reared back on hind legs and rammed his body into the ice. The door shattered.

As the door burst into shards of ice, Neeren lunged into the space. His body quaked from the loss of blood and the exertion of holding his element so long. He shook his enormous body, throwing bits of ice and water across the room.

Maria lay strapped to a bed against the far wall. Chains bit into her ankles and tubes protruded from her delicate flesh. Her beautiful mahogany hair, the hair he'd rested his cheek against, lay in tangles against her head. Dried blood caked her lips and smeared across her cheek. Her right eye swelled with an angry purple bruise.

Pain ruptured across his chest. Rage coated everything in the room in red. A naked roar ripped its way out of his throat. The sound so agonized, for a moment Neeren wondered where it came from. His giant paws slashed the marble floor. Terrified human nurses huddled in the corner. A female vampire with hair as black as oil lay strapped to the bed next to Maria. A pale-yellow plastic tube, heavy with coagulated blood, hung between them.

As Maria's torn and bloody lips formed words, he strained to hear her whispered, "Neeren?"

Her voice sent waves of strength deep into his gut. He locked eyes with her gorgeous hazel eyes. Her fierce strength burned bright searing him.

"Neeren," she screamed as a massive weight slammed into his side.

The impact knocked him to the floor. The spikes on his back digging deep grooves in black marble. A large male vampire screamed mangled obscenities and kicked him in the throat. Neeren hacked up bile and scrambled backward. His giant claws slashed at the slick marble floor, looking for purchase. He shook his head trying to knock the pain from his throat. To gain his breath back. Digging in, he raised his battered body. Stilled. Measured the man before him. The vampire was stronger than the others. Bigger. Older. It didn't matter. Neeren was done playing with his prey.

Neeren roared and reared back. The roar shook the very foundation of the building they stood under. Ignoring the pain in his shoulder, he launched himself at the vamp.

A maniacal light lit the vampire's eyes as he straightened and rushed Neeren. As they met head on the vamp raised his arms, clasped his hands into a fist, and slammed them back down against Neeren's head.

Blood loss slowed Neeren's reflexes. He roared again. Guttural, deep from his chest. He swung a massive paw against the vampire's face, slashing his cheek open. The vampire kept coming. Bewilderment and blood loss stunted Neeren's response time. Fists pummeled his face.

The vampire flung himself against Neeren, then swung onto his back and gripped his neck. Neeren howled. Reared back. Smashed his adversary into the wall. As he fell forward Neeren's left front leg faltered. The Vampire latched on to his neck. Teeth bit through fur and muscle, driving fire through his skin.

Neeren raged and shook his shoulders. Tried to force the vamp off his back by ramming him again and again into the wall with little effect. Inky blackness tried to claim him as blood drained from his body.

"Neeren!"

The scream brought him back from the edge. He raised his head to see Maria ripping tubes from her arms, scrambling off the bed, and falling to the floor.

"Freeze him," Maria screamed.

Her voice slid over his skin like cool rain, breaking through the haze of pain clouding his mind. Neeren swiveled his large body and tore at the vampire with his powerful hind legs, trying to dislodge him before his blood loss was too severe. He dug claws into the legs wrapped around his waist and dragged the vamp screaming from his back. The vampire refused to let go and took a chunk of Neeren's neck with him.

Blood poured down Neeren's wounds and dripped to the floor, coating the marble with the slick smell of pennies. Using the last of his physical strength Neeren smashed the vampire's skull against the wall. The vampire crumpled unconscious.

Fighting against blood loss and delirium, Neeren focused his thoughts on creating a shield of ice. Water came first in a slow trickle along the floor. Pulled out of the earth and old copper pipes, and filling in through cracks in the walls. Soon flowing like a river, flooding the room, and reaching his knees. Water bubbled. Frothed like the ocean. The waking vampire lashed against the water covering him.

Here, Neeren held the power. Each time the vamp tried to rise a wave knocked him back. Slowly water churned. Crystallized. Cracked like ice cubes freezing. Each time the vampire broke through the frozen surface, ice reformed. Hardened. Thickened. Water flowed over the ice forming, adding layer upon layer. Within minutes the man was frozen solid in a block of ice two meters thick. He wasn't dead of course. The undead could not die that way. But for now, Maria was safe.

As his strength gave out, Neeren collapsed. He'd lost liters of blood. Unable to hold his panther form any longer, his body shifted, knitting itself back into his male body. Soft hands cradled his cheek. Soft lips kissed his forehead. Hazel eyes, the color of life warmed his broken body as Maria draped a blanket over his nakedness.

"You came," she whispered.

Gravel coated his voice like rust. "I will always come for you."

Tears glistened in the corner of her thick eyelashes. "Gimme one minute. Okay, kitten?"

Heavy lids dropped over his eyes as he nodded. "Always, Maria."

Chapter 19

Behind Mar, the ice cracked. Her mother sat up on her hospital gurney but made no move to help Jason or hurt Neeren. Isabella's voice coaching her, still echoed in Mar's head.

Cool water rushed over her feet, calming her. Mar was as weak as Neeren. Her blood loss almost as great. There wasn't much time. She stood and placed her hands on the ice imprisoning Jason.

The spell came hard and fast. Fed to Mar from ancestors outraged a vampire tried to harm one of their own. This is where her true strength came from. Family. Centuries of family. Locked on to her since birth. Mar's channeling of the old ones set her apart from regular witches playing with spell books. Her ancestors flowed through her like her own blood. Now their forms surrounded her like beams of light.

Words spilled from her lips like white hot energy. "As he has risen, so shall he fall. What the undead have granted, let life take away."

The ice encasing Jason melted to his waist and pooled around her feet before slowly disappearing from wherever it came. As it did so, blisters appeared on Jason's face, arms and chest. Red hot, angry blisters filled with puss. Within seconds, boils covered his body.

"What have you done?" he screamed while scratching his upper body. The flesh decimated with disease.

Mar shrugged. "Tough break, dude. You're no longer a vamp. This is how you should have died before you were turned. From whatever affliction, this is."

A light flittered through his eyes—his soul re-entering his body. As it did, great sobs shook him. He clutched his head. Tore at his own flesh. "Kill me. Kill me."

Mar nodded sympathetically. "It won't be long."

A long sigh escaped his lips. "So, the plague will claim me after all."

She listened to the whispers of her ancestors before speaking. "As it should have done, so many years ago. I release you from your pain."

A single tear trickled down Jason's cheek. "Tell Collum I'm sorry."

"Why did you do it?"

"My life was stolen from me. And then Collum asked me to protect humankind. It was too much. I never should have been asked. All I ever wanted was my life back. You"—he grunted against the pain—"were supposed to be the key to finding life again."

With a final sigh, the last of the water melted from his lower body and he slumped to the floor. Human. Finally taken by death.

On shaky legs Mar turned her back and walked toward her mother. "You need to tell me what's going on. I can't protect you if you don't."

A sad laughed escaped Isabella's lips. "You can't protect me at all, darling. I made my bed many years ago."

"Tell me about my past, my childhood. There are so many blank spaces and conflicting memories. Did you block them? Why did you help me?"

"Perhaps I'm looking for redemption." Isabella pulled tubes out of her arm. "If only you'd stayed away. Did you really think I couldn't have reached you somehow over the past twenty years? The memories will return in their own time. I didn't block them, Maria. Look to your ancestors."

Footsteps sounded in the hall, breaking through the haze of death.

"It is up to you now," Isabella continued. "You must let me go. Look to your heart, Maria. You know this wasn't me."

Mar gripped her mother's hand as she climbed off the bed. "I won't let you leave. You gotta give me something, Mom. Why let him"—she gestured to Jason's body—"into our lives?"

A bloody tear glistened in the corner of Isabella's eye. "He was the lesser of two evils. And once he turned me I had no choice. Now you need to let me go. I'm not done yet. There is another threat."

She shook Mar's hand off and chanted familiar words. Behind them, a portal opened in the wall. Beyond it, Mar vaguely made out green fields and a man with long white hair. Music carried on the wind.

Isabella smiled before crossing the threshold. "I'm going back to the beginning. Trying to correct a wrong."

"Don't do this. I need answers," Mar begged.

Isabella backed into the portal opening. One foot at a time, never taking her eyes off Mar. "Trust me when it's time."

A strange urge to follow her mother wrapped around Mar's chest. Her body involuntarily leaned toward the music. Behind her, Neeren groaned her name. The sound on his lips jarred her back to the present. Tears fell from her eyes and she shook her head at her mother.

"I don't trust you."

"That's probably best, dear." Isabella laughed, a melancholy sound.

With a last long look, Mar turned away from her mother as Isabella fully entered the portal and disappeared.

Neeren called her name. Mar wobbled over to him, sitting on the hard floor as he pushed himself upright. The holes on his flesh already knitting back together. He cradled her hands in his.

"Did you see?" she asked.

"I saw. That was your mother?"

Mar grimaced. "In the flesh."

"If I'm not mistaken, she used the same type of portal you helped Domhall create."

"I think it was. There was a figure waiting for her."

He kissed her cheek. "No one else needs to know until you're ready to tell them."

Weak and fading, Mar leaned into the hard heat of his body and grinned. "You kicked his ass."

Neeren's thick arms wrapped around her like a protection spell. He kissed her hair. His lips like soft rain after a storm.

"Hardly," he said with obvious pride. "You obliterated the bastard. I just threw a few punches."

~ ~ ~

Moments later Alex and Collum raced into the room. Well, Alex did. Collum strode in wiping vampire dust off his pants. Alex dropped to the floor next to Mar. She hugged her brother first. Then squeezed Mar so hard she thought her ribs might break. Collum looked between her, and Neeren, and the dead man on the floor. Even though Jason had been a friend of his, no remorse crept into his eyes. Mar shivered a little. The dragon was a cold one. He was also the brother she'd never had.

"He wanted me to tell you he was sorry," Mar said while pointing to Jason's dead body.

"Who gave you the bloody lip?" was Collum's response.

"You know it was Jason."

Collum grunted. "I'll burn the body later." He bent down and punched Neeren in the shoulder. "Knew you two could handle it."

Neeren nodded. "You took care of the rest?"

"Yeah, they're dust." As Collum grinned like it was the best joke ever told, the rest of them groaned in unison.

"Seriously though," Collum asked. "You okay, Mar?"

"I'm a little tired. I lost a lot of blood."

Neeren's grip on her tightened.

"What about you?" Collum asked Neeren. "You need a doc to look at those bullet wounds?"

Neeren raised a single brow. "I am fine."

"Was he working alone?" Collum asked.

Nurses crying in the corner interrupted Mar before she could answer. Their terror resonated deeply with her. She searched Neeren's face. "We have to help them. None of this was their fault."

He nodded to Collum. "Now might be a good time to do your thing."

Mar's heart skipped. "What thing? We don't need any dragon fire."

Neeren squeezed her hand, sending warmth through her palm. "Easy, Maria. It is a mind control thing. Not a fire thing."

"Like a Vulcan mind meld?"

He looked at her plainly confused.

Alex spoke up and patted Mar's hair. "Yes. Like a Vulcan Mind Meld. Do you want to close your eyes? You lost a lot of blood."

"Neeren lost more," Mar replied.

Alex nodded at her like she was a child. "He did. But he's immortal and you're not. You need to sleep."

Collum walked back over and laid a blanket over Mar's shoulders. The two nurses skipped away laughing about the terrible dates they'd had the night before.

As weakness began to claim Mar again, Neeren's voice sounded loud in her ears. "We need to move. Now."

"You good to carry her?" Collum asked.

Neeren tilted his head with a sneer on his too handsome face. "You did not just ask that question." He wrapped a blanket tightly around her frame and stood in one graceful movement, lifting her like she was a feather. Cocooning her in blessed heat. "I have you, little witch. It is time to go home."

Collum grinned. "A plane is waiting at the Madrid airport. Glenn will meet us in Vancouver with more intel."

Mar felt herself drifting. Shadows collected behind her eyes. It wouldn't be long before she faded out completely. "Glenny? Tell him to bring some coffee, okay?" She snuggled into Neeren's warm chest and stroked his arm. "I'm going to sleep for a bit now. Love you, kitten."

Chapter 20

Her hair was a disaster. Alex pushed the tangled mess out of her eyes and studied herself in Collum's bedroom mirror. They'd arrived in Vancouver about twenty minutes ago. His apartment took up the top floor of a building with amazing views of the Pacific Ocean. A set of stairs in the far corner of his bedroom led to a private rooftop patio. Her hands shook a little as she wiped dirt off her face.

Glenn paled momentarily after seeing her and Mar. But only momentarily. He pulled himself together damn quick. Alex wondered if anyone else noticed. The man was as fierce as anyone she'd ever met. Composed. Quiet. Resilient. As soon as they arrived he'd ordered Neeren and Collum to put the ladies directly to bed.

Surprisingly, or maybe not, her brother did as Glenn asked without question. Neeren's eyes barely straying from Mar's pale, sleeping face. She'd lost so much blood. Alex was terrified for her. They all were.

Glenn followed Alex into her room with Tylenol, warm tea and cinnamon buns. When she'd asked for coffee, he responded with, "You drink tea after a traumatic experience. You may have coffee tomorrow morning."

He'd patted her cheek. Anger flashing behind his parental demeanor. She hugged him before he pulled away. He smelled like cinnamon. The scent wrapped around her like a wool blanket. Like home.

She stood in front of the mirror now, sipping her tea, waiting for Collum to return with contraband coffee. When she'd asked him to find them coffee, he blanched.

"You want me to steal coffee? From Glenn's kitchen? Princess," he'd said with a groan, "you're asking me to take my life in my hands."

He'd gone though. She was so in love with him.

Her dress was ruined. Her hair a mass of knots. A fine layer of grit covered every inch of her skin. Her fingernails were chipped and broken. Rust mixed with blood from scratches she'd given herself trying to claw open the bars. Her ring sparkled against the dirt. Thankfully they'd hadn't taken it from her. As she studied it her hands began to shake. A cold, clammy tingling crept up her chest to her neck. Alex grasped her chest. Her breath came out in short bursts. Behind her, the door opened and she turned to Collum in a panic.

The smell of caffeine filled the room. Steam rose from a cup in his hand. He walked to her and calmly set the cup on the dresser. His large, warm hand covered her smaller cold one. He stroked her fingers. His thumb rubbing over her ring. Over and Over. Slowly he lowered himself to his knees and rested his head against her stomach. Tears spilled down her cheeks.

"I'm so sorry, princess." His shoulders shook. The words spilling out in a guttural cry full of remorse.

Startled, Alex lifted his head. "This isn't your fault."

Collum sat back on his haunches, gripping her hands. "It is." He continued before she could say more. "I'm not asking for forgiveness. Won't put that on your shoulders. You, my beloved, were taken to lure me to Madrid. Who I am, places you in danger. Every. Damn. Day. I should have remembered this. I'll never forget again."

Heat poured through Alex's chest as she studied her lover's face. Images of him tearing apart her cage like it was made of chopsticks, flooded her mind. His face had been hard as stone. Fire burned in his eyes, but he'd still smiled at her. Told her to "stand back, princess," and winked at her. His wink kept her sane. Kept her from falling apart until they got home. He was perfect. He was everything.

"I love you," she said simply.

He lifted her in his arms and carried her to a bed covered in charcoal gray sheets. It was a man's bed. Two pillows. No bed skirt. Built from distressed wood. Massive windows looked out over Stanley Park from the twenty-ninth floor. How many times had she walked past this building before she'd known about this world? Had he been looking out the window when she'd wandered by?

Collum placed her beside the bed. Stripped her out of her torn dress. Removed her bra and panties. They were black lace. She'd picked them especially for him. She remembered feeling sensual when she'd put them on, thinking about how he'd tear them off her. He removed them gently now. Did not touch her with passion, but with care, like she was broken. Her thoughts cleared. She grabbed his hand. Forced it to her breast.

"I'm not broken."

His gaze stroked over her. She felt his fire like a heatwave. Burning away all trace of her fear.

He nodded. "You are not broken."

"I'm not a doll."

"You are not. You're a fierce warrior."

"And what happened isn't your fault. It's Jason's." She cupped Collum's face in her hands. "Do you believe me?"

His slow sensual smiled ignited a fire in her belly. "Yes. I believe you."

"Good. Now carry me to the shower, lover-mine."

~ ~ ~

He massaged her scalp with magic fingers. Warm water pelted them. She'd laughed when he set her in the shower and she'd seen Head and Shoulders shampoo.

"I like how it smells." He'd teasingly pinched her butt.

"Show me," she'd flirted back.

He did now with firm fingers, lathering soap in her hair. Massaging suds through her scalp, across her neck.

"Under the water, princess."

He placed her head directly under the shower spray. She closed her eyes and groaned in approval. His hands wandered over her breasts. To her waist. Over her hips. Soap slid down her skin, mingling with his hands, like lotion. With increasing pressure, he massaged down her thighs and legs. She kept her eyes closed. Water tickled under her nose, across her lips.

Slowly he made his way back up, leaving a trail of fire as he went. He ignored her most sensitive spots. She whimpered. Tried to force his hands back below her aching belly. His laughter vibrated through her body.

"Not yet. I promise you'll be rewarded."

He kissed water from her eyes, wiped a few remaining drops off her face as he pulled her out from under the water. His hands, full of conditioner, massaged her scalp. The smell of apples filled the small space.

Alex leaned into him, purring. Little claws poked out of her fingertips.

Collum growled in the back of his throat. "Put those away, princess."

Instead she reached behind her and scratched his upper thigh. Her flame tattoo, already vibrating, crawled along her arms and wound its way around her hands and his upper legs. His hands stilled in her hair. He growled again. Trailed love bites along her shoulders. She rotated her hips, grinding into his growing manhood.

"Collum? Do you remember when I said yes to marrying you."

He stilled. "I remember."

Alex fully released her fire tattoo. It crawled along Collum's legs and wrapped around his chest. She stepped back, turned, and watched. Fascinated. Able to feel every sensation.

Jason had played on her weakness. Her confusion about not being human anymore. Her unwillingness to let go of that part of her life. She wasn't human. She'd been imprisoned by vampires. Her dragon had saved her. Her best friend was a witch. Her brother controlled every drop of water on earth. And right now, she was bringing her lover to orgasm without even touching him.

She smiled. "I don't need a human ceremony to prove we're married. I want a dragon ceremony. One befitting your queen. I am now, and always have been, yours."

Fire exploded in his eyes and poured off his skin to mingle with her flame. Steam burst from shower pipes.

Collum grabbed her by the waist, lifted her, and thrust himself inside. Fire against fire. She wrapped her legs around his waist, letting his fire claim her. Her head fell. Back arched. She came as quickly as he did. They hadn't started this for a gentle lovemaking.

As waves of passion washed over them, he kissed her cheek, her eyelids, her neck. Held her against the wall, stroking her to further heights.

He growled against her hair. "I will claim you at the mouth of a volcano and the entire fucking world will know we are one."

Chapter 21

The ocean lapped against Neeren's feet like a lover. Several locals commented it was the quietest they'd ever seen the Pacific Ocean.

Normally waves crashed against the beach. But Neeren was in town and Maria had said she loved him. For the first time in his life he felt utterly at peace. He knew she'd been delirious with shock from blood loss. She might not even remember saying the words. But he knew.

They'd arrived in Vancouver that morning. Mar slept through most of the car and plane rides. She was now safely ensconced in Collum's penthouse with Glenn fidgeting over her like a mother hen. Neeren liked Glenn instantly. His energy was kind. Confident. Old. Easily as old as Collum's.

Alex filled them in on most of what happened. How Mar's mother was the Vampire Queen they'd been searching for. How Jason was her mother's lover. They still didn't know why the vampires wanted Maria so badly. They could wait until she woke up.

Frankly, Neeren didn't give a shit about any of it. All that mattered was Mar.

He'd slept enough on the plane, so once he knew Mar was safe he'd wandered. It was the first time in his life Neeren had experienced true freedom. He didn't have to hide. If he saw an immortal on the street, he simply nodded and walked on.

Vancouver was beautiful. Wilder than his island paradise. Rocky. Gritty. There was a fascinating deepness to it. Vancouver was a town for indie music and growing a beard. For drinking craft beer. It was a town where mountain met ocean. Where evergreen trees grew out of cracks in rocks. Where men wore hiking boots with their suits.

A city bursting at the seams with buildings and people. Congestion, crime, and poverty ran rampant. Yet at their feet sat a vast ocean. And beyond—mountains that touched the heavens. It was a city of contrast.

Neeren absorbed everything like a sponge. Alex told him her city of Victoria was a smaller and even wilder version of Vancouver. Neeren loved his island. He also grieved how much he'd missed during his many years of solitude.

Neeren kept Collum's penthouse in sight as he walked the seawall at Stanley Park. Dogs of all sizes and shapes roamed everywhere. Some gave him a wide berth. Others dragged their owners near to smell him. The animals knew he was different. He laughed it off as people apologized for their pet's behavior.

"You have a way with pups," Collum said, appearing out of nowhere.

Neeren pivoted to head back. "Is Mar awake?"

"Nope." Collum handed him a steaming cup of coffee in a maroon travel mug. "Still out. Glenn figures she'll be down a few hours more. She lost a lot of blood. It will take a while for her body to recuperate."

Neeren accepted the cup gratefully. He took a sip and moaned. "So, this is the good stuff everyone keeps talking about?"

"Glenn's coffee is a drug."

"Does he know any more about what Jason was up too?"

"You need to sit down, man."

Neeren stiffened. "Tell me."

"Glenn dug a little further. But I gotta say man, most of Mar's history is sketchy. Glenn called in a few favors. Word is Mar was born from both a vampire and human. There is a prophecy."

"You are kidding."

"Nope."

Neeren wandered to the nearest bench to sit. "Okay. Let me have it."

Collum sat beside him. "A lot of info is fuzzy. Mar's coven worked hard to cover her history. We have no idea who her dad is but the story goes, because she's a born vampire—not a made vampire—she is destined to be Queen. Another interpretation is whoever birthed the child is the true Queen. For only a true Queen could carry the child of a Vampire to term. Bet her mother is leaning toward that one."

Neeren whistled low in his throat. "How does Glenn find this stuff out?"

Collum leaned back, crossing his arms behind his head. "Glenn has friends in high places. But even they aren't 100% sure about Mar's story here."

"Higher than you?"

"I'm a heathen compared to Glenn." Collum grinned. "You ever hear of Odin and his Ravens?"

"Norse mythology is not really my thing."

"Well in Norse mythology, Odin has two ravens named Hugin and Munin who are his eyes and ears on the mortal realm. Hugin represents thought and Munin, desire."

Neeren's lip twitched. "That's a story."

"You're a story. I'm a story. All stories come from somewhere. From a place of truth." Collum lifted his hands in surrender. "Look, Glenn's been in my life forever. If I ask him to find something out—he does. Every time. And this time he's telling me to dig deeper with Mar and her family."

"Is he one of your Guardians?"

Collum's shoulders rocked with mirth. "Nah. Glenn likes staying at home, cooking for his people, and making us all feel safe. Fighting ain't his deal."

"He cares about Maria."

"Those two bonded over making fun of me, and Mar's ability to praise Glenn as often as possible."

Neeren leaned forward, taking a deep breath of salty sea air. The clean liquid like an elixir in his lungs. Because he was only half-water elemental he needed to be near the sea to remain healthy. Without access to large bodies of water for long periods of time, his lungs would dry out and his blood would harden.

"Do you believe it? The prophecy?" Neeren asked.

"I don't know. Seems like every time I turn around there's a new prophecy to be fulfilled." Collum stared out to sea. The look in his eyes reminded Neeren of how close they'd come to loosing Maria.

Collum continued, "What we know is your lady ran from that family her entire life and hid her past from us because of some misplaced shame."

"We need to find her mother."

Collum turned his steady gaze on Neeren. "What happened in that room? Alex thought for sure her mom would be in there."

The memory of Maria strapped to a gurney with her mother beside her still burned like a hot poker in his brain. Neeren doubted he'd ever forget the image or his failure at not reaching Maria sooner. But the other images? Of her mother remaining passive while he and Jason fought. Of her leaving through a portal. Those were equally important. They needed to know what game she was playing. It wasn't his call though. He wouldn't step on Maria's toes on this one.

Neeren met Collum's gaze with a steely one of his own. "You'll have to talk to Maria. All I know is there were tubes in her arms and it looked like Jason was trying to extract her blood."

Against Neeren's hip his phone vibrated. Maria's name flashed on the screen as he fished it out of his pocket. His heartbeat raced against his chest.

"She's awake."

~ ~ ~

Neeren wrapped his knuckles on the bedroom door. The knock echoed in the expansive hallway. A windstorm whipped through his gut, churning the coffee into a tornado.

Maria's voice telling him to enter sounded strong and healthy. He entered quickly, a cautious smile plastered on his face, prepared to be calm, aloof even. The intensity of his feelings would be too much to put on her shoulders.

Her glorious mahogany tresses trailed over soft white pillows. Her delicate fingers skimmed over cotton sheets. His eyes locked on her fingers, momentarily forgetting everything else. Short, clean nails tipped fingers bare of all jewelry. He frowned. Her hands were those of a worker, a nurturer. Not a party girl. How had he missed it?

An image of her fingers tracing a line from his mouth to his cock jolted through his mind, driving fire over his skin. The image changed, replaced with his fingers tracing over her silken flesh. Skimming across her nipples. Gripping her tiny waist.

She grinned. "Up here, big boy."

He locked eyes with her and winked. "You have beautiful hands, Maria."

"What?" She laughed.

The sound of her laughter was a smoky elixir. He caught her off-guard and he loved it.

"Your hands. You don't wear nail polish?" he asked.

"No, you can't mix herbs with nail polish on. I won't risk contaminating a spell."

The lilt of her voice delighted him. He strode across a plush, cream carpet and reached down to stroke her fingers. Her flesh as soft as he remembered. Achingly soft. Brutally soft. He slowly caressed further up her arm to her shoulders and back down to her fingers, while staring into her eyes.

"Your skin is warm." His stomach summersaulted as she licked her lips.

"It's hot in here." She pushed hair off her neck.

Her wrist, wrapped in pale bandages, glared up at him with recrimination, dousing his desire, and filling him with self-remorse. A yellow bruise covered one cheek. A small cut on her lower lip, sliced through him. Unable to look at her, he stood and closed his eyes.

"I am so sorry, Maria, for not reaching you sooner. You put your faith in me and I failed you. I should have run faster. Should have . . ."

His voice trailed off as warm arms wrapped around his waist. Startled, he opened his eyes to see Mar kneeling at the edge of the bed. Her body against his. Her head fitting perfectly under his chin.

"You reached me in time. No one else could have done what you did. You came, even after I told you to stay away."

Her fingers gripped his back. Desire poured from her eyes. Slammed into him with the force of a goddamn ocean. Heat flooded his chest. Not a gentle heat. Not controlled like passion had always been for him. A raging inferno. For this little witch. Her strength, her chaos—for her. The thought struck him like a tsunami. Everything about Maria burst with light and energy. She drowned out dark shadows.

Neeren ran his fingers over her lip. A slight bump from the cut reminding him to be cautious. He leaned his head down, placing his lips quietly against her own. Curling his fingers in her hair, he massaged her scalp. She moaned. The sound like a purr to his soul. After a long moment, he leaned back and smiled at her.

"Lay down on the bed."

To his utter delight, she crawled backward. Her eyes burning into his as she lay back.

Neeren left her to search for lotion in the adjoining bathroom. He needed a minute to clear his head and gain self-control. The look Maria gave him as she crawled across the bed filled his mind with visions of ripping her clothing off and taking her from behind like a feral animal. He wanted to bite her shoulder as he gripped her hips and thrust into her. Wanted to force her to submit to him. Have her panting beneath him, begging him to claim her.

His cock throbbed against his pants. Claws pushed against the tip of his fingers. He rushed to the sink, turned the tap on, and splashed his face with water. Had to get his shit under control.

Neeren rooted under the sink until he found lotion. Maybe it took him few extra minutes. But, fuck, his cock wasn't backing down and he couldn't go in there with a raging hard on. Not when his beautiful Maria finally trusted him. He gripped the sink and stared hard at himself in the mirror.

"Get a goddamn grip," he bit out to the man staring back.

The bed creaked. Her delicate footsteps padded across the room. He pictured her tiny toes sliding over the carpet, then tightening on the cold bathroom floor. Her smell ripped through him as she entered the bathroom. Like cherries and lust. Passion, like static energy, followed her. He dug erupted claws into the porcelain sink.

Her fingers touched his lower back, scalding him. "Turn around, Neeren."

A growl tore from his throat. "Ah, Maria, if I turn around I won't stop."

She maneuvered her hands around to his waist. Pushed her lithe body under his arms, sliding between him and the sink. Her breasts burned against his chest through her flimsy nightgown.

"I don't want you to stop."

Lust cut his throat like agony. "You are hurt."

With aching slowness, she undid each of his shirt buttons. Her touch weaving a spell of fire and lust. She slid her fingers through his chest hair, over his nipples, and up to his shoulders. Gripped his chin and pulled his eyes down to meet hers.

"I am a goddamn sorceress and I want you. Don't you dare tell me, no."

The need in her eyes shook him to his core, letting lose a passion building up for weeks. He ripped off his shirt, gripped her waist, lifted her onto the sink, and slammed his mouth down over hers. Their tongues met and he leaned over her until her back rested against the mirror, then pushed between her legs. Her night shirt stretched over her thighs. Using one claw, he tore the fabric up to her waist.

The scent of her arousal drove him mad. He placed his palm over her mound, rotating against her hard nib. Her head dropped back against the glass. Forcing his claws back into his flesh, he shoved his hand into her pink panties and thrust two fingers inside her. She screamed, arching her back, nearly falling off the sink.

Maria gripped his head and raked fingers through his scalp, driving a heat he'd never felt before, under his flesh.

Panting, ready to devour her, he ripped his mouth away. "Is that what you want, sweet Maria?"

"Yes," she begged. "More."

He thrust his fingers in and out of her tightness. Heat surrounded him as he watched her. Her back arched, lips parted, eyes half-closed. Her flesh, flushed with desire. Her thighs quivering. Wanton. Unashamed. Wild. She was, fucking glorious.

"No," Neeren said softly, everything in him crying out to take this woman and make her his own. "You want more."

He dropped to his knees, tore her panties off, and lapped at her heat. His head swam with her scent, the smoky taste of her.

Chapter 22

Maria thought she might die. Neeren's tongue felt like silk against her flesh. She groaned with unconcealed pleasure as he flicked his tongue back and forth. His hands gripped her hips, holding her in place. She tightened her fingers in his hair and pushed herself against his mouth.

A slight stubble on his chin and upper lip scratched her sensitive flesh. She squirmed closer. A swirling hunger churned in her belly. Her orgasm started at her ankles, arching into her back and flowing out the top of her head in a slow vibrating wave.

Neeren's tongue never stopped. He licked her in slow circles and fast circles as waves poured through her. Maria had never taken drugs, yet knew for certain sex with Neeren would consume her. Like an addiction. And he wasn't even inside her yet.

As the waves subsided he carried her to the bed. She was languid, satiated, yet still so hungry. She wanted him to push her body against the wall. To feed her. She wanted him to make love to her. As he lay her down, his eyes studied every inch of her flesh. She felt worshipped. He needed to know what he was getting in to.

She sat up, and he sat beside her. In no rush. As though they had all the time in the world. He seemed content with whatever she wanted. It made her want him even more. Mar's heart pounded hard against her chest.

"Neeren, you need to understand something."

"Yes."

"If we do this, my ancestors will call me to them."

He nodded. "Okay."

"Okay?"

He cocked his head to the side as though genuinely confused. "Would you like to tell me more? Do you think this makes me want you less? Or more?"

Maria grinned. "The truth is, there's a bit more to it."

He sat cross-legged before her and began to rub her feet. "Tell me."

She sighed. The pressure of his fingers vibrating up her legs. "It's stupid and old timey. But like, if I willingly give myself to you, my connection to my ancestors become stronger. I'll have access to the other realm. And, you know, ghosts and stuff."

"Why does being with me matter?"

She shrugged. "Cause, you're important to me. And once they sense that . . . It's hard to explain, but if I open myself up to someone the way I know I will with you it opens me up more to them."

A wolfish grin curled his lips upward. He stroked her cheek briefly before going back to rubbing her feet. "You are not sure if you're ready to face them?"

"I feel so deeply connected to them already. Sometimes I feel their light surrounding me. I don't know how much more there will be."

He held her hands in his own and gently stroked the inside of her palms. It was incredibly erotic. "They were with you in the cave. Even in my depleted state, I saw shadows surround you as you cast the spell making Jason human again."

She ducked her head, letting hair fall over her eyes. "I'm just making sure you know, like, I don't know if they're gonna pop up mid make out session."

"They never have before?"

"No one has ever been important enough to matter before."

As she spoke, the look in his eyes nearly undid her. Neeren leaned over her until she fell back on plush pillows. He held his powerful frame above her on muscled arms. Then slowly lowered his body, stopping half an inch from her lips.

His hot breath tickled her lips. "Well, we should probably give them a show. Yes?"

His eyes shifted. Black slits in yellow-green eyes burned into her. His gaze slid over her chest, driving the vision of his tongue on warm flesh into her mind. He lowered himself the last half inch until his bare chest lay against her torn night gown. The warmth from his skin penetrated her flesh. He fit his mouth against hers and kissed her like they had all the time in the world. Licked her lips. Kissed her eyes. Her nose. Her lips again.

She opened her mouth on a groan and he slid his tongue inside. Slowly. Achingly slowly, he tasted her. Mar squirmed beneath him. Her night shirt scratched her skin and she whimpered with the need to remove it. Neeren pushed himself up on one arm. The other arm curled around her neck, bringing her upright with him. As he sat back he lay his hands on her legs and pushed her shirt up her thighs. When it stuck under her behind, he simply tore the fabric in half removing it from her body.

As he looked his fill, Mar thrust her chest forward. She'd never seen anything like the look on his face. He studied her. Selfishly took his time touching every inch of her. She quivered, aching with an unknown need.

Neeren turned her on her stomach and caressed her neck. Her spine. Her ass. Rubbed down each leg and along the ridge of her feet. She cried out in passion. He never wavered. Each touch measured. Controlled to give her what she wanted. He flipped her onto her back and did the same to her breasts, her stomach. When he reached her vagina, there was no hesitation, no deviation. He traced her clitoris. Softly pushed fingers inside her warmth, then pulled them out to stroke her clit with a master pianist's precision. She cried out when he pulled his fingers away and traced the rest of the way down her legs to her toes.

He controlled her flesh like water. Every inch of her body malleable. Every bone in her body turned to jelly. He'd been touching her for hours. For days. Mar clawed against the bed sheets. Thrust her body against his hands. Begged him to take her. He said not a word.

Next came his tongue. Tears pooled in her eyes as he tasted her. Licked her breasts, her stomach, her hips. He sucked on her fingers. Even her pores ached. Her hair. The hair on her arms. Her fingernails. She thrashed below him. Swore at him to take her. He moved lower. Lapped up her juices. She screamed his name, on the verge of coming, needing him inside her.

He released her clit and pulled himself up to her mouth. He kissed her again. Hard this time. She felt plundered. He pulled away and removed his clothing, never breaking eye contact. On a shaking breath, he leaned his forehead against hers.

"I'm going to make you come so hard it will drown out everything else. No ancestor will touch you when you are with me." He thrust into her and she exploded around him.

Wave after wave of power flowed through her. She felt alive, full of craving, of white energy. She gripped his contoured shoulders as he thrust in and out of her. Hard muscles bunched beneath her fingers as the waves of orgasm beat on.

Mar held on to him like a lifeline.

Neeren rode the waves with her until they passed. Until they began again. He spoke against her mouth. "We're not done. I'm taking all of you and you're giving it to me."

He wrapped her hands around his neck. Her legs around his waist. Wound his hands in her hair and pulled her up with him. Stood with her impaled on his body. Pushed her back against the wall.

He fucked her then. Maria leaned into his body. He was different now. Raw. He growled against her neck. Bit her. She wrapped her hand in his hair and forced his mouth to hers. Bit his lips. Begged him to go harder. Deeper. And he did. He gave her everything she wanted and took everything in return. It was rough. Urgent. Dominating. She screamed again and again. A low keening in the back of her throat.

The orgasm started at her feet. She knew Neeren felt it begin. His thrusting became frantic. Like he could barely control himself. He latched on to her shoulder as the world exploded around them both. His feline teeth pierce her flesh as she came. He thrust his hand between them and rubbed her clit as waves poured over them. Maria thought she would pass out. But he kissed her then, while he continued to rub her, as rough waves subsided to gentle rolling waters. She kissed him back with everything she had.

He carried her to the bed. Laid down with her, pulled covers over their sweaty flesh. She kissed him again as her eyes drifted quietly closed. Safe.

~ ~ ~

A familiar stirring curled around Mar's chest, waking her. Neeren's quiet breath tickled her neck. She rolled over and stared at the texture of his face. His high cheeks and strong jaw. As she moved her hand to touch his face, someone snickered.

"Knew your cat would be a good lay. About time you two got down to it."

Maria groaned. Her ancestors were here. Pulling her hand away, she sat up to look at them. Six women of varying ages and sizes crowded near her feet. Each of them stared at Neeren. Maria gasped when she realized the covers had come off sometime in the middle of the night. She hurriedly pulled them over his magnificent body.

"Stop staring. It's rude," she admonished.

"Rude, is having to listen to you two go on and on for hours without even acknowledging our presence," huffed an older woman in a navy frock. Her gray hair hung down her back.

Mar rolled her eyes. "Well I'm sorry to disappoint you, but I didn't even realize you were there."

The first lady who'd spoken stepped forward from the pack. She was middle aged with thick mahogany hair like Maria. "No sense arguing about it now. We have more important things to talk about before your cat wakes up. I'm Xiomara, first of many. You met Sofia," she said while pointing to the first woman who'd spoken. "Next is, Luciana, Emily, Zoe, and Juanna. Only Sofia and I speak English. The other birds refuse."

Mar grinned as Xiomara threw her hands up like it was an old source of frustration. She gazed at each of them in turn. Xiomara was clearly the leader. Luciana was downright ancient. Deep grooves marred her skin. Her hair an ivory white. Her hands covered in age spots. She smiled at Mar with a mouth full of perfectly white, straight teeth.

Mar winked at Luciana before speaking to Xiomara. "A bit awkward under the circumstances but it's nice to finally meet you all. You've been swimming around in my head for so long I feel like we already know each other."

Xiomara smiled. "The feeling is mutual."

"So how exactly are we all related anyway?"

Xiomara answered for the group again. "I'm your great, great, great, great, etc. grandmother. Sofia is my great, great granddaughter, and so on down the line. The conduit comes once every fifth generation. You're the next."

"Sounds impressive. Do I get more of my witchy powers now?"

Xiomara laughed. "You kids. Always wanting everything so quickly. First you become a conduit. You must learn more so when the darkness falls you're ready."

Mar snapped her fingers. "Right. Damn darkness. You birds gonna teach me how to defeat it?"

"We would've but you already slept with it," Sofia said with a sneer.

Anger launched in Mar's belly. "Neeren is not dark."

"Like mother, like daughter," Sofia replied.

"What's that supposed to mean?" Mar asked.

Sofia barked out her words. "Why couldn't you fall for some nice, naïve, human kid? The cat is going to be trouble and you have to concentrate on more important things."

Mar stood up from the bed. "I didn't ask for this, you know. Every time I turn around someone wants to use me. Isabella. Jason. Now you."

Xiomara stepped forward as fast as lightning, gripping Mar's hands. "Your mother is following her own destiny. Yours is greater."

A low vibration flowed over Mar's hands from Xiomara. "And what is my mother's destiny?"

"Beast is stirring," Sofia said interrupting them.

Without letting go of Mar's hands Xiomara replied to Sofia. "Don't worry. He's in a deep sleep. I made sure even he, great dream walker and mind stealer that he is, cannot hear our conversation." She continued speaking to Mar. "Your mother was a great disappointment to us. We never understood her craven need for power over the undead. The only good thing she ever did was lie about how you were conceived."

Mar's blood pounded behind her ears. "What are you talking about?"

"Isabella brought that vile vampire into her home and her bed to fulfill a prophecy even she didn't believe in." Xiomara shook her head. "But your mother wanted to be queen. So, she lied. Jason had come along by then and latched on to her. She followed through with his stupid plan and claimed you as the vampire child."

Questions piled like book pages in Mar's mind. A migraine flitted against her temple.

"Your real father," Xiomara continued, "was a wild sorcerer who played with dark magic. He was banished by the coven shortly after Isabella conceived." Bitter glee tinged her words. "Surprised it took as long as it did for his shit lifestyle to catch up with him. Honestly, what your mother saw in him is beyond comprehension. We've kept your lineage hidden so the other covens wouldn't paint you with the same brush."

Mar held on to her ancestor for support. Xiomara seemed to have no understanding of the crap she was laying at Mar's feet.

Xiomara sneered. "Jason turned her while she was giving birth to you. By then she'd cast every spell she could think of to make you appear half-vamp to every being who thought to look."

"Are you guys for fucking real? I'm not half-vampire? My dad was a dark sorcerer?" Mar pulled her hands away, jumped off the bed, and gulped air into her lungs. "My entire life is a soap opera."

Xiomara rolled her eyes. "Don't be so melodramatic. Your grandparents were real. Once they suspected Isabella of her treachery, they tried to stop her. Morath, the vampire that supposedly fathered you, was a buffoon. He killed your grandparents."

The group of women hung their head for a moment in what Mar assumed was an act of remembrance.

"Jason killed Morath when he discovered him trying to feed off you. Only good thing the man ever did." Xiomara grimaced, like even saying the words hurt her. "The death of your grandparents affected your mother though. Isabella fell into despair and tried to kill herself. Jason stopped her. She begged us to save you. We carried you to the coven in America. We've hidden you from vampires since then."

Mar sat on the edge of the bed. "I always thought I was on the run from her. That she was trying to steal my magic to become stronger."

Xiomara's voice was kind, sympathetic even. "Well, in part she was. Or someone was? We're still trying to piece this together. Look, we needed you to stay away from your mom and everyone around her."

"But if I'm not even the so-called vampire child, why not simply tell the vamps and be done with it."

Xiomara shook her head. The sadness in her eyes told Mar more than she needed to know. "There is more to this tale than we have time for right now. Your sorcerer father is banished . . . somewhere. Your mother has her own end game on this one, kid."

"Why didn't anyone tell me this shit?"

Xiomara looked at her like Mar was stupid. "Dead, remember? We couldn't talk to you until love opened you."

Anger whipped Mar's voice into a squeal. "I want to put pants on. I'm not having this conversation in a sheet."

~ ~ ~

Mar pulled on a hot pink wrapper left at the foot of the bed by Glenn. Once covered, she glared at her ancestors. They alternated between giving her looks of condolence and annoyance. Sofia was big with the annoyance face.

Mar moved closer to them hoping not to disturb Neeren. "You're telling me my mom wanted me hidden this whole time because she's been conning the entire vampire race."

"Yeah." Xiomara shrugged. "What a bitch. Truth is she might be super smart. I mean once she died she'd be out of Olorin's view—That's your dad's name. A fresh start. No soul for him to track."

"But you don't know for sure. My mom might be trying to keep me hidden from him, or she might be on his side?"

Xiomara grimaced. "Bet you wish you'd stayed buried in America now, hey?"

Mar lashed out. "Really? What about you folks? My ancestors. My protectors. Not one of you thought to tell me before now?"

"I did, Sofia retorted.

"Oh, shut up, Sof," Xiomara muttered.

"I want you guys to leave." Mar pointed to the door.

"We can't." Xiomara replied.

"You most certainly can."

Xiomara raised her hands in surrender. Bangles clinked together like bells. "Look, I get you're pissed. But a darkness is coming. And it might be Daddy. Your lover, and your buddies Collum and Alex, will be called to fight. So will you. You need to be ready. We can't leave unless you're with us. Training starts today and you're doing it with us by your side."

Mar's shoulders slumped. Physical and mental exhaustion made it difficult to form words. "This is all a shit show. I hate my mom. I'm not liking you guys much right now either."

"Can you hold your rage in until we have more time to talk about everything?" Xiomara asked.

"Can't I have a night with a great guy before making any more decisions?"

"Nope," Xiomara replied. "You're destined to be sorceress to the guardians. And a fight with the darkness is coming soon."

"Fine. Then I make the decision to train here. We'll start tomorrow."

Sofia cackled. The other ancestors snickered.

Xiomara sighed. "I was afraid you'd say that. See, we really need you to come with us. There are spells you need to learn from the other realm."

The women casually circled Mar as Xiomara spoke. Their soft voices chanting a chorus. Beneath Xiomara's feet, blue light swirled.

"What are you doing? Stop." Mar's angry gaze sliced each of the women in the circle. She glared at Xiomara as panic began to set in. "Tell them to stop."

"Can't, sweetheart. You really do need to come with us."

The chanting increased. Behind her Neeren stirred.

"Big man's going to wake up soon," Xiomara said. "It's better for him if you keep him out of this."

"Fuck you, Xi," Mar spat. She spun in the circle, kicking away light creeping toward her feet. Raced through spells in her brain. A weight pushed over her mind like a window shutting out all the fresh air. She had no idea how to stop this. "Make them stop. I don't want to go."

Xiomara placed hands on her hips. She leveled a glowering look Mar felt right through to her bones. "Look, cupcake. This is bigger than you. It's time to join us. Like it or not."

"Well, I don't like it. My body, my choice." The light rose to Mar's knees. Her legs felt numb. She tried to pull away, but the light held her captive. "Let me go," she cried.

Through the mud in her brain, Mar heard her name. Hope gave her enough strength to turn her upper body toward the sound. Neeren stood beside the bed in full glory. He was huge, towering over them even from across the room. Muscles tight, ready to pounce. His calculated glance swept over her and her ancestors.

"Do you see them?" she asked.

He tilted his head slightly. "I see them."

"You need to stay out of this, big man," Xiomara warned.

"I do not respond well to threats."

Mar saw the control in his jaw.

He looked her in the eye. "Do these ones have human souls, Maria?"

She knew what he was asking. He'd kill them if Mar asked it. Without question. Without blinking. A strange quiet swept through her. She smiled at him. "I'm falling in love with you, Neeren."

His smile blinded her. The brightness outshone the light crawling up her waist. "I know, my queen."

She grinned and rolled her eyes. Trust him to behave like a pompous ass, while offering her the world. "They're ghosts. Already dead."

He sighed, like he was genuinely disappointed. "Very well. Another way then."

"Um, hello. We're on a schedule here." Xiomara huffed before flinging her arm back. Neeren flew across the room and smashed through the bathroom door.

Mar laughed out loud. "Well, now you screwed up."

"You're making this more difficult than it needs to be. It's not like we're trying to hurt you."

Mar glared at Xiomara. "I just found him."

Xiomara shook her head. "You have a destiny to fulfill. And parthen-boy is not one of the good guys."

"He is good. He saved my life!"

"He'll be here when you get back," Xiomara quipped.

The chanting reached a crescendo. The voices of the women combined in an age-old song. Sweat glistened on Mar's skin. Music overpowered every thought in Mar's head. She grabbed her hair, trying to focus her mind.

Roaring erupted in the bathroom. The witches shifted nervously.

"Don't stop," Xiomara shouted over the sound of walls giving way.

A low growl preceded the sound of the bathroom wall collapsing. Neeren, King of the Panthers had shifted. Drywall and cement rained down on silky black fur covering legs larger than tree trunks. Each movement, each step, controlled. A thunderstorm brewed in the beast's eyes.

The witches' voices whipped into a crescendo. Urgency pounded through Mar's own mind.

Neeren's panther stalked the ghostly woman. Sniffed each of them. Sniffed the light. The women's voices became a single mass of sound. An echo older than time.

Neeren snuffed at Xiomara. Leaned his huge body against her non-corporeal one. Lifted his paw and pushed it through her into the light. Tested it with his claws. The light pushed back. Scorched his flesh.

"The other realm, Neeren," Mar choked out as light wrapped around her neck. The pressure against her throat raw and urgent. Her body paralyzed. Her mind nearly shut down. "They're taking me to the other realm."

Neeren forced a paw into the circle. She watched, stricken, as the light burned his paw.

He remained unflinching as the hair on his paw curled and disintegrated. As the flesh bubbled and melted. Held her gaze until she could see no more. Until the light covered her own eyes. Until the light was all she saw. Until she disappeared.

Chapter 23

When it was over and her body faded from the room, Neeren shifted back into human form.

The smell of burnt flesh assaulted his nose. Looking down he realized the skin on his left hand was seared to the bone. He wandered to the bathroom to inspect the damage. Rinsed the flesh methodically, ignoring the pain. Re-washed with soap and water. He searched the bathroom cupboards for a few minutes before finding a jar of Vaseline, lathering what little flesh remained, then wrapping it in a hand towel.

His bones ached. Exhaustion crept up his neck. Along with something else.

He stepped through a gaping hole in the wall. Drywall and busted boards crunched under his feet. A nail sliced into his heal. He looked down. Blood trickled out the bottom of his foot to the floor. He studied the bed covered in tangled sheets.

Something had happened there. Cobwebs lay heavy in his mind. He shook his head. Tried to unplug a memory. Maria. Yes, Maria wasn't in the bed.

Neeren unwrapped his hand. Studied the bone and scalded flesh. A soft light sparked in the dark corner of his memory. Anxiety tried to cut off his airwaves. He breathed deeply of the heavy hanging, chalky air. Coughed. Fought for control of his own mind.

He flicked the light on in the room. Rubble from the wall covered everything. The bed, floor, a layer of dust on the dresser. The light made the floating dust look magical.

Magic. Something involving magic. He shook his head again. Breathed again. A slight scent of fear assaulted his nostrils. A stronger scent of anger. Of frustration.

Shadowed memories surged in so hard it dropped him to his knees.

They took her.

Moments later he wrapped his knuckles on Collum's bedroom door. It was one in the morning. Collum answered immediately.

"Maria is gone. I need Glenn."

Opening the door, Collum backed into the space to let him enter. Neeren vaguely noticed Alex sitting up in bed, wiping sleep from her eyes. Neeren sat in an oversized armchair by the window and stared at the moonlight.

Light. Blue light.

Collum's voice pulled him back from the moon. "Where'd she go? Is she looking for Glenn? She shouldn't be out of bed yet."

"What? No. They took her."

Alex joined them and reached for his bandage. "What happened to your hand?"

Neeren snapped his hand back. "Don't touch that. It's healing."

Collum's gaze narrowed. "Is Maria in this apartment, Neeren?"

Neeren shook his head. "I'm fuzzy. They did something to me."

Collum's firm hands gripped Neeren's shoulders grounding him. Pulling him back from the light into the room. The dragon spoke, "Focus. You need to start from the beginning. Alex, go check the room."

A she ran from the room, Neeren furrowed his brow trying to concentrate on something important. He knew he needed Glenn. "I need Glenn."

Collum handed him a glass of bourbon. "I'll call him now. You drink this and don't move."

He nodded. "I will not move until I speak with Glenn."

Alex raced back in the room skidding to a halt directly in front of Neeren and Collum. "The bedroom is destroyed. No sign of Mar." Panic made her voice sound unfamiliar.

Neeren's chest tightened.

Collum swore. "You need to wake Glenn. Right now. Do that for me before you lose it."

She nodded and raced back out of the room. Neeren drank his whiskey. It burned down his throat. He squeezed his eyes shut and gritted his teeth. This was important. He needed to remember.

"You able to talk, buddy," Collum prompted him.

Neeren fixed his gaze on the man's steady eyes. Focused on the pupils. Breathed fresh air into his lungs. Words flitted through his brain and began to form sentences. "She's the conduit."

"Good, what else?" Collum prompted.

Neeren grabbed the bottle of bourbon and took a long pull from the bottle. Concentrated on her scent. On blue light.

"There were six witches—ghosts. Her ancestors." Neeren growled. "They said something about needing her to fight the coming darkness."

Neeren shook his head again as shadow memories took shape. Became three dimensional. His hand throbbed and he shook his wrist. Pinched the mangled flesh. The pain broke through whatever they'd done to him. Vivid images flooded his brain. He felt the burning on his flesh. Heard her voice as clearly as if she sat in front of him. Neeren hissed, all pretense of being tame removed. Holding his hand in the light as long as he had, offered him a glimpse of their destination.

He knew where they'd taken her. "She's in the other realm."

An immediate sense of peace crawled over Neeren's skin as Glenn entered the room wearing a fuzzy pale peach dressing gown. The man walked straight to Neeren and handed him a cup of coffee. Alex followed. They all listened intently as Neeren filled them in.

"What is the other realm?" Alex asked.

Holding Neeren's steely gaze, Glenn responded, "The other realm is where immortal warriors rest after they are killed on this earth. Essentially, it's heaven on earth. Though witches are technically not immortal they pass on to the other realm when they die. They are offered eternal life in death so they may continue to serve."

"Like Valhalla?" Alex asked.

"Yes, exactly like," Glenn replied. A quiet intensity rung in his voice.

Neeren paced the room with the bourbon in his hand as he recited the story his mother and father had shared with him at birth. "When an immortal warrior passes from this plane he is taken to the other realm so he may live the rest of his days in peace. Norse mythology calls this place Valhalla. Humans call it Heaven." He smiled at his sister. "Our father rests there."

She swallowed. "How do we find a way into this realm?"

Neeren sipped his coffee before replying. "A wise man—a raven of some influence, has the answer we seek."

Glenn interrupted him before he could say more. "You have to die to pass over, Neeren."

An easy smiled covered Neeren's face. "Then you'll kill me."

The room exploded around him. Alex freaking out. Collum trying to talk him down. Glenn saying maybe he should have brought tea.

Neeren sat on the edge of the bed and waited for them to finish carrying on. His feet were cold against the floor. Dried blood coated the bottom of his left foot. Shivers ran up his legs. He needed to soak in a warm bath or stand under a burning hot shower. Anything to take away the chill of losing Mar. No, he hadn't lost her.

He didn't think the witches were out to hurt her, but they greatly underestimated connection in this family. As soon as Maria declared herself Alex's best friend, she became his family. Or maybe it was before. Maybe it was the first day they met. When she'd brought the dragon to his island through a portal. When she'd head butted him in his own kitchen and called him kitten.

"Are you done yet?" Neeren asked as he casually sipped his coffee.

"What do you think, big dummy," was his sister's reply.

"If you would let me finish I can explain how easy it will be."

"Easy to kill you?" Alex yelled before rounding on Collum. "What did you put in the bourbon you gave him?"

"Hey, don't blame me for your brother's death wish," the dragon replied while raising his hands in surrender.

Neeren would have laughed if they had time. Watching his sister take on the dragon was something he hoped to see many times throughout their very long lives. But not now. Now they needed to pay attention. Neeren stood. His roar shook the rafters. "Sit down and listen to me."

The three beings clamped up and sat down.

"Thank you. Now, I have a plan. Glenn. I believe if you kill me—" He put his hand up to stop Alex before she could speak again, "in your dream, then I can travel to the other realm to find Maria."

"If someone dies in the dream they die in the real world, Neeren," Alex told him as though he'd forgotten.

"True. But only if the dreamer wakes up. We all know your boyfriend here can manipulate minds." He nodded to Collum. "It's very simple. Collum keeps track of Glenn's dream until I bring Mar back. Once she's out, he steps into the dream. Then he manipulates it so I come back to life in the dream. Viola, I'm alive again and Glenn wakes up."

All three stared at him like he'd lost his mind.

"What? It will work."

Collum was the first to respond. "Not Glenn. We'll use me. I won't risk Glenn."

"Glenn knows more about the other realm than anyone in this room and I think if I die at his hand, I'm guaranteed entrance."

"Don't push this, Neeren," Collum growled. "I won't risk Glenn."

"Too late. I'm pushing." Neeren stared into Glenn's magnetic eyes." I think you were born there, Hugin. And I'm damn sure you can get me in."

When Glenn said nothing, Neeren tried again. "She loves you. And I love her."

Glenn sighed, seating himself in the chair nearest Neeren while arranging his dressing robe. "I haven't been called that name in a very long time."

"Maria has been taken against her will and I believe you know exactly where. If you are truly one of Odin's Ravens then I am asking you to help me find her."

"Long ago I chose to be where I am—serving who I serve."

"And who is that exactly?" Neeren asked.

Collum interrupted him before he pushed further. "Stop it, Neeren. You're overstepping."

Neeren glared at the dragon. "You have the power of a God on earth. A God's raven sits at your side. Help me, for fuck's sake."

Collum heaved a huge sigh. "Do you think her ancestors would harm her?"

Neeren looked at Collum like he was daft. "They took her against her will."

"I understand . . ."

"I don't think you do. Maria has been used as a pawn her entire life. She has been beaten and controlled by everyone who ever claimed to be on her side. On the very night she finally felt safe enough to trust someone, her ancestors once again took her free will away. I am going to retrieve her."

Glenn wiped his palms on his robe before standing. "Neeren is right. Maria has been through enough. I will help. But you don't need to dream walk."

The man stared out the window to the Pacific Ocean below. "All you need do is drown long enough to stop your heart. The water will protect you as it always has. Hold you in a form of stasis. I can open the door to the other realm the moment you die, and you will open your eyes on the other side."

Chapter 24

Mar opened her eyes to find herself laying on a lounge in garden overflowing with sage and gardenias. Her kidnappers sat in wicker chairs, drinking ice tea, or leaned over flower beds weeding. Wind chimes tinkled in the air. Water trickled from a moss-covered water fountain. Incense burned in the corner.

Mar groaned. Fucking great. They were hippies. Could they possibly have veered from the stereotype?

When she tried to sit up, Xiomara rushed to her side. "Easy. You'll be a bit dizzy from the trip. Don't move too quickly."

Mar pushed her hands away. "Now you're worried about my welfare? You drowned me in some ritual white light after I explicitly said I didn't want to come with you."

"Well, yes. But you were being difficult."

"Me? I was being difficult?" As Mar prepared to blast then with the full extent of her anger she looked down and realized she was still in her wrapper. "Hold up. One of you witches better of brought my clothes with you."

The women looked at each other, and her, with confusion written clearly on their treacherous faces.

Mar exploded. "Do not tell me you brought me here without my clothing! What am I supposed to wear?"

You can borrow something from Sofia. She looks close to your size," Xiomara offered helpfully.

Mar pushed herself up from the lounger, shaking off Xiomara's hands when she tried to help her stand. "I do not wear borrowed clothes," she spit out between gritted teeth.

"And I'm sure as hell not wearing some hand me down hippie rag."

"Hey," Sofia shouted from the flower bed.

"You're being ridiculous," Xiomara said.

"If you'd given me the chance to pack I would have my own clothing. I would have my spell casting shoes. I'd have my Saturday hat. I'd have my makeup bag. Fuck," Mar screamed. "Why couldn't you wait one goddamn day and give me the tiniest bit of control over my life."

Exhausted, Mar sat down, tightening the wrap around her shoulders. "I'm cold. I need a blanket."

As Xi sat beside her, Mar gave her the stink eye. The woman had the audacity to laugh. It was a kind laugh at least.

"Look, I know this isn't how you wanted today to turn out. I also know if we'd given you time to think about it you'd have pushed us off a day, and then another, and another."

"No I wouldn't."

"Yes, you would. You're freshly in love with your cat. He'll protect you, save you, make all the bad people go away. And you'd end up letting him. You don't have time. You need to study."

"You don't know what I would have done."

"Of course, I do." Xiomara pointed to the other witches. "We all do. Because we've gone through exactly what you have. Waiting for the one. Never wanting to leave them. Your training is more important."

Sofia wrapped a second blanket around Mar's shoulders. "My guy was a carpenter. Goddess he was amazing. He died two years before I did. We had a long happy life together. He made me leave to practice my training when I tried to refuse."

Xiomara smiled. "Mine was a farmer. Built like an ox. When I disappeared, he thought I'd left him. It took me years to win his trust back."

"Neeren is not a farmer," Mar said.

Xiomara rolled her eyes. "He's only a man. Besides there are many handsome warriors in this realm to help take your mind off him while you're here."

Annoyance colored Mar's voice. "He's the king of the Parthen. He can walk into the dream of every living creature in existence. He controls every drop of water on earth and the precipitation in the sky. He isn't only a man. You should have waited."

Xiomara waved off her rebuke. For a moment, Maria felt sorry for her. But only for a moment. Her ancestors were a little too high on themselves for their own good. It didn't matter how powerful they were. If she was going to join their ranks they needed to start listening to her.

"I'll train, but you better come up with a better plan for clothing me. You better tell me more about my father. And you also better be prepared for my lover to show up."

"We are in the other realm," Xiomara replied. "He can't reach us."

Mar reached for her iced tea. She sat, crossed her legs on the chair, and let the morning sun soak into her weary flesh. "Sure, you birds keep telling yourselves that."

~ ~ ~

Later that afternoon—after a warm shower and a hot lunch—Mar joined her ancestors in their spell room. Ancient texts lay in piles among tables covered with bottles of herbs, potions, and elixirs. Fire burned in the soot covered corner wood stove. Though chaotic, the room was meticulously clean.

The women lived in a place Mar could only describe as a commune. One large house held the kitchen, dining room, living room, a couple guest rooms with showers, and a spell room. Smaller cottages surrounded the main house, offering each of the woman their own space to retreat too. The main garden connected to the main house, but each cottage had its own mini garden as well.

It was beautiful. If you went in for the whole hippy dippy thing. For Mar though, a house was not a home without access to Saks Fifth Avenue, the corner jazz bar, and a gym with a sauna.

Sofia found a decent pair of jeans and a T-shirt for her to borrow. Mar's skin itched but at least they hadn't tried to pawn off a linen Mumu on her. She shivered thinking about it.

"Are you paying attention?" Xiomara asked, interrupting her thoughts.

"Of course, I'm paying attention."

"Let's start with a simple volume of transferring spells."

"Actually, let's start with a simple conversation about my father."

Xiomara grimaced. "We've told you everything."

"Um, nope. I don't think you have. Tell me about my mother's past."

"Very, well." Xiomara laid the text on the table and gestured for Mar to sit beside her. "Your father, Olorin was well known as a skilled sorcerer. He and Isabella dated for many years. They were thick as thieves but your mother never had his skill with magic. None of us thought it would last.

"Go on," Mar prompted.

"We were wrong. Over time the relationship changed. Olorin became stronger, more competitive. Isabella followed him like a puppy rather than a lover. Next thing we know, he's gone, she's pregnant, and she's hooking up with a vampire. We watched. We listened. Isabella was ambitious and committed to whatever path she was on. But also, scared. More scared of a missing ex-boyfriend than hooking up with the vampires."

Mar spun the name around in her head. Placed it in a little pocket to bring out later when she was alone. "Do you think Olorin's dangerous?"

"We do. Obviously, so does your mom."

"Will the vampires figure out I'm not the prophesized child?"

"Maybe? The jig is probably up now. Which means your mom will be a vampire without a coven."

"You all think he's still alive?"

Xiomara nodded. "We do. We believe he was banished to the demon realms and is still bound within. Sadly, we don't know which one. The way the runes are behaving, we wonder if someone found him."

"You think my mom did?"

"Maybe. She never could say no to him."

"But you just said she feared him."

"Your mom always had bad taste in men. With Olorin? Sometimes love can blind you to the truth."

"Does she have enough power to help him?"

Xiomara simply shrugged, leaving Mar dissatisfied, verging on pissed.

"I truly think I grew up in the most dysfunctional family in the world."

"It's certainly possible," Xiomara replied.

Mar burst out laughing. "This sucks so hard. My mom sucks. She sure knows how to pick them."

"Isabella is a complicated woman."

"What am I supposed to do with all this information?"

"Be ready. Train. Be wary. Become stronger than your adversaries. Watch and wait. That's all you can do for now.

The image of Isabella lying beside her on the hospital gurney flitted through Mar's head. The image shifted to her mother opening a portal and the man waiting for her in the shadows. Was Isabella evil? Confused? Playing them all or helping them? Mar had never been so confused in her life. Xiomara was right. If Mar wanted a life outside of Isabella's mistakes she needed to train. She needed her ancestors now more than ever.

"Okay, let's do some learning."

Xiomara grinned while grabbing books and plopping them on Mar's lap. "Good. Study all the ancient texts in this room. These books are why you're here. They can't leave this realm. We can't risk them falling into the wrong hands."

Mar ran her fingers over old leather bindings. Energy pulsed beneath her palm. She sighed as light filled her chest.

"The books recognize you already. This is good," Sofia said from the corner.

"Is my father the darkness that I'm supposed to fight?" Mar asked.

"We don't know." Xiomara lifted her hands in a sign of frustration. "The runes have shown darkness sweeping across the land. It will cover the earth in shadow and devour everything in its way."

"Yeah. Not vague at all," Mar complained. Behind her Sofia snorted. She was also sure Juanita smirked.

"It's only vague if you want it to be," Xiomara replied.

"Whatever. So even though you suspect my pops is somehow involved, you have no idea what or who the darkness is, or exactly when it's coming. But it's going to devour everything in its path. About, right?"

Xiomara sat down and sighed. "Yes."

"And when did the runes tell you this?" Mar asked.

"We've known for many years. Every time we throw them the same thing comes up. Shadow. Power. A month ago, the runes became urgent."

"What happened a month ago?" Mar asked.

Shadows flitted across Xiomara's eyes. "Many things. Your new best friend came into her power, setting in motion a landslide of power shifts, including the death of two very old and powerful elementals. Your mother's ambition resulted in the deaths of at least half a dozen high level immortals. This has culminated in the Guardian, Collum Thronus, recruiting new members such as yourself and setting even stricter restrictions over the Vampire kind. And finally—Domhall Taleisin has been opening doors to realms he shouldn't."

"Domhall? What does he have to do with anything?"

"The man has no boundaries at all. I swear." Xiomara tossed her ghostly hair behind her shoulders.

That was the other thing Mar needed to remember. Her ancestors were ghosts. In this realm, they remained mostly corporeal but when they became angry or annoyed they'd waver a bit like an old TV screen during a power surge. To be fully corporeal would take tremendous amounts of power.

Xiomara continued. "He showed up here last week to tell us to check the runes. Like we don't know how to handle our own magic—thank you very much."

"Domhall *is* very old and powerful."

"We know," Xiomara snapped. "We don't need him to tell us how to do our jobs."

"He's pretty good at manipulating things the way he wants them to turn out," Mar said. "His ends usually justify the means."

"You're sounding more and more like your Cat."

"No. I'm sounding more and more like a woman who is sick of making excuses for assholes or turning a blind eye to murder because it doesn't affect me."

Xiomara wrung her hands together. "We owe you an apology. We hid the truth of your past from you. We were protecting you, but we went about it the wrong way."

The words slid over Mar's skin like a cruel promise. "A little late to the apology game, Xi. I mean I had no idea what was going on. I find out I'm a vampire—that sucked hard by the way. Only to find out a day later it's another big lie."

"Many things happened to you that a child should never have to endure. We wanted to protect you."

The other ancestors crowded around Mar nodding their heads and looking remorseful. Remorseful but still selfish, she thought.

Xiomara continued. "We need you to see what's coming. You won't be able to do this if you can't let go of your anger."

Mar exhaled a long slow breath. "I'm not angry."

Xiomara shifted. Sofia looked away. Juanita placed a hand on her shoulder.

Tears burned at the back of Mar's throat. She was angry. Livid. Everyone she'd ever loved or believed in as a child had lied to her. She had a father who might possibly be the darkness she'd have to fight. She was so angry her teeth hurt. Domhall had probably known too. At least she knew Neeren hadn't lied.

Mar flopped back in the chair and stared at the ceiling. "Fine. I'm angry. I'll get over it. Teach me what I need to know."

Laughter burst out of Mar's chest at the looks on her ancestors faces. "What? I don't hold grudges okay. If I did I'd have no friends. Brew up what you need to and tell me what book to read." She snapped her fingers. "Let's move. The sooner we finish this the sooner I can go home."

The witches jumped to attention. Rushed about the room gathering supplies. A small, green glass bottle. A dusty burlap sack filled with dried herbs. A knot of sage. They were concise and efficient.

Xiomara handed her a leather-bound book of such substantial age, cracking it open felt spiritual. Yellowed pages as delicate as bird feathers lay inside. Ancient spells, many written in a language older than human language, competed for her attention.

"Do you feel it?" Xiomara asked.

Of course, she felt it. Mar was no fool. The essence of the goddess imbued the book. Her ancient wisdom inscribed on the pages in hopes the light would always overcome the dark. "How old is this text?"

"No one knows," Xiomara replied. "It rested in this place

long before I came. And I have rested here for over fifteen hundred years. The spell you must practice is on page fifty."

Maria turned brittle pages. When she came to the page she wanted, she gasped. A bright white page of fresh parchment covered in crisp ink lay in front of her.

"Tell me what you see," Xiomara said.

"The page is brand new. It shouldn't be in this book."

"Thus, it has ever been. New witch. New spell. The goddess offers a spell meant for you alone to weave. Her gift to each new conduit."

Maria reverently stroked the paper. A new spell. For her. From the goddess. It was almost better than sex. A thrum of energy vibrated from the page to her fingers. Energy that felt like hope and home. The one constant in her life had been magic. Whatever shit came her way, Mar always knew the goddess had plans for her. Kept her going when nothing else would've.

She settled into the corner with the book in hand. Sofia handed her a cup of green tea.

"You ladies have rum in this realm?" Mar asked.

Sofia grinned. "Rum is for sissy's. Moonshine is the elixir of champions around here." She pulled a small clay bottle from the pocket of her linen dress and discretely poured a splash in Mar's tea before putting a finger to her mouth.

The stuff smelled like dirty socks. Mar grimaced but kept her mouth shut. She made herself comfortable in the large burgundy lounge chair and prepared to spend the afternoon studying. For the first time since being ripped away from Neeren, excitement flickered in her chest.

Half an hour and the cup of toxic tea later, one of the witches screeched. Shocked out of her studying, Mar bolted upright. Her feet landed in water and she squealed at the contact. Around her the witches panicked. Xiomara and Sofia yelled at the others to pick everything up off the floor. They grabbed books and bottles, threw pillows on top of tables, and papers on top of pillows. Water slowly covered the floor, reaching their ankles. Water filled the space, rising to knee length. The liquid shifted, consolidating into a deeper pool in the middle of the room.

Xiomara called for the women to help her cast a protection spell.

Mar watched awestruck as the water covered everything in its path. Watching her ancestors scramble filled her with an odd sense of delight.

The book in her hand began to quiver as though looking for attention. Words appeared below the text already on the page. Crouched on the edge of the chair and keeping an eye on the pool forming in the center of the room, Mar read the words forming on the paper. A glow started in her belly, weaved up to her chest, and settled around her heart.

The pool in the center of the room formed into a chest high cylindrical shape. It pulsed as more water poured in from nowhere. The witches joined hands, creating a protection circle around it.

As though they could stop this.

The book on Mar's lap rattled. She placed bare feet on the floor and coughed to draw her ancestor's attention.

Mar's voice resonated with power as she read the words on the page out loud. "He who fights shadow shall be rewarded with light. We open the door to he who offers himself to death. For death in the service of love, we bid him entrance to the realm."

Pale light surrounded the water. Pulsed. Mar repeated the spell again and again. Until the pale light shimmered purple. Until her ancestors dropped their hands.

Fingers, blistered and raw, pushed through the water. Heat spread over Mars chest.

Neeren was here.

A hand followed the fingers. Then his forearm speckled with dark hair. His foot slapped against the floor. Mar's mouth watered as a defined calf appeared. Then an upper leg thick with muscles built from years of training.

Mar's heart quickened. He'd come for her again. How had she ever thought he was a player? She walked to the edge of the swirling pool. The last bits of water on the floor tickling her toes. Her ancestors scattered as she approached. Actually, they'd scattered before then, as soon as her words filled the room, resonating with the voice of the goddess. They backed away till spines met wall.

As Neeren's head and chest pushed out of the water she met him. The look in his eyes when he saw her almost brought her to her knees. A savage growl carried across the room as he stepped from the water and enveloped her in his hot arms.

As soon as their skin touched the water fell to the floor and disappeared. He kissed her head. Her forehead. Her eyes. Squeezed her so fiercely she thought she might break. She'd never felt so safe in her life. She loved him so hard it physically hurt. She kissed his chest. Rubbed her cheek on the arms wrapped around her. The quiet storm churning in her gut calmed. For a moment, they stood like statues. An island in the middle of chaos.

His hot breath against her ear whipped up a storm of another kind in her belly. She pushed her body against his while wrapping her arms around his neck.

Staring into her eyes, he asked, "Do you wish me to destroy them for you now, Maria?"

The hopeful tone in his voice caused a genuine smile to curl her lips. Her ancestors sputtered angrily behind her, but none approached. The goddess had given her the tool to help Neeren come through. None of them would fight his right to be there.

She chuckled. "No. I've decided I like them."

He sighed. "Very well."

He stepped back slightly, gripping her shoulders at arm's length. As her ancestors gasped, awareness prickled her skin. Neeren stood in front of them all, completely naked. Mar immediately jumped back into his arms.

"Um, maybe we should try and find you a wrap or something."

A wicked grin revealed pearl white teeth. "Are you embarrassed, little witch? Or are you trying to find an excuse to take me to your room?"

She swatted his behind. He growled in her ear. Behind them her ancestors coughed. One of them, probably Xiomara, groaned, "Get a room."

Sofia loudly exclaimed. "A worthy male."

Maria ignored them. She should have known Neeren wouldn't be able to.

He spoke directly to the women. "You took Maria against her will. Family or not—with her permission or not—should you think to do so again, I will hunt you down and harm you in ways you cannot yet imagine."

Xiomara glared. "We don't answer to you. We exist on a higher realm."

He sneered. "And yet I'm here aren't I? It seems I have friends in even higher places."

As the two stared each other down Xiomara looked away first. Mar stifled a giggle.

"Do you wish to leave, Maria?"

Both her ancestor and Neeren asked the question at the same time. Neeren's question sounding as though it weren't a question at all but rather a negotiation of when. Xiomara sounding as though she were asking for confirmation the kidnapping had been warranted.

Mar grabbed a green wool blanket off the wooden rocking chair nearest her and wrapped it around Neeren's waist before answering either of them. She'd been blushing since he'd crossed the threshold, trying not to look down, while Neeren smirked. His "manhood" on display and growing at an alarming rate.

"Can we please put a hold on this conversation until I find you something to wear?" Mar refused to look at Xiomara. "Sofia? Any chance there's male clothing lying around?"

Her ancestor laughed. "Kid, this is a realm full to the brink with warriors. There's male clothing available. I'll just go pay Ragnar the Ravisher a little visit."

As she skipped out of the room, Xiomara yelled, "Back before dawn, you hussy."

Neeren's unexpected laughter curled Mar's toes. She kissed his cheek. "I missed you."

He winked at her, leaned in, and growled in her ear. "Show me your room, little witch. I only need your body to warm me."

~ ~ ~

Maria shut the bedroom door and leaned into Neeren's rock hard back. Heat from his skin seeped into hers. She turned, burying her face into his chest once again.

"How did you find me? A spell was gifted to me, to let you through, but only because you'd already started the journey." As the reality of what she'd said set in Mar hit him. "Did you kill yourself, you idiot?"

She gnashed her teeth together at his chuckled response.

"I did. Glenn and I had a solid plan." He gripped her chin in his hand, forcing her to look into his eyes. She melted as he spoke again.

"I will always come for you. Death is inconsequential."

She sighed. "Only you would say such a thing."

His presence overwhelmed the space. Nothing could stop him. Neeren was a mass of power and energy, and she ultimately realized, love. This man who seemed so cold, so calculated, in truth was the most emotional person she'd ever met. His emotions controlled everything he did. Seething just below the surface. He burned with emotion, with his devotion to his family, and now to her. My goddess—he'd manipulated death to reach her. He was a Tsunami.

She pulled away slightly, rocked by the revelation. "I love you."

He grinned. "Yes."

She smacked his chest. "Say the actual words out loud."

He shrugged as though it were tedious. "Very well. If you wish it. It changes nothing. My heart said this long before. You know this, Maria."

"Say them anyway."

He lightly kissed her forehead, her eyelids, her cheeks, her nose, her mouth. "I love you with all I am. I give my life and my death to you. I am yours. I was yours the moment I met you."

Tears streamed down her face and she swiped at them with the back of her hand like a child would. He laughed at her tears.

She rolled her eyes. "You're so melodramatic."

He snarled and licked her ear, sending shivers up her spine. "Yes, witch. I am. Now, are you ready to leave this place?"

Her heart pounded in her chest and she struggled to give him an answer. He'd come to save her, but she knew she couldn't leave yet.

"Honestly?" she stuttered. "Not yet. I actually have a lot to learn and I think maybe I need to stay a bit." Mar looked up at him sheepishly.

He stroked her hair. "Are you certain?"

"I think so." She cleared the nervous tick in her throat. "I mean, I know you risked everything to come for me. And my ancestors totally were losers, but I kind of think I need to be here for a bit."

Butterflies churned in her stomach. She hesitated only a moment before relaying the entire sordid story of her life. To Neeren's credit, he stood patiently, hands resting beside hers. He flinched once but otherwise remained stoic. No trace of his thoughts on his face. When she finished, he rubbed the side of her cheek with his thumb.

"Very well." He ripped the blanket from his waist. "This room is a hovel. How could they think to place you in here? We may need to find another cottage with appropriate space."

Two reactions burst through her chest. First, her lover was a total snob. Second, her lover was a total hottie she utterly adored. She decided to run with the second. "Shut up and kiss me."

As he grinned his wicked grin, she licked her lips and grinned back. One good thing about having a legendary lover was she reaped the benefit of years of practice. She ran her hands up his rock-hard chest, reveling in the feel of him. His muscles jumped beneath her touch. Static energy sparked from her fingers as she traced a trail down his waist. Laughing at how deliciously wanton she felt, Mar slowly let her fingers trails over the tip of his cock before dancing away and racing to the four-poster bed.

Neeren's breath was hot on her neck as he chased behind her. He grabbed her around the waist as she launched herself in the air to jump on the bed. Spinning, he fell so she landed on top of him on the lumpy mattress.

Heat seared through her groin as he groaned. She pushed up, using his chest as leverage, rotating her wetness into him. He smelled so good. Like sandalwood and ocean salt.

Like sex.

She'd never been one for holding back. Refused to do so now. Reaching down, she pulled her dress up her legs and over her head. Straddling him in her panties, she gave herself over completely.

"No bra, little witch?" he growled.

She stuck her tongue out while trying to ignore the heat spreading through her body. His hands, secret weapons, slowly stroking across her flesh.

"They kidnapped me with only a night shirt on. And I'm sure not borrowing one of the hippy sister's bras." Mar groaned and bit her lip as he pinched her nipples, lightly twisting them.

"Ride me, Maria." He released her breasts and gripped her thighs. Gently squeezing before moving his hands to push aside the fabric of her cotton panties.

She cried out as he rubbed along the edge of her clitoris. "Do that again."

"Ride me as you've been told, little witch and I'll give you all you ask for tonight." He removed his hands and gripped her thighs again. He waited, still as the moon.

She whimpered for more.

"You're so wet. Put me inside you."

Reaching down she grasped his cock and slowly slid it inside herself.

He grabbed her waist, holding her tight. "Don't move yet."

She pushed against him and he slapped her ass. "I said don't move, witch."

Maria whimpered again. Fire spread from her stomach to her breasts. She desperately wanted to arch her back or rotate her hips but Neeren held her so tight she couldn't move. His hand wandered to her clit and she moaned. Jumped at the unexpected current of pleasure.

He pulled his hand back and smacked her again. "Move again and I stop, Maria."

"I have to move," she begged.

"You do not. Control makes it sweeter." She smacked his chest and he chuckled. "Hit me again and I end this."

"I hate you."

"And I love you." His fingers strayed near her clit.

She held herself rigid. Chewed on the inside of her cheek as he found her nub and started rubbing with his knuckle. Exerting just enough pressure to make her scream. With his thumb, he played with the folds of flesh. Twisted his hand and inserted two fingers into her next to his cock. She screamed but held herself still. Sweat broke out across her upper lip. He ground his knuckle into her clit hard, almost painfully. But beautiful pain. Sinful pain. She wept, and her legs quivered on the bed.

Removing one hand from her leg, he pulled her chest down to his mouth. Lifting his hips, he pushed himself into her with aching slowness. "I'm going to make you come now. Do you want to come for me?"

She moaned and cried at the same time, unable to talk as his hands and body filled her with sensuality. A connection to the Aphrodite. This was a hostage taking. Her body no longer her own. Controlled like it was his instrument. They hardly moved. She never been more wet in her life. More aching with need.

As he moved—releasing and pushing slowly into her again, he twisted her clit and nipped her nipple. An orgasm rocketed through her with no warning. Her body gave out, surrendering completely to Neeren's control. As the waves swept over her again and again, he slammed her body on to his and groaned his own release.

Chapter 25

Neeren gulped back air and rolled them over until Maria rested against his chest. He stroked her hair, her back, her ribcage. Kissed her shoulder as she rested her head on his arm.

"I'm sorry it took me so long to reach you."

"What? Don't be stupid." She pushed herself up on her shoulder. The loss of her heat left him bereft.

He grinned. "What do you insist on calling me stupid?"

"Because you're acting like a dummy." She jumped off the bed, grabbed the blanket thrown on the floor earlier, and flung it over them as she settled back on the bed.

A peace he'd never known settled in his bones.

"I can't believe you allowed yourself to die to reach me."

"Collum is watching my body on the other side. As soon as you are ready to return, he will pull me from the water and revive me. It is not a big deal."

"It is so a big deal. How did you even think of it?"

"Glenn is useful for more than baking muffins and making coffee. Now, how long do you think we will remain here?"

"We? You can't stay. You have a Kingdom to manage."

Neeren sat up, growling at her. "I am not leaving without you. How can you think such a thing?"

"Well I mean, when you said '*very well*' earlier, I assumed you were okay with me staying."

"I am okay with you staying. As long as I'm with you. Besides, I'm long past due a vacation." Neeren laid back down pulling her tight against his chest. There was no goddamn way he was letting his little witch out of his sight again.

"We will stay until you are ready to return. When we do, you need to tell Collum and my sister everything about your past and what happened in the catacombs."

"I know." She sighed. "They're going to hate me."

"They could never hate you." The scent of lemon and bourbon wafted from her hair to his nose. She'd forever be a dichotomy. Sweet and free spirited. Tough as nails. Using whatever means necessary to get what she wanted. She was wicked. Hot. Wild.

"Collum needs to understand your history, your family, the relationship your mother has with the vampires. It is necessary to building a proper plan for protection."

Mar flopped against the bed. "You're right. I'm not going to let Isabella ruin another life. I need one week to train. Then we'll go back."

He admired her utter lack of artifice or guilt. With Maria, you got what you got. And once she made up her mind she ran with it. She was every breath of fresh air he'd dreamed of as a child.

He tweaked her nose affectionately. "Very well. Now do you think those ancestors of yours can get word to Alex to let her know we are safe?"

Mar winked. "Those birds are brimming over with magic. Sure thing they can send some kind of magical note to BFF and Dragonballs."

Joy exploded out of his throat. Control slipped away. His hardened shell cracked. A grin split his cheeks open as he laughed at the absurdity of the situation. He was dead, and yet he'd never felt more alive. "Excellent. Now can we please find a different blanket. This thing stinks like stale incense."

~ ~ ~

Neeren nursed a heathen drink Sofia handed him called Moonshine. Across the field, Maria sat cross legged on thick green grass. Her head bent over a musty spell book. Long mahogany hair covered her face. He knew she'd have her brows scrunched and she'd be chewing her lip. They'd been there four days. Each morning she spent studying in the field. Each afternoon practicing spells with her ancestors. Sometimes she'd land on her ass from the force of energy exerted. He'd jumped every time, ready to run to her, only to hear laughter ring out across the field.

He hadn't realized how powerful she was. It shamed him, if he was honest with himself. Watching her whip up whirlwinds and energy fields, light bursting out of her body. She awed him. She was a force of nature and will. Her magic capable of swallowing him whole.

"Finally realizing you're in the presence of greatness?"

Xiomara's voice grated on his nerves as she positioned herself next to him on the wicker sofa. She refused to maintain a healthy distance. He'd given no indication he wished to speak with her. But still, she bothered him daily.

"Cat got your tongue?"

He rolled his eyes while gritting his teeth. He wouldn't tell her to piss off. He wouldn't. "Very funny. I, of course, have never heard that before."

The woman smelled of sage. A scent he'd had about enough of. The entire building reeked of it. There was no logical reason witches needed to smell like sage. Should Maria burn it incessantly, as these women did, he would install an air filter in the castle. He sipped the moonshine, doing his best to pointedly ignore Xiomara.

"You're going to have to talk to me eventually."

"No. I will not."

"Oh for goddess's sake. I get it. You're upset we took Mar. She's over it. What can't you let it go?"

Anger burned in his chest. "You fucked with my memory. You stole her from me."

"We needed some time alone with her. You think we didn't study up on you? We knew you'd come for her. We needed her to understand the seriousness of what's coming and her role in it."

He uncurled his legs, standing to his full height and looked down at the woman. "You don't apologize?"

She shrugged, apparently unintimidated. "Nope. I did what I had to do. As you'll do what you must. Look, you can be mad all you want. I hope you get over yourself soon. We have a common interest in keeping her safe."

As she pointed to Maria, some of his anger drained. After speaking with Xiomara and Sofia it was easy to guess where Maria got her attitude from. Her ancestors spit sarcasm for breakfast. Being among them the past days tested his patience in ways he hadn't thought possible. He'd laughed a lot too though. Sofia was a cantankerous old bat. He preferred her company.

Maria's voice rang out across the field, swearing to the winds as a vortex she'd been spinning collapsed in on itself. Light filled his chest as she stomped her feet in frustration.

"I would give my life for her."

"We know, big guy. It's why we could come for her. True love and all."

He nodded but said nothing more. Sitting back on the couch, he waited for Xiomara to continue. He rested his feet on the footstool. One of the legs was shorter than the others and it rocked as he shifted. "You need to remodel."

"We like broken things here. We have no interest in perfection."

There was meaning under her words. He studied her face, finally. Waited for her to continue speaking.

"Her mother plays a dark game. We don't know if Maria is strong enough to win."

He nodded. Waited.

"You know the darkness is coming. You must feel it."

"I do not feel what you witches' feel."

"C'mon. It's creeping in everywhere. Touching all the light places."

"And you know it rests inside me as well." He glowered at her. "What is it you want, Xiomara."

She glanced away. "Yes. We know it resides in you. But you've controlled it all these years. You searched for light instead of falling into dark. I need you to be willing to help Isabella . . . or kill her."

His heart pounded in his ears and chills raced up his spine. The words came out quick. Brittle. "I'm not killing Maria's mother."

Xiomara rushed on. "I'm not saying you have too. We don't want you to have too. But right now, we don't know where the darkness is coming from. Someone's wielding it. We can't find Isabella. We can't read her. Someone or something very powerful is protecting her. We think Olorin may be pulling strings from wherever he's locked away." She dragged her foot in the grass. "Mar won't be able to stop Isabella if she comes for her."

"Do not underestimate her," he growled.

"Don't be obtuse. Mar might be a tough ass witch, but Isabella's her mom. There's no way she'll be able to take her down if it comes to it."

A weight settled in his chest. Of everything he'd done in his life. Everything he could do. What Xiomara asked would destroy him, because it would destroy Maria.

From the corner of his eyes, he caught sight of her twirling on the lawn. His chest collapsed. He dropped his head into his hands.

"She would never forgive me."

Xiomara nodded. "Doesn't matter. You said you'd give your life for her. Will you give your love?"

He stood, intending to walk away. Her voice stopped him.

"Answer the question."

Rage clouded his vision as adrenaline rushed through him like a wave. Claws burst from his fingers. He spun on his heels, seething, ready to rip her head from her shoulders. When she stepped back it pleased him. He clenched and unclenched his fists. Breathing deeply, he forced his mind clear before speaking through gritted teeth.

"I will do what is necessary to protect her. Whatever the cost."

Xiomara sighed. "I take no pleasure in asking this of you."

He grabbed his forgotten drink off the floor by his chair. Chugged it. Let the moonshine burn his throat and cloud his mind. "And still you ask it. You ask me to kill a woman. A mother."

"I ask only because of how deeply I'm certain of your disgust. I also know you'll keep your word. Do you give me your word?"

He moved slowly. Deliberately. Each step measured. Each thought measured. His jaw brittle as he answered before walking into the cottage. "I give you my word."

Chapter 26

"Has Glenn heard anything?" Alex stormed into Collum's office without knocking.

Neeren and Maria had gone over to the other realm five days ago. Alex received one brief communication saying the two were fine and would be staying for a week while Mar trained. The ancestors warned of a coming darkness and they would fill them in when they returned. Meanwhile, Neeren's lifeless body lay in a pool in the basement under the watchful eye of another guardian, Idris Bolaji.

Alex met Idris briefly only a couple of times. The first time as an enemy. The second as a trusted friend. Collum shared that Idris had been a guardian for over two-hundred years. He also worked with Lachon Findel an elemental elder and one of her grandfather's oldest friends.

Collum jokingly described Idris as a freelancer. He was a huge man. Almost as bulky as Collum. The story went that Idris, a Lion shifter, was brought to America as a child slave in early sixteen hundred. After transitioning and discovering his true power he'd killed the slave trader and escaped. Then made it his mission to root out and destroy as many slave owners as possible. Collum found him near death in 1792, after being shot in his lion state. Idris agreed to join the guardians but refused to stay in one place for long, or to take any job he disagreed with.

Maybe Idris felt an affinity with Neeren because they were both shifters? Alex couldn't fathom why a man so fierce agreed to babysit a corpse. Whatever his reason she thanked him from the bottom of her heart.

Each day though, Alex became more concerned. None of them knew what this prolonged state of existing between life and death would do to Neeren. Mar had been guided by her ancestors. Neeren's entrance to Valhalla was a different story all together.

Collum sighed and pushed himself back from the desk. "Nothing yet. You know I'd come find you if we received any word."

"It's been too long. I don't like leaving Neeren down there."

"He's a water elemental. I don't think marinating in liquid for a few days is going to hurt him."

She scowled. "What about his brain? It can't be okay for his brain to be in stasis for so long."

"We're monitoring him. We'll see any alteration in his brainwave pattern immediately. Besides, Idris never lets people die on his watch."

Collum gently cupped her elbow and led her over to the couch by the window. The warmth from his hand soothed her as nothing else could. She leaned in and breathed deeply. Nothing on earth smelled like her dragon. Alex's head swam with visions of the two of them wrapped around each other. His knowing grin annoyed her.

"Have you discovered anything else about this darkness hinted at?" she asked.

"Not much. Glenn's looking into it." He paused, and she knew he was about to say something she wouldn't like. "I skyped with Quinn about an hour ago. With her knowledge and research abilities, I think she'd make a great asset to the team. With your investigative journalism background, I think the two of you would work well together as researchers. What do you think?"

Alex covered her face with her hands. "Did you tell her about Neeren?"

"Yes."

Alex groaned. "She'll call my mom. Gray will be here on the next plane."

"So?"

"So? Do you think Gray is going to be okay with her son being chained under the water for a girl he just met? I may not have been with my mother long, but it was long enough to know she'll rip him out of the pool as soon as she gets here."

"Idris will keep her back."

Alex laughed and patted his shoulder. "You keep telling yourself that. You better warn Idris."

He pinched her and pulled her in for a quick kiss. "Your family is going to prove the bane of my existence, isn't it?"

"You're the one that keeps reeling them back in."

"You'll work with Quinn?" He asked the question between nibbling her neck. Little love bites that would turn to so much more if she let it.

"I'll work with Quinn . . . if she accepts."

"She's out of a job. Why wouldn't she accept?"

"Because you're asking her to be a guardian. Quinn wasn't a fan of the secrets my grandfather kept. She prefers a life free of subterfuge."

"Hmm." Collum nuzzled further and pulled her on to his lap.

She let him of course. Ran her hands over his shoulders and dug her fingers into muscles carved from rock. His skin jumped. Hers tightened in response. She pressed her breasts against his chest.

Collum's phone buzzed. The sound like thunder interrupting the quiet of their breathing.

"Ignore it," he growled.

She tried. After the third round of buzzing she knew it wouldn't stop just because they wanted it to. "You better see who's so desperately trying to reach you."

He shoved his hands through his hair. Alex laughed at the forlorn look in his eye as he stood and fished the phone out of his pocket. He turned back after reading the text with shock clearly written on his face.

"It's your mother."

Between bouts of hysterical laughter, she replied, "have fun," before leaving him to deal with the scariest thing in the world. A mother on the warpath.

~ ~ ~

At two that afternoon Alex found herself on the roof looking out over Stanley Park. Glenn—she assumed it'd been Glenn—had created a serene escape from the city below. White wood, lilac pillows, and thriving pots of lilies filled the space. She leaned against the patio railing watching people far below walk along the seawall. A slight ache filled her belly as she accepted she wasn't one of them anymore. She'd never be able to walk blissfully unaware of the immortal world.

Salt spray coated the lower windows of buildings. The world smelled fresh here. She'd always loved the Pacific Ocean. The depth of it. Today it seemed smaller.

The door to the patio slammed behind her. "Tell me where you're going next time," Collum bellowed as he walked onto the roof.

The scent of his fear reached her. "What happened?"

"It's Idris. Neeren's back. Idris hauled him out of the water when his body began convulsing."

Terror sliced through her chest. "Is he okay?"

Collum rushed to her and laid his hand on her shoulders. "He's fine. I promise you. But he's freaking out. Mar was supposed to be back before him."

"What are you talking about?"

"He watched the ancestors send Mar back before he

agreed to return. She's not here and he's threatening to drown himself again to find her."

"He can't do that again? Can he?"

"Glenn's advising against it."

"We have to stop him."

Alex pushed past him, racing down the stairs to stop her brother before he did something stupid. Collum's hot breath tickled her neck as he followed. She reached the room in the basement of the building within minutes.

If she wasn't freaking out she'd have laughed out loud. Idris held her brother on the floor in a head lock. In front of them stood Glenn in his favorite pink track suit trying to reason with her brother. "You need to calm down. You're safe."

Neeren raged. "I told her I wouldn't leave her again. She should be back already."

"I'm sure she's on her way. Her physical body may simply have reanimated in a different location. Give her time," Glenn said.

"Or you could simply give her a call, brother," Idris replied sarcastically while struggling to hold Neeren down."

Alex sensed there was more going on. Neeren was pale and shivering. "Can we get him a towel or a blanket?" she asked no one in particular.

As the shivers grew worse Neeren began rambling. "The darkness may have her. It's too soon. We should have stayed longer. But my body was giving out. We swore we'd stay together."

Neeren struggled against Idris, physically weakened from his time in the pool. Chains wrapped around one wrist. His voice took on a dark quality "Let me go before I can't hold myself back."

"Not happening until you calm down," Idris replied.

Neeren's voice became frantic, cutting. "I'm losing control. I'm not in control. You need to stop, now."

"You elbow me one more time, brother and I'm knocking you back in the pool."

The air in the room shifted. Neeren closed his eyes. When he opened them black pools of deliverance peered back at them. Idris screamed in agony and flung his head back. His body twisted like a broken doll. Alex stood rooted to the spot unable to understand what was happening. Collum swore and rushed Neeren. He swung his fist. Connected with Neeren's jaw. Her brother slumped. Out cold. Somehow still held in Idris's arms.

Breathing heavily, Idris released him and stumbled back on hands and knees. "What the fuck did he do to me?"

Neeren lay on the cold floor, dripping wet, his skin tinged pale and lifeless. Alex shivered as fear for what he'd been through crawled along her spine.

Idris rubbed shaking hands over his face. "He was in my mind. Screaming at me to die or let go. Then it felt like my head was going to explode." He turned to Collum. "Literally going to explode, man. Not figuratively."

Alex glanced between the three men in the room. No answers would come until Neeren woke up.

Chapter 27

The early evening dusk whispered along her skin as Maria opened her eyes. The scent of freshly mowed grass filled her nostrils. Equally strong was the smell of mint tea. Like her Nonna used to make. A multi-colored plaid blanket lay beneath her back. A wicker picnic basket rested near her feet. Just beyond, in the shadow of a large Elm tree, sat a figure in shadow. A hood covered her mother's face.

Mar launched a barrage of foul language to the wind before sitting up and screeching, "You're kidding. It's one thing after another with this goddamn family. Where am I?"

Isabella remained in shadow. Her voice grated on Mar's nerves like nails on chalkboard. "You needn't be rude. I simply wanted to make sure you were all right after the ordeal Jason put us through."

Mar rooted through the picnic basket. Her stomach felt as empty as her mother's heart. "Jason? Really, Isabella?"

"I don't like your tone. I even brought you a meal."

Mar ripped into a hunk of bread, smearing jelly on it. "I know everything. The ancestors told me everything. My entire messed up life story."

"Well then they must have told you how I protected you all these years."

The bread dropped from Mar's hand as nausea crept up the back of her throat. "You didn't protect me. You used me in your sick game. I was a child."

Maria wiped her hands on her dress and stood. She reached her mother in three quick strides. Poked her in the chest. "You're a bad mother. I think you are a bad person. I don't want to know you."

Isabella's loud gasp echoed in the shadows. "How could you say such a thing? I saved you in that cave. I've been saving you for more years then you'll ever know."

Hysterical laughter bubbled, fighting with the nausea. "You put me there. I saved myself."

"I knew this wouldn't work, but he told me I should try."

"Who told you? Domhall? My father?"

Finally, her mother looked at her with some semblance of reality. Fear curled the white of her eyes. Like a terrified colt, Isabella stepped back. "Do not mention him."

"Why not? Why are you so afraid of him?"

"I devoted my life to keeping him from you. I lost everything. Even you." As Isabella reached for her Mar jumped back.

"You have everything you wanted, Mother. Power. Immortality."

Isabella's voice came out in the barest whisper. "Not you. I never had you. Everything got so messed up."

Mar curled her hands into fists at her sides. "Talk to me. Explain why I should trust you."

Isabella shook her head side to side like a marionette doll. "It doesn't matter now. I'll find another way."

Lifting a single eyebrow and tilting her head, Mar simply replied, "Honestly. If you would just answer one of my questions with something other than riddles I might be able to believe you. But you can't. You never could. You know what? You keep on being Vamporilla and stay away from me. I have bigger fish to fry. The ancestors. The guardians. They need my protection. I don't have time for your particular brand of crazy."

As her mother waved her away like a petulant child, Mar's blood boiled under her skin.

Isabella's next words turned Mar's blood to ice. "I know Xiomara claims to have seen a great darkness. It's always the way with her. Vague predictions. Possible outcomes." Isabella pointed to her chest. "I know real evil."

Mar felt certain the forest stilled around them. Birds stopped chirping. The sound of the ocean quieted in the distance. The wind calmed. Her voice caught. Tears burned the back her throat. "What do you know about it? Just tell me. For once. Is my father evil? What happened to make you choose this existence over me."

"Maria child, the darkness was always coming—*for* him. As it would have come for us if I hadn't made the choice I made." She laughed. "There are only two constants in this world. Battles among the immortals never end. Humans always shrivel and die."

"I'm human."

Her mother's eyes glowed red under her hood. "You don't have to be. You could join me. Be with your Cat forever. He could protect you from Olorin."

"I don't need protection. Maybe you haven't figured it out, but I'm a badass."

Isabella smiled. "I'm a badder ass."

Disgust made Mar's voice come out on a shriek. Her stomach clenched at the thought of becoming like her mother. Of being the kind of woman who could abuse her own child. "I'm still trying to figure it out. Why the Vampires. Why let them take me?"

Isabella's shoulders slumped in resignation. "I thought I was doing the right thing. Was given bad advice by someone I trusted. I realized too late I'd have to obey my maker in every way. I messed up. I couldn't defy Jason. The only thing I could do was manipulate things to keep you safe and try to keep my mind intact."

"You broke my wrist a week ago."

Isabella took an involuntary step back and stumbled on protruding roots. "That was a mistake. You know it's true. I was confused . . . It happens sometimes."

Mar knew what came next. Her mother would ramble for a time. Falling in and out of lucidity. She'd blame Mar for how things were. Then she'd apologize. They'd never get around to the end of it. Mar had places to be. She put her hand up to stop her mother from speaking further.

"I don't care anymore. Somehow you manipulated my re-entrance to this realm. I'm assuming we're at least still in Vancouver?"

Her mother nodded.

"Stanley Park?"

She nodded again.

"Okay, well Neeren is probably freaking out by now. Hand me your cell so I can text him."

"Cell?"

"Don't play stupid. I need to call him."

"Maria, I'm going to need your help soon. I can't hold him back much longer."

"I don't owe you my help." Mar flicked her finger. "Hand me the phone."

"For goddess's sake listen to me."

Magpies flew out of the trees, startled by Isabella's high-pitched demand. The sound startled Mar. For a minute her mother sounded lucid. But she knew better. Mar sipped the mint tea. It soothed her throat. To some extent it soothed her anger. Seeing her mother like this reminded her of why she studied as hard as she did. Mar would never be at anyone's mercy again.

The deep red of her mother's lipstick brought back a flash of the night Jason had attempted to drain her blood. Mar had watched her life leak from her arm into the tube. But Neeren had come. She didn't give two shits if her mom had secretly been on her side. Isabella would always look out for Isabella. Period.

"No. I'm not listening to you anymore. We're done—forever. Olorin? The Vamp Pack? They're your problem."

"Maria . . ."

"No. Not another word. And you can keep your stupid phone. I'll borrow one off a nice, non-psycho tourist."

Mar spun on her heels and walked away from her mom into the light. She refused to feel guilty. Refused to acknowledge the small pebble of doubt sitting heavier on her chest with every step.

~ ~ ~

Thirty-five minutes later Mar reached Collum's apartment building. She'd tried calling Neeren but his phone was either dead or off and she couldn't remember Alex or Collum's numbers.

After leaving her mom in the park she'd found her way to the sea wall. From there it had been easy to simply walk back to Collum's apartment rather than hire a cab. She'd asked a few locals for directions and found her way. Standing on the front stoop, she buzzed the main building number and waited for someone to let her in.

When she saw Alex step off the elevator through the glass doors Mar almost broke down. Alex rushed to the door, unlocked it, and pulled Mar in for a bear hug of the finest order.

"Don't you ever disappear again," Alex sobbed into her neck.

Mar sobbed right back. "I won't. I swear."

"I was so worried about you." Alex pulled back. Looked Mar over.

Warmth tingled over her entire body. Mar felt real, true love for her friend. If she could've picked a sister, she'd pick her inquisitive, mothering, judgmental, Alex. Every damn time.

Mar kissed her cheek. "I'm okay. I promise. Had a little unexpected pit stop on re-entry but nothing I couldn't handle."

"We've all been worried. Neeren re-entered over two hours ago and had a meltdown after discovering you weren't here."

Mar cringed. Part of her loved hearing how much he cared. The other part felt sick that once again her mother's machinations caused someone she cared about pain.

Alex grabbed her hand, dragging her to the elevator. "C'mon. Everyone is waiting upstairs. I told them I needed a minute with you and kyboshed them coming down."

Mar laughed. "Thanks, friend."

Alex winked. "I've got your back."

Instinctively Mar hugged her again. "You're the best friend I ever had."

As Alex squeezed her, Mar felt love all the way to her toes.

"Same here."

The two women held on to each other for a few minutes soaking in the bond of sisterhood. Finally, Mar pulled back. "Where's Neeren now?"

"We had to knock him out. He went a little nuts. He's sleeping it off in his room."

Mar nodded. "How nuts?"

"I don't really know. One minute Idris was holding him down. The next Idris heard Neeren's voice in his head and his brain felt like it was going to explode." Alex sighed. "His physical body didn't react well to being held in stasis for so long. We're worried it might have caused temporary neurological damage."

Mar grimaced. She couldn't tell Alex the truth until Neeren woke. Wouldn't betray his trust. Not even to her bestie. Besides they both had truths to tell. They'd be stronger together.

"Okay, I'll go check in on him right away. But, any chance I can take a hot shower and change before I meet the gang?"

Alex gave her a sideways look but said nothing. Mar knew she must sound flippant, but she wasn't going to risk Neeren's story coming out until he was awake to defend himself.

"Sure. I'll take you up to your room and you can shower and change. I'll let you know as soon as Neeren wakes up. It shouldn't be long."

Mar touched her friends arm. "Thank you. I know we have a lot to talk about. I need a minute to breathe first. Okay?"

The elevator dinged and opened its doors and they stepped into it together.

"I understand. I'm here when you're ready. You need a minute. You get a minute."

~ ~ ~

Mar wiped the steam off the mirror, giving her reflection the once over. She refused to acknowledge how her hands shook.

How powerful was her mother? Sure, Mar blew off their interaction with bravado, but the truth was when she'd woken up in the park, with Mom standing in the shadows, she'd been terrified. It meant her mother was strong enough to manipulate the ancestors magic. If mommy dearest was strong enough to find Mar anywhere, then Mar's attempts at hiding from her all these years had truly been a joke.

Either that or Isabella had a powerful ally none of them knew about. Mar smacked her hands on the sink counter before walking into her room to dress. Anxiety cut off her air. She gulped in patches of oxygen as she sat on the edge of the bed. Could she trust her mom? How many times would she be played for a fool?

True, Isabella helped her in the catacombs, but she'd put her in the cage to begin with. She'd become a vamp to protect them both from a dark sorcerer. Then gotten Mar away from the vampires as a child. But she was the one who claimed Mar was the prophesied child to entice Jason to turn her. And now her mom, never a stellar witch, could make portals and interrupt the ancestors spell?

What the hell had the picnic basket been about? Did Isabella think they were going to sit down like a regular family? Mar in the light, her mother in the shadow. That they'd eat cheese, drink wine, and talk about the weather? Goddess her head hurt. She really needed a drink. Maybe a foot rub. Definitely retail therapy.

A quiet knocking on the door reminded Mar where she was and who she was here for. Neeren stood on the other side of the door. She knew it as she knew her own breath.

"Enter, kitten," she joked.

He did. Pushed the door open, stepped into the room, and closed it firmly behind him.

She gasped. He looked ill and wan. She jumped from the bed, still only half clothed, and rushed to his side.

"What happened to you?"

He embraced her. His long arms enclosing her fully. "Nothing to worry about, little witch. I was dead for five days. It will take my body a few days to recover."

Mar smacked his chest and pulled back. "You big jerk. You didn't tell me we had to worry about your physical body while we were in the other realm. I thought you were safe?"

"I was safe." He sighed before pulling her back into his arms. "I was watched over both here and there."

He petted her hair. Forgive her feminist heart, she loved it.

"I'm not leaving you, ever," he vowed.

The deep timber of his voice vibrated to the base of her groin. But also in her heart. She snuggled further into his chest and inhaled his masculine scent. Every moment they'd spent together in the other realm had been perfect. His presence, once so overwhelming and intrusive, had become her island. He'd never once interfered in her training. Never once lorded over her. He remained near enough she always knew where he was. His nose in a book and his bare feet up on a lounge. Or talking to one of her aunts about his ridiculous dog.

Each night he'd kiss her. Touch her. Love her until she whimpered in his arms, begging for more. Until she screamed her release. Then he'd wrap her in a blanket and kiss her quietly goodnight. Mar sighed. Remaining angry with Neeren was going to prove difficult. She totally needed to gain the upper hand and knock him down a peg or two. Just to keep things real.

"Where were you?" he asked.

"Let's sit down."

"Sounds ominous."

"Well it isn't. Now sit down."

He raised an eyebrow but did as she told him.

"Alex tells me you lost your shit on Idris."

He growled. "I wish she did not tell you."

"She's my best friend and she's worried about you. What happened?"

He shoved hands through his hair before speaking. Sensing how difficult it was for him she gripped one of his hands.

"When I re-entered this realm, I was disoriented, cold, looking for you. It's no excuse . . . I was confused, being held down by a mountain of a man, trying to find you, but you weren't here."

He paused, and she wrapped both arms around his chest.

"My base instincts took over. I wanted him to let go. He refused. Forgive me. For the smallest fraction of a moment

I thought, if only he'd die then I would be free to search for you."

"Idris watched over my body while I was with you. I owe him kindness. Instead I almost took his life." Neeren bowed his head. "Collum stopped me in time. I will be forever in his debt."

"I'm sorry I wasn't here when you woke up."

He gripped her chin. Forced her to look into his hypnotizing eyes. Their deep mix of green, black, and yellow soothed her.

"This is my fault, Maria. Not yours. You will never blame yourself for my failings. Do you understand?"

She smiled and nodded. "I understand, lover."

"Good. Now that we have this settled, tell me where you were."

She kissed him briefly and began. "I was with Isabella, in Stanley Park, enjoying her version of a family picnic."

Chuckling, he pulled her onto his lap. "Tell me everything from the beginning."

~ ~ ~

It was late by the time Mar and Neeren made their way to Collum's dining room. Glenn stopped by her room earlier, and after hugging her, told her they had fifteen minutes to get their butts to the dining room. As he put it, *the family has waited long enough.*

Mar dreaded the coming conversation. It meant she'd finally have to come clean about everything. Her entire messed up life. She'd been hiding from everyone for so long. The thought of her friends faces changing when they heard the truth haunted her. Like it had her entire life. It's why she was such a loner. I mean how do you tell people your mom is a psychopath vampire? With all the other revelations from the past week she felt ready to disown herself.

The stress bubbling out her throat almost choked her. She ended up gagging. Neeren looked down with a raised eyebrow.

"What was that noise?"

"Hysteria?" she offered flippantly.

"Right there with you, darling," he replied.

She burst out laughing. Grabbed him for a quick kiss. "I adore you, kitten."

"I adore you, little witch. Now, shall we meet our fate with heads held high?"

"It is the only way one meets fate," she countered with a wink.

Still smiling Mar pushed the door open and came face to face with Quinn and Gray Taleisin demanding immediate access to Neeren. She stepped back involuntarily. Bumped into Neeren's solid chest.

"Courage," he whispered as he kissed the top of her head.

"Mother. Aunt Quinn," he said, bringing the attention of the room to the two of them.

Mar groaned as the women rushed to Neeren. She moved aside until she found herself standing beside Alex.

"Why are they here?" she asked her friend.

"Sorry. Collum called them. I told him he was stupid. But he wouldn't listen."

"Ugh. He's such a frickin' dragon."

"Tell me about it," Alex replied. "I've been holding them off for the past hour. I finally had to send Glenn after you two or they would've broken down your bedroom door."

For the first time, Mar noticed dinner laid out on the table. The scent of fresh baked corn bread and spicy chili tickled her nostrils. It felt like ages since she'd eaten. There'd been food in the other realm, but after re-entering this realm she felt exhausted and twitchy. She couldn't imagine what Neeren must be feeling.

"Should we eat?" she asked Alex.

"Don't see why not. They're going to fawn over him a while and he'll let them. Collum is hiding in the corner. He has no idea how to handle an irate mother. You should have seen him when they first arrived."

Mar laughed out loud but cut it short when Gray's narrowed eyes flicked to her. "Hurry up and get me some booze. I'm not gonna be able to handle this sober."

Alex grabbed her arm. Dragged her across the room. "Come on. We'll fortify and then deal with the parents."

Chapter 28

Neeren let his mother hug and berate him in equal measures. He smiled softly. She smelled of love and home. Out of the corner of his eye, he noticed Collum leaning against the far wall looking decidedly uncomfortable. Neeren knew that as a dragon Collum would have received little to no affection as a child. Overbearing mother's and aunts would be new to him. Glenn stood near him. Likely talking about something mundane like Netflix or hockey. The bond between the two was something special to watch.

Neeren grinned as Quinn playfully smacked his shoulders and gave him hell for worrying them, while forcing food into his hand.

"You look weakened," Gray said while plucking at his shirt.

"I'm fine, Mother. You worry for no reason."

"Alex said you had an episode."

He glared at Alex. She stuck her tongue out at him. Maria pointedly ignored the entire situation. He'd have to remember that just like the dragon, his lover wouldn't know how to deal with normal mothering.

"I did not have an episode. I assure you I am well. My journey was safe."

"Yes. Your journey. Would you care to tell me more? How did you come to volunteer for this task?" She glowered at Mar.

He bit his lip to keep from laughing as the little witch took an instant interest in the floorboards.

"I wasn't volunteered. I chose to go." He stroked the side of Gray's face. "Please understand, Mother. I have found my mate and she needed me. I could do no more than go to her."

Neeren paused as his mother and aunt gasped. Mar choked in the corner. Alex smacked her back to dislodge whatever blocked her windpipe.

He continued, "As you would have gone to father."

Gray stuttered. Neeren let her find her way. "Your . . . Mate?"

"Yes." He said nothing else. Simply let the room settle into acceptance of what was meant to be.

Finally, his mother replied, "I see. And you both are fine now?"

"We are both fine now. We do need to talk about all that has transpired in the past week. Would you and Aunt Quinn like to be a part of the discussion?"

He didn't ask Collum in advance if the dragon would approve of their presence. There had been enough secrecy between them all.

His mother, bless her, recovered like the true warrior he knew she was.

"Yes. It is time we all spoke about what is next." She dismissed him. Neeren smiled again as she turned her attention to Collum. "Dragon," she commanded. "It is time we lay all cards on the table. Pour wine and let us begin.

Neeren's estimation of the King of Dragons rose again as the man straightened from his spot on the wall and nodded to Gray before saying. "Of course. As you wish."

Neeren watched with barely concealed delight as everyone in the room rushed to do his mother's bidding. She directed Collum's staff to start the meal. Even Glenn let her guide the distribution of plates and cups.

He stopped Quinn as she walked by him. "Thank you."

"For what?"

"For giving my mother her fire back. I know it was you."

"Your mom always had her fire. She just had to move through grief for a while."

Gray commanded Alex and Maria to sit beside her. "You two, over here." She didn't snap her fingers, but she might as well have.

Maria looked stricken. Holding in laughter, Neeren seated himself on her other side. Gray took a place at one end of the table. Collum the other. Quinn sat beside Collum. Idris entered and sat across from Quinn. Finally, Glenn sat between Idris and Alex.

Neeren nodded to Idris. They hadn't spoken since the incident.

"You okay now, brother," the man asked.

"I am. I am also deeply ashamed for any harm I caused."

Idris waved his hand. "Yeah. Fuckin' hurt whatever it was. We're good though. Just keep a lid on your shit next time."

"Lid sealed."

Collum cleared his throat. He raised his glass. "To family—blood and bond."

"Blood and bond," they all replied.

They ate in companionable silence. Neeren's mother asked Alex and Maria questions, making sure to include him as well. By the end of the meal Neeren felt his little witch relaxing by his side. Glenn passed the bottle of wine, then rum, around. Both liquor and the conversation flowed. As the staff finally cleared the plates away, Neeren stood.

"We have been through much these past few weeks. I think we all know more is coming. I know you all want to hear about what happened in the cave with Maria but first you need to hear my story."

"Neeren," his mother began. But he waved her into silence.

"My mother and Maria know what I am. What I can do. Idris experienced the beginning of it earlier today."

He told them all of it. How as a young child he'd almost killed his father. About his years of training with Monks and Buddhists. With anyone who could teach him control. About how his power over the mind worked. Killing with thought any shifter or human whether they were awake or sleeping.

When Neeren finished speaking, Collum stood.

"You're not alone, Neeren. Few in the immortal world possess the power to control another's mind. I'm one of them." He raised his glass to Neeren. "We're not so different. I'm glad your parents had the foresight to train you. But you can let the weight of this go. We'll help keep you steady."

Under the table, Maria squeezed his hand. Neeren felt at ease for the first time in a very long time.

"Now," Collum said. "Can we discuss your situation, Mar?"

Neeren's beloved witch squared her shoulders and told the story of her mother. Her father. Of her childhood. Of her ancestors. Collum and Alex asked the occasional question for clarification.

"So, if I condense this," Collum began. "Your mother used you to become queen of the vampires to protect you from a sorcerer the magical world believes is evil. Once Jason turned her she basically jumped from the frying pan into the fire and was forced to carry on the charade so Jason wouldn't kill her. Correct?"

"You got it boss," Mar quipped. "Then there is the part about me being a conduit to stop the coming darkness. And mommy dearest trying to convince me something else is coming."

"Why didn't you tell us before?" Alex asked.

Neeren understood where Alex was coming from. She and Mar had become fast best friends. He also knew how much pain and guilt Mar carried with her every day because of her mother. He was surprised when Collum spoke up before Maria had a chance to answer.

"I suspect many of us in this room wish our parents could have been different. My father killed my mother and abused me daily in the name of making me stronger. Gray, Quinn—I'm sure there are many things you would like to say to your father if you could. We all know Domhall made mistakes."

Staring into Maria's eyes, Collum said, "I always knew your mother was a member of the vampire race. You never had to hide that from me. You're not your mother. You won't be judged by the guardians for her mistakes."

"You knew?"

He nodded. "That she was a vampire, yes. The rest, no."

The tears welling up in the corner of her eyes rocked Neeren. His appreciation of the dragon grew. At this rate, he'd be calling the man a friend.

Collum continued, "But as part of this team you can't keep things from us again. We're strongest when we're united. If we hope to defeat the darkness your ancestors spoke of, we must be united."

Mar tremble beside Neeren. Her face betrayed nothing. "Deal. No more secrets. Good to know you aren't gonna kick me out of the super-secret club."

Everyone at the table laughed in relief. Years of secrets laid before them all. A sense of peace covering the group.

Neeren raised a glass in toast. "To Maria."

~ ~ ~

Near three in the morning, Neeren finally climbed into bed with Maria tucked into his shoulder. They'd spent the better part of the night with the family in Collum's study. They'd finished off another two bottles of Merlot before his little witch pulled out the whiskey. He chuckled quietly thinking of how his mother's eyes lit up when Maria challenged her to shots. He and Collum had happily stretched out in arm chairs as the four women in the room outdrank them. Even Glenn had a few shots after Maria called him a chicken.

Maria woke him up while laughing hysterically as Alex tried to drag her stone-cold sleeping dragon off to bed. Apparently, his mom and aunt Quinn called it a night about half an hour earlier. By the time they made it up to the room Maria was half asleep in his arms. He'd stripped her to her panties and bra while she snored and giggled.

He sighed as she curled against him snoring loudly in his ear. Maria fascinated every part of him. Her wildness. Her strength. Her self-sufficiency.

Deep in his bones, he knew she didn't need him. It was the fact she chose him anyway. He'd love her forever for that. This mighty woman. His little witch.

She snorted in her sleep and his heart flipped. Like an electric current jolted through him. *I can't live without her.* The thought hit him like a freight train. He'd known the truth of it for a while.

He nudged her. "Maria?"

She groaned and turned on her side.

"Maria." He tickled her neck.

"I'm sleeping. Go away."

"I need to talk with you. Wake up."

"Can't it wait?" She elbowed him and scrambled to the other side of the bed.

But this was something he couldn't wait on. If he didn't get it out, he might falter. And this time he wasn't going to be patient or careful. He wasn't going to think it through.

"Maria. Look at me. I'm going to ask you something. You need to be awake for it."

She grumbled something about him being a tyrant before turning over and staring at him with bleary eyes. "Fine. What?"

Touching her cheek, he smiled before saying with all the seriousness he could muster, "Will you marry me?"

She stiffened. Pushed herself up on her elbows, wiped the sleep from her eyes, and sat cross-legged in front of him. "What did you say?"

Still smiling—he wondered if he'd ever get the smile off his face—he replied. "Will you marry me?"

As she stared back with a dazed look, he sat up, matching her cross-legged stance.

"I know this isn't romantic. I promise to rent out the top of the Eiffel tower for a private dinner overlooking Paris, and to ask you again with all the pomp and circumstance you deserve. For now, I simply need you to know this truth. You are my every waking thought and sleeping dream. I cannot live without you by my side. Will you marry me?"

She hitched in a long breath. "I'm mortal."

He shifted. "I know this."

"You're not."

"This I also know."

"You'll live for a thousand years. I've got another seventy-five max."

"Maria. Immortality has offered me nothing but tragedy. I gladly give it up to stand in the light with you."

As she tried to speak he gently interrupted her. "You are a powerful witch. I suspect you'll live past the ripe old age of human mortality. And if you don't?" He shrugged. "I don't. I've thought about this. Your ancestors must have a spell capable of linking us. To make me age as you age."

"You would do that?" she asked in a halting voice.

"Immortality is overrated. My legacy will last in other ways."

His witch grinned. "You're insane."

"Possibly."

"What if you regret your decision?"

"Before you I existed for duty. For family. You offer joy. Abandon. Real life. How could I ever regret a life with you?"

She touched his cheek. "Yes."

It surprised him, how quickly his heart stopped. "Yes?"

"Yes."

"Really?"

"Did you think I'd say no?"

"I hadn't gotten that far yet—what to do if you answered yes."

"Well I did so you better figure it out."

Clutching her face with both hands, he kissed her like his life depended on it. Put years of waiting and wanting into the kiss. It was a kiss that tasted of freedom and future. They kissed until they were both panting. Disoriented. Euphoric. Complete. They kissed until they were soothed. Until a steady calming sensation took them over.

Neeren kissed her cheeks. Her eyelids. Her hair. He kissed her until they were full and laughing. A kiss meant for friendship. For a lifetime. To signify a bond beyond today's lust. That welcomed old age and holding hands while watching grandchildren play in the park. It was perfect. She was everything.

He pushed stray hairs off her face and pulled the thick quilt over her shoulders. "You have said yes. I will let you sleep."

Maria grinned and yawned. "I love you, kitten. Don't you dare tell Alex until I do."

"I promise," he said as she drifted off to sleep.

He stroked her back until she calmed and her breathing evened. As she slept beside him, he made another promise to whatever beings were listening. If anyone tried to take her from him again, their death would be slow and painful.

Neeren would strike without a moment hesitation.

Chapter 29

Alex poured Collum his second cup of coffee before topping up her own. The thick brew, Glenn's elixir of the Gods. Her hands wrapped around the olive-green mug in supplication. If she never saw alcohol again it would be too soon. Sunlight poured in through the open kitchen windows. Below the building the sidewalks filled with people making their way to work. A steady stream of morning chattering and hurried footsteps reminded her of the mornings she'd raced to the newspaper. She would not miss morning rush hour.

The smell of the ocean helped clear her mind almost as much as the coffee. She still hoped to get a run in along the sea wall before the rest of the house stirred.

"You should have some protein," Collum said shaking her out of her reverie.

"I will. Glenn is poaching me an egg."

"You really think you're getting a run in? You should have gotten up by six."

"Maybe I would have if someone hadn't kept me up half the night," she scolded.

Trust her dragon to wink at her and pinch her bottom.

"Barbarian," she teased.

He smirked. "If you wanted tame, you should've waited for a wilting wallflower. We need to talk to Quinn today. I want the two of you to start researching this new threat right away."

His lighting fast subject change was too much for Alex this early in the morning. She sipped her coffee before responding. The scent of dill and paprika wafted through the room as Glenn walked in with their breakfast.

Collum nodded in thanks as he set a plate of eggs in front of him. "Have you heard anything, Glenn?"

"My sources offer differing opinions," he answered. "Lachon Findel has access to oracles. Perhaps Quinn could approach him? See if he's heard anything."

At the mention of Lachon, Alex jump in to the conversation. "I'm not sure that's a good idea. Aunt Quinn isn't a big fan of his."

Collum scowled. "Your aunt is a professional. She'll get over her dislike of Lachon if it means stopping a deadly opponent."

"I wouldn't be too sure," Quinn said as she sauntered into the kitchen.

Alex stuck her tongue out at Collum before hugging her aunt good morning. Quinn was the calmest, most reasonable, and logical person she knew. Except when it came to her father and Lachon the Law. Because of a decision they'd made twenty-six years ago, Alex had been ripped apart from her family. Quinn hadn't even known Neeren existed until a month ago. She refused to speak to her father or Lachon.

Once they'd been reunited, Alex, Quinn, and Gray talked at length about the whole sordid affair. They'd talked about Alex's grandmother, Kaylen. Learning she'd been murdered by the elders had been too much for Quinn to bear. She blamed Domhall. She blamed Lachon.

Alex doubted Quinn could ever forgive them.

Alex shoved half her eggs on to a plate for Quinn. Her aunt smelled of lemon and mint. She wore jeans and a yellow cotton T-shirt. Her shower-damp blond hair hung halfway down her back. Alex leaned over and hugged her again.

Quinn raised her eyebrows. "Why am I expected to deal with Lachon?"

Collum spoke as Glenn handed Quinn a cup of coffee. "That's part of a bigger conversation."

"We have time. I think you can begin," Quinn replied.

"We were going to talk to her about it anyway. Might as well be now." Alex hid her grin behind her coffee cup. Her domineering dragon was quickly becoming outnumbered by strong women.

He sighed, and placed his cup on the oak table, leaning back in his chair. "I have a job offer for you, Quinn."

"I'm enjoying retirement right now. It'd have to be a good offer."

Alex burst out laughing and jumped in to save Collum. "Aunt Quinn, Collum wants you to join the Guardians."

Quinn sat straighter in the chair. "Guardians? As in plural?"

Collum crossed his arms on the table before launching into an abbreviated explanation. "A thousand years ago I realized I needed a team. I asked the four strongest warriors from differing races to join me. Rule one—they must never speak of their involvement."

"Like in Fight Club?" Quinn joked.

Alex laughed at Collum's confused look. He ignored them both and continued. "Your father was one of us, but he lost his way. Recently I asked Alex to join us. Now I'm asking you."

Quinn slumped in her chair. Sipped her coffee. Remained silent.

Alex rushed to fill the silence. "There's a new threat to all the races. One we can't pin down. The witches are calling it the darkness. Mar's mother is suggesting it might be a dark sorcerer. Collum's heard from other groups saying it's something else entirely. We thought it was the vampires but now . . . we don't know. We're hoping you'll join us as head of research."

She touched Quinn's shoulder. "You're good with details and keeping records."

Quinn grimaced. "More secrets, Alex? Haven't we had enough secrets?"

Quinn turned to Collum. "My element is wind. I'm not meant to hide things. For me, transparency and honesty are at the core of who I am."

Alex noticed the respect in Collum's look as he spoke to her aunt. "Then don't become a guardian. Work directly for me. As my assistant. My researcher. This doesn't have to be a secret. All the races should know about whatever you discover."

"Is it that bad?"

"I believe so. The witches believe so. This threat affects all races."

Quinn sipped her coffee. "What does Lachon have to do with it?"

"The Law of the Elemental has access to oracles. They may be able to see something. The man is also known for his vast knowledge. I want you to ask for his help."

"Why can't you ask him directly?" Quinn asked.

"There's only so much of me to go around. Hence the reason for a team. I need help and you need a new job. What do you say?"

Alex forced herself to keep from laughing out loud as her aunt groaned while rolling her eyes.

"Lachon probably despises me," Quinn said. "I left him drugged on my kitchen floor a few weeks ago to keep him from following when I traveled with Domhall to meet Neeren. I'm not too keen on him either."

"We all have to make sacrifices. He'll deal with it. Like you will to secure the common good."

Quinn studied the ceiling before speaking. "Fine. But I expect to be paid double what I'm worth. And I'm worth a lot."

Collum pushed his chair back, the feet scraping the floor. He strode to Quinn. Towered over her while grinning like a child with a lollipop. Or a cougar that had taken down a gazelle. "Done. You start this afternoon. First I want you two to find out everything you can about Isabella Del Voscova."

Chapter 30

Mar cracked one eye open hoping to see who was trying to cut her head open using a dull blade. Maybe an old fork. Rusty. Yeah, it was definitely rusty. She groaned and covered her eyes with her hands. A thin strip of sun found its way through a slit in the yellow curtain. Wouldn't you know it, the beam pierced directly into her cornea.

She shoved her head under the covers to go back to sleep. Neeren's slight snore buzzed through the covers. How come she hadn't noticed before? He sounded like a freight train. Maybe she could smother him with the pillow? Mar pushed two thick pillows between them hoping to dull the sound. He snorted and threw an arm over her.

"Holy crap." She threw the covers off and scrambled out from under the weight of his arm.

Now she was wide awake and hungover as all hell. She tiptoed to the bathroom. Groaned while staring at the dark circles under her eyes. She snapped her fingers. Sweet cool air circled her head. The headache subsided. Her dark circles disappeared. A healthy pink glow filled her cheeks.

"Magic, one. Booze headache, zero."

She grabbed last night's outfit off the floor and dressed. Neeren burrowed further under the covers, like he was also trying to hide from the sliver of light.

Goddess, she loved him. And she was going to marry him. Last night had been a revelation. The word 'yes' burst out before she could stop it. Like her entire soul craved him. It made no sense. Marriage to Neeren? Babies with Neeren?

Little black kittens running around the island. A built-in family. A real family that didn't try to kill you every time your turned around.

And he was willing to give up hundreds of years, maybe even thousands, to be with her. Her hand shook. Her heart raced in her chest. Was it fair to him—even if it was something he offered? She needed to be alone. To think it through.

Through the window the sound of the waves crashing beckoned her. Mar blew her sleeping lover a kiss and quietly opened the bedroom door. She snapped her fingers before firmly shutting the door. A tube of lipstick popped open, and wrote, in perfect penmanship on the bathroom mirror— Gone to the seawall to clear my head. Back before ten, babealicious.

She wandered downstairs and found Glenn whistling cheerfully while glazing cinnamon buns in the kitchen. "Morning, Glenny."

The way his eyes lit up when he saw her, made her heart smile. She should have had a father. Should have had someone like Glenn in her life. Maybe if she had, her mother wouldn't have . . . Mar shook her head. It didn't matter now.

Glenn hugged her and she melted.

"Well, look at you." He held her at arms-length and inspected her. "You don't look worse for wear. It's been quite the adventurous week."

"It has." The next words burst from her mouth before she could stop them. "Can I tell you a secret?"

He handed her a cinnamon bun. The sticky icing dropped on to her fingers. "Now, you must," he demanded.

"Neeren asked me to marry him last night."

Glenn whistled. "Doesn't waste any time, does he."

"Nope. Look at me though. Who would?"

Glenn released her arms to grab a coffee. He added two sugars and one milk, exactly how she liked. His kitchen smelled like lemon. Every surface gleamed. A young staff member stood on the corner texting.

"I thought you would've left for England by now?" she said.

"I like Vancouver. Besides, I think I need to keep an eye on you."

"Well, you'll have to keep an eye on me later. I'm going for a walk by the seawall with the best cup of coffee in the city. Got a to-go mug?"

"Are you sure you want to disappear so soon after the last time?"

"That was nothing. Only a little visit to my ancestors to learn the tricks of the trade."

"If you say so."

She swatted him. "I left a note for Neeren. Besides. "She pointed to her chest. "Powerful witch, remember."

"As if any of us could forget."

"You'll tell the others? I really need a minute to myself."

He glanced at the exit before he nodded hesitantly.

"You worry too much."

"No, just enough." He poured fresh coffee into a fluorescent pink mug with diamonds glued on the base.

She clutched her chest in her best impersonation of Scarlett O'Hara. "Glenny, is this for me?"

He blushed. "I saw it a few days ago on Robson Street and I thought of you."

Mar threw herself into his arms and hugged him for all she was worth. "I actually love you, Glenny."

"And I you, Maria Del Voscova." As he pushed her toward the door, her feet slid across the polished surface. "Now don't be long. I'm making French Toast for breakfast."

~ ~ ~

Mar wandered the sea wall aimlessly for a bit. Most of the work crowd were in their offices by now. The few people left on the sidewalks looked her up and down. She laughed. Her hair was a mess. Her outfit wrinkled. It totally looked like she was doing the walk-of-shame. She giggled, feeling lighter than she could remember.

Sneaking behind a large tree she snapped her fingers and changed into a hot pink yoga outfit tailored perfectly to show off her tiny waist. With another snap she had on hot pink runners. Her hair piled high in a pony-tail. Her face makeup free with a light pink gloss. Diamond studs in her ears. Goddess, she loved being a witch. Mar held the cup Glenny had given her against the sweater. Yep. Perfect damn match.

Before stepping out from behind the tree she glanced around to make sure no one noticed the change. Satisfied all was clear, she stepped out and sauntered along the sea wall.

The smell of salt hung in the air. Waves crashed reminding her of Neeren. Her breathing slowed. She moved with delight. The energy of the morning flitted over her bones. This was perfect. This being alive inside her body. Being in love without fear. Neeren was willing to give up a thousand years of this to be with her. Was that fair? She'd be willing live a thousand years to be with him.

She tapped a perfectly manicured finger against her lips. Swallows twittered above, questioning her right to join them. She stared into the horizon. Water below—air above. Human existence in between. A wood bench beckoned her to rest a while. She plopped down. Gulped Glenn's glorious coffee. Closed her eyes and simply breathed.

They'd figure out the immortal thing later. They both deserved a bit of happiness. And the darkness? Her mother? A father? The future wasn't something any of them could hide from. She'd lost the first century of her life to lies, manipulation, and hiding. She didn't want to waste any more time. Real love found her. She couldn't walk away from it.

She was a powerful witch. If she looked long enough, she'd find a way of extending her life. A way not involving vampires, or blood sacrifices, or any other ancient Wicca stuff. Maybe technology.

Maybe vitamins?

Laughter bubbled out of her chest. She was going to marry Neeren. She'd live on his island and make babies. In a real home. One she'd protect with her life.

A shadow crossed in front of her, blocking the view of the sea. A gentle voice that sounded like honey and wine asked, "May I sit with you?"

Chapter 31

Cold air slid over Neeren's chest. He cracked open his eyes, while stretching out his hand to touch Maria's shoulder. Connected with cold sheets instead. He jolted up in the bed. Croaked her name through lips dehydrated from the night of drinking. He swallowed a couple times and tried again.

"Maria?"

Neeren padded to the bathroom on silent feet and found the message written in pink lipstick on the mirror. He splashed water on his face and strode to the window to throw open the light cotton curtains. Sunlight spilled over his flesh.

He loved how the early morning sun felt against his skin. Warm. Tingling. Soft. They would marry in a pool of sunlight. He'd watch the sun glisten on Maria's hair as he committed himself to her.

Determined to join his little witch at the ocean he threw on a T-shirt and fresh track pants. Before he stepped over the threshold of the door a slight wind tunnel kicked up in the center of the room. Seconds later a fissure split the tunnel in two. The only sign of disturbance, the slightest sway of the curtains. Assuming it was the ancestors he stepped back to give them room in the small space. A minute passed. The portal hung open ominously. There was no chaotic tremor of voices. No high-pitched laughter.

Neeren called ice to his fists. Power radiated through his body. His pores filled with moisture. Dew settled on his skin. He held himself at the ready. A delicate foot swathed in red stepped over the edge of the opening. Her body followed. He swore under his breath, fists clenching at his sides.

Maria's mother spoke before her foot hit the floor. "Before you strike me down, listen to me. Maria is in danger."

The portal closed as quickly as it opened. She stood before him dressed head to toe in blood red silk. Every inch a vampire queen.

"Where is she?" he demanded. Red hot anger clouded his vision.

"I do not have the answer to your question. I can only tell you what I sense."

He lunged toward her. "What game are you playing?"

Isabella stood her ground. Looked him in the eye. "We don't have time for this. My daughter is in trouble. She wouldn't listen to me when I tried to warn her yesterday. Now I fear we're too late."

Terror vibrated clearly in her voice. His vision cleared, and he took a moment to study Isabella. Greasy hair hung down her back. Her dress was torn in several places.

He rotated his shoulders calling on calm. Control. "Tell me what's going on."

"An old being—ancient, wants her. He knows how powerful she is. Seeks to control the conduit." She gulped a breath between each broken sentence. "I started this. Have been trying to end it for over a century. If only . . ."

She stopped mid sentenced and grabbed his shoulders. "There's no time. Maria won't stand a chance alone. She doesn't have enough magic to stop him. We have to go now."

Images of Maria tore through his head. Silky skin. Mahogany hair. The freckle on her left nostril. Her dancing on the ridge below his office window.

A tight pain gripped his chest. "She left over an hour ago for the seawall."

"We have to go now. I'm begging you."

He stepped into her space and grabbed her arm. "If you are lying to me. If this is another ploy to take her? I'll kill you myself without a moment's hesitation."

She waved him off. "Yes. I know. I'm not unfamiliar with threats to my life. Can we go now?"

He shoved his feet into a pair of black converse and threw the bed quilt at her face. "Cover yourself and keep up. I won't wait for you because of the sun."

~ ~ ~

Mar grinned at the man standing in front of her. Dude was gorgeous. His skin weathered like a man who spent his life at sea. Thick mahogany hair covered his head. His bright blue eyes full of life and intellect. He wore layers of navy wool on top of layers of navy wool. His kind smile held no flirtation.

He lifted his muffin and paper. "You've found the best spot for morning paper reading. I usually have this bench to myself."

Mar waved for him to sit beside her. "Did I steal your spot? I need to go home anyway. Enjoy it. It's a beautiful morning." It seemed her time of quiet contemplation was over. Breathing deeply, she prepared to stand.

As he sat, his legged brushed hers. Waves of sorrow washed over her skin and clouded her vision. Mar tried to stand but her body felt weighted down. Held in place by an invisible force. Her quiet bench became a prison with no walls. Bonds tightened around her arms. Her feet glued to the cement beneath them.

The honey of his voice reached through the heavy fog in her brain. "Thank you, my dear, for allowing me to join you. I've been looking for you."

Mar could do nothing but stare at him. Her lips glued shut. Her mind heavy. She tried to flip through spells in her mind. Struggled to turn the pages of her spell book. The ease with which she'd always been able to find what she looked for fled under this stranger's gaze.

"Twenty-five years I've been trying to outrun your ancestors. I never wanted to hurt you. You're my blood. I brought your mom the damn prophecy book and she betrayed my trust. I make one stupid mistake and how did she repay me?" His fingers tightened on the bench. "She listened to Xi. Stole you. Betrayed me."

He stroked her cheek with gentle fingers. "I'm not here to hurt you. No matter what they say. You've had enough hurt in your life. I need to make sure you won't scream for your mother. Can you promise me that?"

A single tear trickled down her face. The few people around them walked by oblivious.

"Don't cry. Shit. Don't cry. This isn't what I want. I'm going to release your hands and feet now. And you can talk. Please don't call Isabella. I am not ready to deal with that woman yet." He snapped his fingers.

Mar wiggled her hands and toes, and licked her lips. "For fucks sake," she yelled in his face. "I have had enough of this kidnapping crap. You let me go now or I will rip your cock off the minute I have a chance. I am so sick of this shit!"

She took perverse pleasure watching the blood drain from his face. When pride replaced the confusion, she punched him. "Do not tell me you're my dad."

His glowing smile blinded her.

"Ah, fuck. Let me go."

"Sorry I missed watching you grow up. But the women in your family leave a bit to be desired in the sanity department."

She hit him again. Her mind fully cleared. "You're evil. What the hell?"

He replied through gritted teeth. "I'm not evil. Never have been. Try explaining that to your mother and your hellion coven of ancestors though. I make a few bad decisions, call forth a couple demons by mistake, and suddenly everyone's calling me evil. I'm left to bounce from realm to realm, chased by shadows, for twenty-five years trying to clear my name."

"Dude. The magical community calls you a dark sorcerer."

"Really who's that? Xiomara? She's a bitter old witch who hates any hint of rebellion to her authority." He copied the sarcasm in her voice, and she prepared to hit him again.

Mars head spun.

"Your mom fell in love with me. She became pregnant. Xiomara was pissed. Next thing I know I'm being called this great evil sorcerer and your mom's gone nuts."

Mar shook her head. Uncensored thoughts surfaced. How the ancestors forced Mar away from Neeren. Xi watching her every move in the other realm. How they never stepped in to help her as a child. How they let Jason turn her mother. Surely, they could have stopped it.

"Keep going," Olorin prompted. "Fill in those blanks. I'm not the bad guy."

A hard shout interrupted them. Mar whipped her head to see Xiomara mere steps away.

"Olorin. Step away from the girl. You'll not take her while I live."

Her father jumped up. "Stay the fuck away from me, Xi. I deserved to meet her."

"You. You don't deserve a thing. You're disgusting." She motioned to Mar. "Come here, child. He won't hurt you while I'm here."

The anger in Olorin's voice was crushing. "Look at me. I'm not here to hurt you. I risked everything to meet you."

Xiomara's voice rose an octave. "Maria. Take my hand. I'm your family."

"Don't do it."

She studied her father. Indecision split her head open.

"I . . . I'm sorry. I don't even know you." Mar reached for Xiomara's hand.

Pain racked her body as soon as her fingers connected with Xiomara. A black stain spread up the flesh of her arm. Her skin began rotting. Her life force draining.

Xiomara shook her head. "The life of the conduit belongs to me. You do not fight me." With her other hand, she magically forced Olorin back while creating an invisible wall blocking him from reaching her.

In the distance, Mar saw Neeren's face in the faces of the humans walking to work. She saw her mother's face. Even Glenn's.

Her father beat against the wall around her and Xiomara.

Shadows climbed up Mar's chest. Visions of all the people she loved swam among her tears. Her hearing shut down. She swore her visions were yelling at her. They flared their arms.

The wind whipped. The ocean surged against the break wall. Waves surged higher and higher. Humans ran for shelter from the impending storm. A storm that hid the immortals from view.

Visions swirled in front of Maria. Swam in and out of reality. Xiomara's face changed. Shifted into something black and haunting. Something oily. Something dead.

An ancient voice echoed from the warped face. "They won't have you. I waited thousands of years for a conduit as strong as you."

Mar's sight began to fade. The visions became shadows. Warping. Evolving. A giant Panther raced toward her.

A raven gained entrance through the top of the wall and flew at the deathly creature holding Mar captive. Began plucking at the oily face. A hand covered in rot released Mar's arm to swing at the bird, magically tossing it a hundred feet out to the ocean.

As soon as it released Mar, pain spilled like wildfire over her skin. Black agony. Her sight and hearing returned. She heard screaming. Her mother's voice. A growl louder than the crack of the ocean smashing over rocks. Then Neeren's guttural voice begging her to hold on.

Darkness raised its arms. Chanting. Erecting a physical barrier. Her father lay on the ground. His hands pushing against the barrier. Magic pulsing between his fingers. The deathly incarnation of her ancestor screamed at him. Whatever Olorin was doing was weakening the barrier.

Her mother began yelling. "You might be able to stop it, Neeren. That thing is a warlock. Once, long ago, a human. You have a small chance as it becomes corporeal."

Glenn flew back. "We can't get through the barrier. It's closed off the top."

Tears fell from Mar's eyes as life began to trickle back into her body. They were there. Her mother. Neeren. Glenn. All soaked to the bone and fighting for her life. Her father on the other side of the wall. His eyes pulsing white. Power surging from his hands into the force field. Darkness screeching that Maria belonged to it. Neeren paced the invisible barrier. His paws stomped like thunder.

He sniffed her father.

Olorin raised one hand in a sign of surrender. "Take it easy. I'm helping not hurting. I need to stay focused on this wall, so if you could step back it'd be a big help."

Neeren glanced at Mar with his glorious cat eyes. She signaled agreement by nodding her head slightly. He growled once then continued to pace.

Neeren ignored the storm raging around them. Focused on the evil holding Mar. Locked eyes with it. Darkness clutched its head with rotting hands. Screamed in agony. Mar prayed to the goddess Neeren's power could kill the thing. But still the wall held.

Isabella's voice rang out. "Maria, we cannot reach you. Olorin can't break the wall. With the barrier in place Neeren is unable to fully manifest his power. Magic will not end this. Do not hesitate, child. That thing is not Xiomara, but it is corporeal. Do not be afraid. You must strike the heart while Neeren batters the mind."

Neeren prowled the barrier. His focus complete. A freight train could barrel down on them and she knew he wouldn't look away. The creature, this warped version of Xiomara, fell to its knees. Death, darkness—whatever they chose to call it, clutched its head and began ripping greasy hair from its scalp.

On hands and knees, Mar searched for anything she could use as a weapon. A battered tree, its trunk ripped apart, lay two feet in front of her. Jagged edges of birch protruded like swords. With shaking limbs, she scrambled toward it. Prayed for strength. She wouldn't die. She had a life to live. A man to marry. She pulled on one of the broken branches. Tore at it till her fingers bled.

Death continued to scream. Neeren never wavered from his prey.

The branch broke, jolting Mar backward. She twisted. Dragged her battered body back. Raised her arms to plunge the stake.

Death raised her head. "No."

One word. The stake fell from Mar's hands and she dropped to her knees.

Neeren howled, throwing his great weight against the barrier.

Mar's knees bled against the sidewalk. Her back bowed. Pain exploded like fireworks in her chest.

Isabella screamed. Smoke poured underneath her clothing as the sun penetrated cloth and burned into her skin.

Olorin rushed to Neeren's side. His clipped words reaching Mar even as she gulped for her last bits of air.

Olorin slapped the giant Panther in the face, getting his attention. "This isn't over great beast. Drown them now while the creature is in corporeal form. I can bring her back."

Neeren roared. The anguish in his howl cascading over her in waves. The ocean crashed against the seawall. Higher. Harder. Beneath her the ground rumbled and shook.

Mar braced herself. She knew what was coming. All around her the earth split. Great slices tore open as though Neeren's claws were creating gigantic gashes in mother earth herself. Water sprayed up from below. Geysers erupted.

Her mother's voice broke through the noise. "We'll bring you back. My darling. It's the only way to keep darkness from taking you. We must destroy it now."

Water rose above Mar's knees. Her chest. She gulped for air before saltwater covered her head. It stung her eyes as she focused on Neeren. As water filled her lungs.

Darkness fought for breath beside her. Choking on water. Clutching at its face. Its throat.

Mar convulsed. Once. Twice. Then sweet oblivion took her.

~ ~ ~

Her throat burned. Mar choked, gulping great breaths of air into lungs starving for life. She smelled lilacs and mint. And cinnamon. Her stomach growled. She cracked open her eyes to see she was back in her room at Collum's.

Neeren sat beside her. His head bowed. Behind him stood her mother. Fresh burns covered Isabella's face. Behind them stood the rest of the guardians, Neeren's mother, and Quinn. She sensed the other ancestors too. Their presence loomed large in the room.

Mar licked her lips. "Kitten?"

His head jolted upright. His gorgeous eyes filled with love. "Do not move. Everything is fine now. You are safe."

His voice flittered over her skin light a gentle mist. Quiet. Confident. Sure.

Mar tested her voice. It crackled and bubbled. "What happened?"

The room stilled.

Pain poured out of Neeren's eyes. "You drowned. I drowned you. Your mother and Olorin rightly assumed that that creature wouldn't think to erect a barrier beneath the earth. I forced water up from below. Because the darkness was corporeal, it drowned as any being would. This forced it to release its hold on magic."

He swept his fingers across her cheek. "Once the barrier dropped, your mother struck true."

Relief flittered across Mar's chest. "It's dead? And not in a sent to Valhalla kind of way?"

"Yes. At least we think so."

Mar looked at her mother. "Where is the real Xiomara?"

"She's downstairs with the other ancestors. She didn't want to be here when you woke up. She was afraid her presence would frighten you," Isabella replied.

"Do we know what that thing was? We can't keep calling it darkness and death."

Neeren handed her a glass of warm tea. She wrapped cold fingers around it gratefully.

"I'm sorry, my love. Not yet. We'll find out. None of us will stop until we know."

She licked her lips. "Where is my dad?"

Neeren glanced at Isabella before speaking. "He left."

"What? Why?"

Isabella spoke, "I'll find him. I promise."

Maria squirmed against the cashmere sheets. "Did I die?"

Neeren hung his head. "Yes."

Fresh tears streamed down her face. "How did you bring

me back? Please don't tell me you made me a vampire. I'd rather be dead."

Neeren clasped her hands around the cup. "Never, my love. I would never allow such a thing."

From the shadows, Sofia came forward. "Please forgive us for not seeing the danger. For not seeing the darkness coming for you."

Mar sighed. "I don't blame you. I thought I'd wake up as one of you. How am I still alive?"

Her mother placed cool hands on her shoulders. "You were born of Magic. Now you are re-born of it."

Fear fluttered in Mar's stomach. "At what cost? Bringing the dead back means taking a life. One for the other."

Neeren removed the tea cup from her hand, placed it on the counter, and gripped her hands in his. Warmth wrapped around her. "I gave you mine, my love."

Sorrow tore at Mar's gut. "Why would you? You can't do that. I need you."

"I can and I did. I had fifty lives to live. I simply gave you half of them."

"But . . . What?" Bees buzzed in her head, confusing her thoughts. Mar glanced at her mother. "You don't have the power to do this."

Isabella blinked once. "It was Olorin. He and the ancestors worked together to unite their power. It was enough. They all agreed. You deserve to live. Too much of your life has already been stolen."

Neeren kissed Mar's forehead. "You are alive and will be for many years to come. There is nothing more to fear."

A soothing breeze stirred the air in the room like a homecoming. Like the goddess welcoming her. Mar had been granted hundreds of years to spend with the man she loved. She forced herself to a sitting position. Kissed her lover. A light butterfly kiss holding a promise of forever. His eyes burned into her, saying without words how much he loved her.

Mar knew before she could start a journey with him she had to understand her mother, her past.

"Mom. Who is Olorin? Why rip me away from him?"

Isabella cleared her throat. "Our tale is one of beauty, manipulation, anger, and sorrow. Olorin practiced dark magic. It's how he knew the spell to give portions of Neeren's life to you. I loved him tremendously and he cheated. Betrayed us while you were growing inside my womb."

Pain colored her next words. "Early on in our relationship, when Olorin was teaching me spells we'd should have never touched, darkness poisoned my mind. Over the years, it took on many forms. Many creatures. Sometimes Xiomara. Sometimes others. I was insane. Believed anything it said. Did anything it asked. Everything made perfect sense. Banish Olorin. Become a vampire so he couldn't find me. I faded in and out occasionally. Thankfully I had enough sense to listen to the real Xiomara when she suggested shipping you to the American coven."

Isabella's voice took on a pleading quality. "I wandered in and out of sanity your entire life. Six weeks ago, Domhall Taleisin found me and began healing my mind. It's been a slow recovery."

"Domhall knew?" Mar snapped.

Isabella sighed. "Not everything. But enough to guess what had been done to me. We've been trying to stay one step ahead for weeks. Jumping realms. He located Olorin."

Mar closed her eyes before speaking. "Thank you for whatever part you had in ending this. But it doesn't make up for years of abuse. I'm not ready to forget everything yet."

Her mother nodded. "I understand. When you are, I'll be there."

She kissed Mar's head and swept out of the room. No one

tried to stop her. Mar swallowed the feeling of loss aching at the back of her throat.

She leaned into Neeren's chest. "Can we please go home to your island and get married now?"

The room erupted with questions. Neeren explained they were indeed planning on getting married. Mar hurried the explanation and then rushed everyone out the door. Her head hurt. She'd been through a lot. She needed time to rest.

As Neeren pushed Alex out the door, telling her Mar would answer questions later, Mar exhaled with relief. Neeren climbed onto the bed and wrapped her up in his arms. She snuggled in, grateful for the warmth of his body. Grateful for him. For his calm ways. His unflinching demeanor. Neeren grinned and her stomach summersaulted in her chest. His grin melted her. The sardonic lift to the right side of his upper lip. She wanted to lick that lip.

He tilted his head like he knew what she was thinking. "Kiss me, Maria."

And she did, for all she was worth.

Neeren broke the kiss off before she was ready. He kissed her cheeks and eyes a hundred times before speaking.

"You are everything to me. The wild heart of you brought me back to life. Thank you."

She wiped a lock of hair off his forehead. "Are you sure about this? You gave up half your life span for me."

Neeren sat up dragging her with him. "I will not answer this question again. I do not live without you." He smashed his hands through his hair. "When I thought I might not reach you. And then the drowning. . . I died with you, Maria."

She grabbed his face. Kissed him again. "How did you know to find me?"

"Isabella. She contacted Olorin and walked through a portal into our apartment to wake me. Your mother saved you."

Mar placed her fingers over his lips to stop him. "You saved me. Mother would never have reached me alone. It was you. Like it's always been." She kissed him playfully. "By the way, when you are in full cat/beast form, you're bloody glorious."

His chest puffed out like she knew it would. Her toes tingled. She shivered with delight.

He wrapped her back up in his arms. "We will leave for the Island tomorrow. The others can join us or not. I'm not letting you off my beach for a long time. We have traveled enough."

She nudged his neck with her nose. Inhaled his unique musky scent. Let it render her lightheaded. She licked along the muscles under his skin. "Well, until Collum has another mission for me."

She felt the breath catch in his chest. "You are not still planning on being a Guardian? Let the dragon solve his own problems."

Mar leaned back. Obviously, they'd have to sort out a few things before the wedding. "Look, kitten. Every single shitty thing that happened to me this past week was because of my family. It had nothing to do with the guardians. I want to use my power to help. I'm not sitting on your island eating bonbons for the next five hundred years."

"Of course not. You'll help me rule."

"Uh, nope. I'm not the ruling type. You do your job. I'll do mine."

"What about when we have children?"

"Children?"

"Of course. At least three. No child of ours will grow up alone like we did."

Her heart melted. At this rate, she was going to be a puddle of mush in the middle of the bed. Mar clutched his shoulders. "Ever hear of maternity leave?"

"Now, I know you're trying to fool me."

Mar flexed her shoulders. "Lover, I'm all yours. Heart and soul. Making babies." She lifted three fingers. "At least three. Being the best momma in the world. But I'm also going to practice my magic and remain a guardian. We don't know if that vile thing is dead or not."

"That doesn't have to be our fight."

"It's already our fight. I can't walk away from it."

He shuddered. "I can't lose you, Maria."

"You'll never lose me, you big suck. You're stuck with me for a couple hundred years at least. Goddess, I'm gonna have fun turning your world upside down."

Neeren rolled his eyes. "You already have. You are the best thing that ever happened to me."

"Bet your ass, I am. Now kiss me until I can't see straight and then make love to me until I forget my name."

Mar squealed with delight as Neeren raised one eyebrow, grinned wickedly, and proceeded to do exactly as she asked.

Also from **Soul Mate Publishing** and **Rayanne Haines**:

FIRE BORN —
Book One in the Guardian Series

Independent, tough as nails, and fierce to her core, Alex Taleisin can't quite believe it when she has to fight for her life against something not-quite-human in the YMCA parking lot.

That's when her aunt lets her in on the family secret. They're immortal—Elementals to be precise, and Alex is the long-lost daughter of the strongest female warrior of their time.

Her guardian (a freaking Dragon!) and the sexiest man Alex has ever seen gives her a choice. Go with him, learn how to control her fire, and find her father's people, or try to survive on her own. It's an easy choice considering she's only twenty-six. And the Elders may already be on her trail thanks to the fight with the nut job in the parking lot kick-starting her dormant DNA.

Enter an insane grandfather, a shifter with a hidden agenda, and a witch with a shoe addiction, and suddenly loner Alex is wishing for a quiet house in the hills with the dragon she's falling for.

But a fight is coming and Alex knows the only way to find her answers is to trust her powers and become the warrior she was destined to be.

Available now on Amazon: <u>**FIRE BORN**</u>

Coming soon:

AIR BORN —
Book Three in the Guardian Series

Quinn Taleisin hates secrets, and shadows, and subterfuge. Which is why she still can't believe she agreed to become a member of the Guardians, an elite force of immortals tasked with keeping the balance between good and evil in the world.

Sounds great, except, to be a guardian you must agree to live in secrecy. Quinn is a wind elemental. Being caged in by secrecy is worse than death for someone like her. She can't imagine a worse fate—until she's asked to work with Lachon Findel, the man she holds responsible for her mother's death and her father's insanity.

Lachon is the oldest living elemental in the world. Known as Lachon the Law, he's an earth element; a man who sees the world in black and white, right and wrong. So maybe once, briefly, a hundred years ago she thought he was a good guy. She knew better now. No way would she fall for his savior of the world shtick.

When the dangers of the past catch up with them, Quinn realizes the only way either of them will make it out alive is if she can put the ghosts of the past behind her and finally trust the flesh and blood man in front of her.

Want to know more? Connect with Rayanne Haines at www.rayannehaines.com

CPSIA information can be obtained
at www.ICGtesting.com
Printed in the USA
LVOW13s1151170518
577491LV00004B/12/P